DEEPLY ROOTED 2

A Novel
by

ICE MIKE

Duffle Bag Books
PO Box 10531
Oakland, CA 94610
www.dufflebagbooks.com

(Paperback)

Deeply Rooted 2

ISBN 978-0-9962840-6-6

Library of Congress Cataloging-In-Publication Data:
LCCN: 2015945748

1. Crips Bloods   2. Thug Life   3. Thugs   4. Kingpin
5. Queenpin   6. Life Sentence   7. Robbery   8. Drug Dealers
9. Black Romance Novels

Senior Editor, Linda Wilson

Second Edition August 2016

Acknowledgments

To my family: A special 'thank you' to you, Mama, for always holding me down, even when I didn't deserve it. My son, **Michael**, thank you for loving me in spite of my flaws. Understand that you have the potential to be GREAT! To my brothers **Choo-Choo** and **Tracy,** some of the best memories of my life have you guys in them, real talk! A special thank you to the woman who kidnapped my heart and is currently holding it hostage. **Jaimie,** you are truly the other half that makes me whole. I appreciate how you hold me down and lift me up. My life is so much better with you in it! I love you!

To my friends: I appreciate everything that you all bring to the table, whether you do it knowingly, or you just do it on the strength. In some way or another I learned something from you, and I am a better person because of it. **Keith Thompson, Angelo "Lo-Lo" Garcia, Jamal El Karaki, Spade, Bam Laws, Vegas** (The Brain), **Truth Stevens, Dario "Cafe" Jackson, Tick-Tock, Roc Boi**, and all the brothas in the **MSG.** Shout out to **Tru Sav Entertainment**.

To the many writers out there: Thank you to a couple of late great "King Pens," **Iceberg Slim** and **Donald Goines**, giants in the literary game! They planted seeds in my young mind that are bearing a brilliant fruit decades later. It's indescribable the impact you had on my life. Thank you to a few other writers who have influenced me, or inspired me to read or write: **Sister Souljah – Tracy Brown – Kwame Teague – Teri Woods – Quentin Carter – Nikki Turner – Joy Deja King – Keisha Ervin – Ashley and Jaquavis – Cash – K'wan – Leo Sullivan – Noire –** and **Zane** to name a few. I have read you all at one time or another, and in some kinda way I absorbed some of your energy, and because of it I am on the verge of greatness!

Wahida Clark, thank you again for recognizing game and

giving me this platform to shine and share my gift with the world. Also, thanks for wakin' my game up and forcing me to see things for what they really are. My motivation to be the best is so *Deeply Rooted*!

Thank you to **Linda Wilson**, the best editor I know. Your insight has helped me become a better writer! I hope this is only the beginning of our partnership. I have big plans in the literary game going forward, and I want you on my team!

Thank you KK for the bangin' book covers!

To the readers: A special thank you to everybody who bought a copy of my book(s). I truly appreciate that you spent your hard earned money to help my dreams come true. You have no idea the vision in which you are investing in . . . A special shout out to the people who reached out to me personally, you know who you are. Your letters gave me added motivation to take my writing to the next level, and I did just that. Thank you for inspiring me!

No matter how you feel about this book, post a review online on Facebook – Instagram – Twitter – Amazon – Barnes & Noble and tell the reading community what you thought of it.

#getdeeplyrooted
#buyreadreview

COMING IN 2016

Deeply Rooted 3

Golden State Heavyweights

Passion Wit' a Pistol

Deeply Rooted 4

To All the King Pens & All the Queen Pens

In 1982 it all began
My fire got lit way back when
Mama came to visit me in juvenile hall and she brought in
Two novels by two authors, two kings of the pen
The late great Donald Goines and Iceberg Slim,
"Whoreson" and "Pimp: The Story of My Life"
Cut deep into my soul like a double-edged knife
At the young impressionable age of thirteen
African Americans, black men, brothas!
Writing about a lifestyle I'd personally witnessed and seen
It moved me in such a manner
Touched and affected me in such a way
I intellectually pillaged that small black village called Holloway
Like so many of the characters those legends built up and broke down with
ink
And as sure as the eye blink
My ship became wrecked and slowly started to sink
My circumstance had me feelin' hopeless, I was on the brink
But like so many other brothas, I was raised up by some sistahs
And with my fire re-lit, I recognized that this was it!
I discovered my gift and realized I too could do this!
It forever changed how I thought, the way that I would think
Sister Souljah, Teri Woods, Nikki Turner, Tracy Brown
Y'all were my connecting structure, my saving link
I have you and so many other raw ass writers to thank
For motivating me to spin tales from the end of my pen
And poke holes in my emotion and pour out my wildest imagination
So, it's from the bottom of my heart that I tip my hat and say with that;
I extend my deepest appreciation
To all the King Pens, and to all the Queen Pens
For without you guys where would I be?
Perhaps just another character
Or quite possibly another sad story

Note to all: The moral of *my* story is, I don't write books as a way of glorifying the street-life. I write books because I made a vow to myself, and to the ones I love, that I would never commit another crime in the streets like a common crook. Instead, I commit crimes writing street-lit between the pages of a book. I create stories and weave tales about a foul lifestyle that I once identified with so much. And I write without fear of being arrested or imprisoned for the *crimes* I commit now. In fact, I am getting paid for the *crimes* I'm committing today. Imagine that. I did . . .

Dedication

This book is dedicated to Gerald Morris Jr. aka Choo-Choo. A piece of me died when you did, Baby Bruh. You are truly missed in a real way, but you will never be forgotton. We love you, Choo.

Rest in Peace Family
Gerald Morris Jr. aka Choo-Choo
Sunrise 5/26/72 – Sunset 11/22/15

Introduction

Born into the world the daughter of a ruthless kingpin, Miko Dunbar woke up every day with a strong sense of entitlement and privilege. After avenging the death of her father, she was finally able to focus all her energy and attention on becoming the queenpin she'd dreamed of. Eighteen months into it, she'd managed to regulate the illicit flow of narcotics' traffic in San Diego by gunning down the opposition and forcing most gangs in the city to play the game by her rules.

The city of San Diego was hers for the taking, and she was taking as much of it as she could. Miko's drug empire was relatively new to the West Coast, but her way of doing business and her approach to the game was old fashioned, cut throat, and ruthlessly brutal. Her dope spots dotted the city, and every one of them was checking major cheese. Also, her stash houses in several hush-hush locations throughout the city warehoused a high-volume of the superior product she supplied to the masses, thanks to her Colombian connection, a brilliant and brutal cartel boss named Javier Mesas.

Miko Dunbar was intent on running the city on her terms, and she was prepared to do any and everything to make that happen, even if it meant turning the drug game upside down and sending the streets into chaos. Her ambition to be 'the best to ever do it' was deeply rooted, and with her two worst enemies, Wahdatah and Baby Shug out of the equation, it was just a matter of time before the streets of the Southeast Planet were hers . . .

CHAPTER 1

Miko Dunbar

Miko Dunbar possessed the face of an angel and the heart of a devil. The curvaceous queenpin set her phone down and slowly walked from behind the elegant, high-glossed African wood table. She faced the two thugs in front of her with the uber confidence of a boss bitch. Her voluptuous backside rested against the front end of the desk, and she placed her palms flat on either side of her widespread hips. The beige Tory Burch dress clung to her curves, wrapping tighter around her thick frame every time she moved. The expensive wool fabric hugged her like it loved her. Her tongue snaked out, moistening her lips, and she cleared her throat softly before addressing Cream and Suspect, her two younger cousins.

"I want to flood the streets with this next shipment, Cream. Only this time, every brick we sell will be at a cost much lower than the next dealer's bricks."

"A lower cost? Are you serious, Miko?" Cream asked.

"As cancer," Miko responded, wearing a look of irritated impatience. She sucked her teeth before continuing. "Every ounce we sell will be cheaper than the next dealer's ounces. Every rock one of our workers sell will be bigger than the rocks our competition is selling. We have a product that's far more superior to the product our competitors are putting out there, and I want our product to be made available at a more affordable price. By doing this, we will essentially squeeze out the competition and render them obsolete, which in turn will force their clientele to spend their money with us."

"I don't think it's prudent to be—"

"I don't give a fuck about being prudent, Cream!" Miko cut

1

him off and mugged him. "Besides, I don't pay you to think, Cream. I pay you to follow my lead, you feel me?" She eyed him until he gritted his teeth and averted his eyes.

A malicious, wicked smile spread across Miko's flawless face as she pushed off the desk and continued to address her two top lieutenants.

"Exactly. Now look here, Cream. I want you to personally select the team who will be accompanying us tonight when we hook up with Javier. I want an escort truck with eight gunners, and I want the truck trailing us carrying six shooters. Once we account for the product and confirm the numbers, I want the trailer truck to be loaded up and armed with six shooters. We're going to exit in the reverse order we entered, understood?"

Cream nodded in the affirmative. Miko shifted her emotionless brown eyes to her other cousin.

"Suspect, I want you to touch base with all our big order purchasers and let them know that tomorrow is their lucky day. Inform them that I'm knocking a thousand off every kilo they buy, in addition to the lovely price they were already getting. Let the lightweights know that I'm knocking a hundred off every ounce, and that too is in addition to the lovely rate they were already receiving." Miko stared hard into Suspect's eyes until he verbally acknowledged her.

"A'ight, I got you, Miko. As soon as we're finished here, I'll be on the phone hollering at everybody who cops weight from us. I'll also let all our block workers know that a change is in effect. Before the sun comes up tomorrow, every D-boy who does any type of business with us will know what the deal is," the angry-looking, light-skinned gangsta with the foot-long dookey braids hanging past his shoulders responded.

When she turned her back and rounded her desk, her two

cousins exchanged bewildered looks, lifting their shoulders and then dropping them, unsure of her motives. Cream cracked his neck, cleared his throat, and then verbalized what everybody in the room already knew.

"Miko, you do understand that once you put this new order into effect it's going to ruffle a lot of feathers. It's basically a declaration of war."

With a steely gaze, Miko snorted disdainfully. She picked up her compact and gazed into the small mirror, casually fluffing her long locks and puckering her full, luscious lips to ensure her gloss had not smeared. Then she looked up at both of her cousins and spoke with an unsettling coldness. "That's exactly what I want to do. I want to shake this bitch up and start a drug war out there in the streets!" she hissed, pointing her manicured finger at the window.

"For too long, people out here have been eating comfortably and checking paper easy, based on the pedigree of hustlers who laid down a foundation before them. This shit was handed down to a lot of those ma'fuckas out there. Most of them never had to put in any kind of serious work to get what they have. They ain't about that life! They don't know what it's like to be violently confronted by ma'fuckas who got more money than them, by people who got bigger guns than they do, and who got more resolve in this cutthroat game than they'll ever have. People like us who murdered and maimed to get where we're at in this world!" She slammed her open palm down on the desktop, sounding like a gunshot went off in the roomy office.

"For the last eighteen months we've been knockin' down any and everybody who refused to conform to our way of doing business, and replacing them with people who bought into the game plan. We removed the old guard and substituted them with young, hungry, obedient goons who're savage about their cabbage. Thugs who think like we think and do as we say. But there are still some nonbelievers out there who continue to resist us—people who are not completely convinced that we are the new order! And until those sonofabitches have been uprooted and removed from the equation, then this city isn't truly mine! These streets ain't truly ours!" She sat down and crossed her legs, eyeing her cousin Cream hard.

"A war is exactly what I want, Cream, because only through war will my true enemies reveal themselves to me, and only then can I truly decimate all those who oppose my rule." She spoke with unwavering conviction. The frosty gleam in her eyes corresponded perfectly with the cold blood running through her veins. "I don't give a fuck how the streets feel about it; that's my plan and I'm sticking to it! If somebody has a problem with it, we can settle it in the streets on some gunplay shit," she mused mischievously, becoming oddly excited between the thighs at the prospect of impending death and destruction.

CHAPTER 2

Baby Shug

For two days, one particular clown had been mean-mugging me every time I walked a lap around the yard, and it ain't been sitting well with me. Today, I was packing an eight-inch ice pick type shank in my waistband like a pistol. As soon as the time was right, I was finna go poke holes in Mean Mugger's midsection until his ribcage looked like hamburger meat. My cellie, a young Crip homie named Devin, was on his spot, ready to play his role. The guard in the gun tower was busy talking sports with a couple of inmates off to his left, so his attention was diverted just like I'd planned it. The full court basketball game next to me was fluid with continuous back and forth high energy action. I hit the joint one more time and filled my chest with purple haze, then looked over my shoulder to see what the guards walking the yard were doing. *They on the other side of the yard. They ain't trippin'. The coast is clear. It's all good! It's about to go down in this bitch!* I thought and turnt up inside, ready to do my thang.

"Watch where the fuck you walkin', cuz!" the young homie Devin barked at the older convict who'd just bumped into him. He was talking to the same dude who'd been mean-mugging me.

"My bad for bumpin' you, youngster, but you need to check your tone and take some off of all that tough talk, potna. Watch your mouth, boy!" Mean Mugger growled at the lil homie and balled both fists.

"What you mean 'watch my mouth?' Man, ain't that a bitch! You bumped into me!" Devin declared angrily.

Left with no choice but to give him his undivided attention,

Mean Mugger frowned and flexed on Devin. "I ain't gon' tell you again, youngster. Check that hostility in your voice, or I'ma—Agh! Agh! Agh!" he screamed like a bitch when the ice pick poked holes in his prison issued T-shirt. The unforgiving steel in my hand repeatedly penetrated the soft area around his ribcage. After my third time stabbing his midsection, the homie Devin hit the older convict in his chin and knocked him out. Dude was sleep on his feet. When he slumped to the ground, I knew I'd bought myself some more time. The crowd of inmates standing on the sideline watching the basketball game inadvertently acted as a wall, preventing the guard in the gun tower a clear line of vision to the violent ass assault. I redirected my stabbing motion, sticking the mean mugger in his neck. The tender meat near his jugular offered little resistance as the ice pick flashed sticky with his blood before digging deep into his neck tissue over and over again. A line of blood squirted out his neck like his throat was pissing. I knew then that I'd hit his jugular vein, and his time on this earth was in serious jeopardy. Sometime between the fifth and sixth stab, he woke up out of the fist-forced slumber, woozy and weak. His body was zapped of strength as his life fluid poured out of every new hole I blessed his body with.

"Give me the knife, Shug! Give me the ma'fuckin' knife, homie!" Devin hollered out. His voice snapped me out of murder mode. I handed the ice pick off and stood up over the mean-mugger as he struggled to catch his breath. The entire ordeal took place in fewer than two minutes.

As previously planned, I pulled the baggy, denim state jacket off and stripped out of the extra shirt and pants I had on. I left that shit next to the dude who lay dying behind the crowd of spectators. I pushed off and started walking a lap around the yard. It wasn't until I was halfway around the track by the water fountain when the guard in the gun tower activated his alarm.

"Yard down! Yard down! Prone out! Prone out! Everybody get on the ground and prone out!" The command came out over the prison's public address system loud and clear.

I hit the button on the water fountain one more time and rinsed my hands of any visible DNA before I followed suit like the other thousand or so convicts on the yard. I got flat on my stomach in the prone position, watching with mild interest as the po-po raced around the yard like chickens with their heads cut off trying to figure out what happened. The yard stayed down for three hours while the prison staff went about conducting their investigation. One by one we were stripped out our clothes and searched for scratches, bruises, stab wounds, or blood stains.

Although I got away, the lil homie Devin wasn't as fortunate. He managed to flush the ice pick down the toilet on the yard, but the bruise on his hand from knocking the older convict out raised staff's suspicions. Upon closer inspection, they discovered blood stains on his clothes. I doubted that a case would stick if it ever even came to that, especially since no witnesses were going to come forward with any helpful information, but the homie Devin was definitely going to the hole pending an investigation.

Having no true 'caught red-handed' suspect meant the prison would be on lockdown for a couple of weeks while the police did what they had to do. I wasn't mad at that, because a potential threat to my life had smoothly been eliminated, and I was able to elude detection. Plus for the next two or three weeks, I had the cell all to myself, a luxury that a convict learns to cherish after being cooped up in a six by twelve foot cell damn near all day every day with another grown ass man. I had Devin's hook up, and I was gonna keep it gangsta and make sure I fattened up his prison account, so his time in the hole would be a little easier to deal with. I hate it went down like it that, but Devin knew the gun was loaded when he picked it up.

Later that night while lying in my bunk trying to settle on a freaky thought to fall asleep to, the reality of my circumstance knocked me off that train of thought, bringing me face to face with the demons of my past. I looked up at the wall and tried to focus on the poster of Blac Chyna and her perfectly caked up ass, but the demons in my head weren't going anywhere.

My thoughts drifted to my father and what he must have endured. I wondered what it was like for pops to be cooped up in one of these concrete cages for twenty-three years straight— his life fucked off because he was trying to make a better future for my brother and me. Then my thoughts flowed to my brother, Wah, and I wondered what he was going through at that moment. Laid up in a coma and nobody there to comfort him, or ease the pain of his suffering. My heartbeat sped up when my thoughts ventured off and eventually landed on Miko, my ex-bitch. There was a time when I used to love her with every ounce of my existence, and the fact I loved her so deep like that made it that much more difficult to deal with. To know that the woman I made love to every day, whom I'd given my heart to unconditionally, was the same woman who caused so much chaos, angered me in a manner that I couldn't put into words. I was sleeping with the fuckin' enemy! My heart banged on my chest cavity like a prisoner trying to escape confinement. The hatred I felt for Miko was indescribable. She took away everything I ever loved on this earth, and then managed to snatch away my freedom in the process. *I seriously underestimated you, bitch. But you can best believe that if the opportunity ever presents itself, I am going to take pleasure in killing you, 'ho! I'ma beat you to death with my bare hands until you breathe your last breath, bitch!* I reveled in the thought of murdering Miko while trying to calm my heart from pounding so hard. I didn't know exactly what I was going to do to her if I ever got the chance. I just knew that whatever I did would be the worst pain she ever experienced, and even then it wouldn't be enough.

CHAPTER 3

Miko

Miko's caravan rolled into the warehouse and fanned out as planned before turning and facing the direction in which they came. Her thought process was, if it became necessary to make a hasty retreat, they would be as prepared as possible to swiftly exit the warehouse. The doors to the Yukon Denali on Miko's left opened, and a group of heavily armed goons spilled out and took up their prearranged positions. The doors on her right opened, and several more heavily armed hardheads poured out and posted up in strategically advantageous spots.

A small army of Colombian thugs stood statue-still with stern-faced determination while cradling automatic weapons. They stood guard around the champagne-colored Mercedes across from Miko. Wearing blank expressions, a smaller group of Colombians stood near a nondescript black van with large caliber guns in their possession. For a full minute that was the scene: Miko's heavily armed goons mean-mugging the group of equally heavily-armed Colombian thugs. Every man's alert eyes took in every detail as the opposing groups eye-balled one another suspiciously. They'd been doing the same song and dance every other month for the past year and a half, and there had never been a problem before. The money was never funny, and the product was always top-flight and exact. But this was the dope game, shit happened and things changed. Those who weren't properly prepared for those changes usually ended up six-feet deep with a bunch of bullets in their bodies. When millions of dollars were present and a truck holding hundreds of bricks were in the same room as a group of greedy-hearted, game-savvy, street savages, anything was subject to happen.

Miko sat comfortably in the backseat of the white X-5 Beamer, patiently waiting for her connection to show his face. In her mind, if something shady was in play on the Colombian's part, then it was a good chance the man calling that shot would not be present, or put himself in harm's way. Javier Mesas' absence would be the first sign that something shady was about to go down. She fluffed her hairdo and repositioned her long flowing silken locks, so it lay perfectly flat down her back. Her ever watchful eyes took in the landscape in front of her through the tinted windows. A small smile finally cracked through Miko's beautiful mask of seriousness when the rear door of the Mercedes opened.

Javier stepped out dipped in an expensive pinstriped black Giorgio Armani suit. A large platinum, diamond-faced Rolex watch weighed down his left wrist.

The intimation of a smile quickly disappeared, and she used her soft hands to iron out the rumples on the raspberry colored Herve Leger dress wrapped tightly around her voluptuous frame. She prepared to exit the X-5 Beamer. Anthony, her driver/bodyguard pulled the door open and waited dutifully with a hand on his heater. She stepped down onto the smooth surface of the shiny concrete and assembled herself. Head high, carriage upright, the queenpin took several elongated strides and met the Colombian kingpin at the midway point between their parked vehicles.

"Miko, it is always a pleasure." Javier extended his arm, and a devilish smile decorated his handsome, light-brown face.

"Likewise, Javier, the feeling is mutual." Miko took his hand and shook it firmly. She looked into his eyes, momentarily holding his stare. The handshake was brief, the greeting cordial. As soon as she released his hand, her eyes hardened and her sensuous mouth pinched tightly with seriousness. She quickly glanced over her shoulder and got Cream's attention. They exchanged a look, and with an imperceptible nod, a signal passed between the cousins.

"Cream, go take care of that." Her instructions were simple. Cream and two of his gunners made their way over to the van loaded with bricks. Her eyes returned to Javier's severe gaze.

"Suspect," she called to her other cousin, motioning him to move with two fingers, without ever taking her eyes off the Colombian drug lord. Suspect dutifully filled both of his hands with thick nylon straps and lugged two fully packed Louis Vuitton duffle bags until he was next to Miko. He placed the bags between the two drug bosses. "Two million dollars, Javier. Do we need to sit here and waste time counting it?" Miko asked with comical sarcasm.

The Colombian ignored her question and took a step forward until he was within arm's reach. He served her with a cocky smirk before bending at the knees and picking a duffle bag up in each hand, as if weighing them. His brows lifted, and the corner of his mouth curled into a sneer. "No, Miko, we don't have to count it. It feels like two million to me." His Spanish accent was thick, and his dark eyes danced full of daring joy. "Besides, if it wasn't two million dollars exactly, you know the repercussions." He took a step backward and put space between them.

Miko's posture stiffened, and her body language changed from one of calmness to one of displeasure. "I don't take kindly to veiled threats, Javier."

A slick, knowing grin briefly appeared on Javier's face before vanishing as fast as it had emerged. His posture changed as well, his body language reflecting hers. "That is not a veiled threat, Miko. Business is business. I don't make threats, I fulfill promises."

The two drug bosses stared one another down. The room in the huge warehouse quickly filled with tension. Cream and his gunners stopped counting bricks, and their hands touched hardware. The Colombian thugs stood up straighter and readjusted their artillery as well. Miko's entire squad got a little taller, and metal could be heard moving. Everybody's hand was on a weapon, every finger caressing a trigger.

Miko, confident in her squad of hitters, took a step closer and spoke evenly.

"Like I said, I don't take kindly to threats, Javier, so keep yours to yourself. My money count has never been in question, so are we doing business or not? Because right now you're wasting my time with all this posturing!" She spat the last word out as if a bug had just flown in her mouth.

Javier laughed softly at her boldness, then he wore that same cocky smirk. He knew his crew of killers was capable of eliminating hers if it came down to a gunfight. He enjoyed toying with the burgeoning queenpin's emotions; it added to the excitement.

"Fair enough, Miko. I can respect that. Tell your people to finish counting the product and load your truck up," he said aloud, before leaning closer and whispering, "If I've upset you, please allow me to make it up to you later over dinner." It was her turn to laugh and smile evilly.

"I don't mix business with pleasure, Javier. It tends to cloud judgment. Besides, I meant it when I told you that I don't take kindly to threats."

"Like I said, Miko, I don't make threats, I fulfill promises." They left it at a stalemate and stood with their arms folded as their people did their thing. Miko tolerated Javier's teasing because she knew what was to come later.

For the next twenty-five minutes, Cream and two of Miko's

gunners transferred the cargo in the van from one vehicle to another, until every kilo of cocaine was securely in place in the back of the Yukon Denali.

As previously planned, Miko and her entourage drove out of the warehouse in a straight line. The Denali full of gunners, the lead truck, and the other Denali full of drugs tucked in the middle with trigger-happy gunners guarding it with their lives. Miko, Cream, Suspect, and her driver brought up the rear in the X-5.

* * * * * *

"Oooh! Hell yeah, baby! Yes! Yes! Yes! Beat this pussy up, papi! Fuck me harder, baby! Hurt this pussy! Hurt this pussy good, you muthafucka! Fuck . . . Me . . . Hard . . . Er!" Miko's beautiful features were scrunched in an ugly sex face. Her expensively manicured hands gripped the headboard tight as she tooted her plump, light-skinned ass in the air and took the long, thick sex stick from the back, her pussy popping and squishing with the sounds of sticky sex juices. He slid in and out of her tight hole, glistening wet with her pussy sauce as he repeatedly rammed his rod into her, plunging into her depths with hard and violent thrusts of his hips. All ten thick inches was twisting her back out in a pleasurably painful manner. "Yes! Yes! Yes! Oooh, fuck yes! Get that shit, ma'fuckah! Get that shit good, papi! Aaagghhhh!" Miko screamed at the top of her lungs as Javier aggressively grudge-fucked her from the back.

"I gon' kill this pussy! I gon' kill this pussy! I gon' kill this pussy good, bitch!" Javier wound her long hair around his fist and slammed into her again and again as he threatened her with every stroke of his dick.

Miko creamed all over the Colombian drug boss's meat. While her body shook with joy, he pulled out of her gushy wet slit, shooting thick spurts of hot nut onto her soft, jiggly ass cheeks as he reached around and furiously rubbed her clit from the back. She looked over her shoulder and laughed teasingly before saying, "I told you I don't take kindly to threats, Javier."

The kingpin laughed along with her, admiring the exquisite beauty of his half-Creole half-Puerto Rican mistress. "And I told you that I don't make threats, Miko. I fulfill promises, mami." Having emptied his excitement on her, he suppressed his lust and thought about her adamant refusal to join forces with his cartel. "I wish you would reconsider my offer, Miko. We could make an unbeatable pair if you joined my team," he said, grabbing his cum-slicked dick and wiping it off with her underwear. Javier tossed the expensive undergarment onto the bed next to her, smiling mischievously.

She looked over at the sex-stained silk and lace panties and then up into Javier's impassive eyes before replying, "That's the problem with you, Javier. Like most men, you want to control everything. No offense, but I don't want to be on your team, boo. I want to have my own team, so I can call my own shots. I'ma boss bitch, Javier. I'm not the type of chick that takes orders from anybody, not even you." She stood and climbed into the soiled panties, immensely enjoying the wetness against her skin.

You're still young and naive to the ways of this wicked world, mamacita. One day I am going to have to show you that you don't have all of the answers like you think you do, mi amor, he thought as he finished getting dressed in silence. When he was done, he shoved his gun into his shoulder holster and watched her get dressed, shaking his head at an intense private thought. *You don't even know that you have a dirty rat within your own ranks. In due time you'll see that you would've been better off with me, if you live long enough.*

CHAPTER 4

Young Glock Gang

One by one tricked out whip after tricked out whip pulled up to the curb in front of the yellow house on La Paz Street. Mean-faced thugs with granite jawlines wearing some combination of green and black colored clothing slammed doors to old school Chevy classics. With thuggish strides, Jayquan, G-Mack, and Goldie strolled up the walkway leading to the heavy, black metal screen door.

A dark brown, grim-faced goon named Bony James opened the front door and greeted the gangstas one at a time with a thug hug. The four street-hardened Lincoln Park thugs, who referred to themselves as the Young Glock Gang, were now present and accounted for. Kush-filled blunts lay splayed out in a black glass bowl at the center of the coffee table along with bottles of Hennessy, Remy, Ciroc, and Patron. Lighters sparked fire to the tips of blunts while glasses of potent liquids emptied quickly before being hastily replenished.

After a few minutes of small talk and bullshit conversation about the latest videos of big booty bitches on Instagram, Bony James insisted on everyone's undivided attention. The 50 Cent lookalike stood in front of his fellow gang members and addressed the Young Glock Gang, one of Southeast San Diego's more sinister cliques.

"I asked y'all here today to discuss a matter of serious importance." He made eye contact with each of them. "If you been payin' any attention to how shit been goin' down lately, then it shouldn't come as a surprise to you that it's becoming harder and harder to move any type of weight in the Southeast Planet. If we ain't buying our work from Miko Dunbar, the new

19

bitch on the block, then we spending more for our shit. And it's moving hella slow because her people got fatter sacks and better product. She's squeezing us, y'all, and our pockets are choking to death as a result." The hard-bodied, heavily-tattooed gangsta pulled hard on his blunt, holding the weed smoke deep in his chest while his words sank in. Seconds later, he blew a white cloud out his mouth. He spoke passionately about the perceived disrespect for several more minutes before growing silent and opening the floor up to whoever wanted to voice their opinion.

Sporting a black khaki suit with a white tee underneath, Jayquan stood up and angrily volunteered his opinion with a swisher dangling from his lips.

"I feel you on that shit, Bony James." He turned his Green Bay Packers fitted hat that sat low over his eyes slightly to the right. "As hard as we had to grind to get this far in the game, it don't make sense that a no-name ass bitch come out of nowhere and start regulatin' the dope game." The wood floor creaked beneath the movement of his black Chuck Taylor's with the thick green laces that matched his belt.

G-Mack cleared his throat and injected his view into the conversation.

"You right, blood. That bitch came out of nowhere. Now she the biggest boss in the city, and she shittin' on us like we some fuckin' peons or somethin'." The pissed off scowl he wore alibi'd his feelings.

"That bitch Miko got shit on lock right now, so it's gon' be hella hard to uproot an organization with the type of manpower she got," the cool, calm, and collected Goldie said, showing his gold fronts. He turned the glass of Henny up and drained its remaining contents before pouring another. He was the chill one of the bunch.

Bony James looked at each one of his homies and donned a mask of rage as he prepared to go on his verbal tirade. He purposely exhaled his frustration before angrily punching his open palm with a heavy closed fist.

"That's exactly what the fuck I'm talkin' about! I don't give a fuck about no Miko Dunbar! Fuck her, and fuck those bitch ass bustas in her crew!" Bony James shouted, repeatedly pounding his fist. He stopped for a second and pulled a cigarette out of the Newport box, successfully firing the cancer stick up on his first try. "This is our ma'fuckin' city. These our blocks that bitch settin' shop up on, blood! I ain't going for it, and if any of you ma'fuckas is cool with how shit been goin' down, then you need to get the fuck up and get the fuck out my crib!" He puffed hard on the cigarette two more times and let the poisonous smoke pollute his respiratory system. Like a caged animal he paced back and forth while pulling deep on the cancer stick.

The uncomfortable silence worked in his favor. The other three thugs in the room were forced to confront and contemplate the reality of their circumstance. They were about to make life or death decisions that could not be undone once the gunplay popped off.

"I feel you on that shit, Bony," Jayquan spoke up and adjusted his Green Bay Packers fitted hat. "It's a classic squeeze move, homie. Put some shit out there that we can't compete with, and we either fall out the game or start fucking with her. We gonna end up holding onto our sacks until we starving in the game. Then we ain't gonna have much choice but to turn to that bitch if we wanna eat."

"I agree with you, Jayquan. That bitch is definitely shittin' on us, but I disagree with that last part of what you said, bruh." Goldie, the tight-eyed, light-skinned TI lookalike interjected, speaking in a low, even tone. His speech pattern was like a Jay-Z flow, cool and calm, relaxed.

Jayquan wore a perturbed look as he dug in his pocket in search of his lighter.

"Whatchu mean that last part? Whatchu talkin' 'bout, homie?" he asked and fired up again.

"The part where you say that we gonna end up holding onto our sacks or starving in the game if we don't fuck with her. We weren't raised to bow down to a bitch, or bust like a pipe under pressure. True, that 'ho Miko shittin' on us hella hard with them heavy ass sacks and them low ass prices. She is tryin' to starve us, no doubt, just like you said. But like I said, we ain't built bitch made!" Goldie handled his pistol and dropped the clip out. He studied the last of the sixteen hollow tips stuffed inside the 9-millimeter's magazine and pushed the clip back in, shaking his head up and down. "I'm with Bony James on this one. Fuck Miko Dunbar, and that fuck squad she surrounding herself with. All them bitch ass ma'fuckas can get it, you feel me? I'ma clack er' one of them faggots out the game!"

The usually reserved G-Mack was turnt up too. He downed his drink and slapped hands with Goldie. "That's what's up then, y'all! Let's go knock some fuckin' noodles out and get paid in the process!" Reserved or not, gunning an enemy down was something he grew up on, a lifestyle he was very comfortable with.

Bony James enjoyed how the drink and the trees were instigating the emotion in the room; their bloodlust was thick in the air. As a wicked grin creased his lips, he thought it was the perfect time to further arouse and agitate their anger. "We need to flip the script on them and put the heat on their asses, literally." Bony James snuffed the cigarette out in the ashtray before pushing it aside.

"Whatchu mean? Put the heat on 'em like how?" Jayquan asked.

"With some of these here." Bony James reached under the table and dragged a large black duffle bag out. He picked it up and set the bag down heavily on the table before unzipping it. One by one he reached inside the bag and pulled out brand spanking new MP5 .40 caliber assault rifles with semi/fully automatic capabilities. Each assault rifle came with foot-long banana clips and nylon shoulder straps that allowed the shooter to move around or run without fear of dropping the murder weapon. He handed a rifle to each of his cold-blooded cronies, smiling wider when their faces lit up with sinister pleasure. After everybody in the room had a weapon, he picked up the roll of black electrical tape, silently took two clips and started taping them together with opposite ends of each magazine exposed, allowing for a speedy reload and more than enough bullets to knock a herd of cattle down.

"That's what the fuck I'm talkin' 'bout! Where you get these bitches at?" Goldie coolly asked as he fondled the assault rifle affectionately, as if it were a pair of soft titties.

"Don't worry about where I got 'em. The point is we have 'em. We have the proper artillery necessary to go to war with that bitch Miko and her whole crew. The question is, are y'all prepared to do this gangsta shit to the death if need be, or are y'all gonna continue to sit back and let that bitch shit on us like the city is hers and not ours?" Bony James knew his well-timed jab would have the desired effect.

"Talk to us, Bony. You sound like you goin' somewhere with this, homie. Tell us what it do." Jayquan played with the MP5 like it was a toy, admiring the killing machine's light weight design.

Bony cleared his throat and said, "Well, it ain't no secret

that she got at least fifteen to twenty dope spots throughout the city, right?" Each man nodded. "And word on the streets is, the bitch got a few money houses too. Spots where workers count, wrap, and pack money into boxes on a weekly basis. I say we start makin' that bitch and her crew pay a stipend for doing business in these Southeast streets. This is our ma'fuckin' city! The Southeast Planet belongs to us!" Bony James had successfully tapped into the trio of thugs' pride and emotions, pushing buttons he knew would turn their savage gangsta all the way up.

Goldie rose up and stuck one of the newly taped double-clips into the magazine hole and rested the rifle against his left bicep in the crook of his arm, finger on the trigger and the barrel pointed at the ceiling.

"I'm witchu, Bony. We all witchu, and since you managed to secure some weaponry of this caliber, I assume you have a plan." He looked seriously into Bony James' cold black eyes.

All thirty-two of Bony's teeth were on display.

"I thought you'd never ask. You damn right I got a plan. I got a plan that can't fail, unless we fail to execute it."

"Run that shit then, Bony. Tell us what the deal is, so we can go lay some shit down!"

The room grew quiet, and the Young Glock Gang's ringleader took full advantage of the spotlight.

"I got a man on the inside who's not only supplying us with these weapons, he's also going to be supplying us with detailed information that will put us in a position to knock down that bitch Miko's dope spots, stash houses, and her money transport trucks. I'm talkin' dates, times, and routes, the whole nine yards!" He rubbed his rough palms together as if trying to start a fire, and then he grabbed the bottle of Patron. "If we play our cards right, we can all be rich beyond our wildest imaginations! We can get money like we ain't ever seen, y'all. Like we ain't ever even dreamed about having!" His face sported a victorious smile as he tipped the Patron bottle and splashed some drink into his glass. "It's going down tomorrow, y'all. We'll be jackin' our first stash house tomorrow night!" He picked the glass up and held it in his huge hand with his thick pinky finger sticking out. He proposed a toast. "In the words of the infamous Curtis Jackson: 'We gon' get rich or die tryin',' homies!" The other thugs in the room stood with a glass in their hands and got raucous, toasting to the thuggery that awaited them.

Bony James slowly put his glass to his lips and downed a couple mouthfuls of Patron. *I'm airin' out everybody in that stash house. I don't give a fuck if they armed or not! Fuck Miko Dunbar and everybody ridin' wit' her! I'm destroying that bitch's whole fuckin' empire!*

CHAPTER 5

Tiyatti

Every thug wasn't a bad person with an innate desire to wreak havoc and destruction on society. Every gangsta didn't have a dark heart with a single-mindedness that rotted and ruled their core value system. As is so often the case, many young brothas have only been exposed to an already broken world where the only tools they've been given to fix their broken lives are the ones handed down to them by people they erroneously consider as role models of their society. The pictures of success in their still young, unseeing eyes are the drug dealers, who pompously flaunt their ill-gained accomplishments in the face of struggling, common black men and women, who are the mortar that cements the community. Or the pimps and players and hood thugs and street-hardened gangstas who breed fear and command respect on the heels of it, as they demonstrate through blatant violent examples, that terror is power.

Tiyatti Jones was an ideal illustration of a young black man left with little choice but to embrace the street life and what it had to offer as a way of surviving. When a child is left alone to make grown folk decisions concerning matters of instant gratification, risks versus rewards, or decisions that will have a profound impact on the rest of his or her life, that child will almost always make the wrong choice, a choice that will lead them down a road few ever escape unscathed, if alive. Children are inherently attracted to 'shiny things.' Well, in the inner cities of America, the thugs, the hustlers, and the gangstas are the 'shining examples of success,' and like any other child in America, the children of the inner city are strongly attracted to the 'shiny things' they see most often.

The twenty-two-year-old high school dropout was forced to take on the colossal task of becoming the guardian and sole provider to his younger brother when their mother was unexpectedly killed in an automobile accident five years ago. At the time, Tiyatti was a seventeen-year-old straight 'A' student about to enter his senior year of high school. His circumstances forced him to drop out of high school, and he worked job after job while struggling to provide for his little brother, Devontay, who was twelve at the time of their mother's untimely death. But as is a common theme throughout America, Tiyatti was let go by his most recent job, and finding steady work without a GED or high school diploma was almost impossible. So he did what most other inner city kids did when faced with such hardship: he buckled under the pressure of being impoverished and destitute, and succumbed to the lure of the streets and its many avenues of ill-gotten success. The expectant father-to-be shared a two-bedroom apartment with Duchess, his pregnant girlfriend and his now seventeen-year-old younger brother, Devontay. Tiyatti loved his little brother more than anything on the face of this earth. He would protect him to the death if need be, and do everything in his power to ensure that his younger sibling escaped the ghetto unscathed and lived to realize his dream of becoming a professional athlete.

The bond and connection he shared with his girlfriend of five years was deep and enduring. She stood strong by his side and supported him every step of the way when he stumbled and struggled to cope with the sudden loss of his mother. Duchess was his strength at his weakest moment, his weakness when he was at his strongest point. She was his soul mate, the other half that made him whole. Often, she acted as a surrogate mother, providing Devontay with a motherly presence as he struggled to adapt to a life without his mother. Devontay and Duchess and their unborn child were Tiyatti's everything; without them he had nothing.

"Devontay, are you any closer to making up your mind, lil bro?" Tiyatti asked as he sliced off a square of butter and slapped it on his stack of pancakes. His stomach growled with anticipation when the thick chunk of butter started melting and soaking into the hot, fluffy flapjacks.

"Not really, Ty. I've narrowed it down to the top ten schools I wanna fuck with, but the more schools I eliminate from consideration, the harder this shit seem to get, bruh," he responded, revealing his angst at trying to settle on which college scholarship offer to accept.

"What you really need to do is watch your mouth, boy, and stop cussing so damn much," Duchess cut in, correcting his foul mouth and bad mannerisms at the breakfast table.

"That's right, baby. Get on his ass!" Tiyatti laughed and instigated the chastising exchange.

She turned and scolded her soon-to-be baby daddy as well. She pointed a finger at the love of her life and served him with a stern gaze. "You need to watch your mouth too, mister."

Devontay got a kick out of that. "Ah ha!" He laughed while fighting to keep his food from spraying out of his mouth.

"Whatever." Tiyatti shook off the two-front assault with a wave of the hand and refocused on his stack of pancakes.

Devontay recovered from his bout of laughter and said. "Real talk though, bruh, I think I'ma end up choosing USC, UCLA, Stanford, or Cal-Berkeley."

"Why's that?" Tiyatti cut his pancakes in squares and quizzed his little brother, a habit he practiced on a regular basis, believing that by making his little brother explain his thought process, it forced him to deliberate more seriously about his decision-making. Devontay was not only gifted athletically, he was also gifted intellectually, and Tiyatti wanted to make sure he maximized his brain power.

"Well, academically they all offer great opportunities, and the fact that they're all located on the West Coast allows me to stay closer to home. But the biggest factor in my decision-making is that all four of those schools agreed to let me play both football and basketball, whereas the other big name schools are adamant that I only play one sport."

"That's what's up, Dee. I'm glad to know that your decision will be a well thought out and carefully considered one." Tiyatti expressed his heartfelt pride and joy toward his little brother.

Duchess interjected herself into the conversation and reminded him of reality for the umpteenth time. "The main thing is that you get the best education possible, Devontay, because the pros are not guaranteed, but having a good education guarantees that you'll have a brighter future ahead of you."

Tiyatti stood and pulled her chair out. "Get off your feet for a while and feed my seed. Sit down and eat something, baby." He massaged her neck and shoulders affectionately after she took her seat at the table.

For the next thirty minutes they ate and conversed as a family unit, before Devontay excused himself and got ready to go to school. He grabbed his book bag and walked to Tiyatti's side of the table. "Stay sucka free, Dee. I love you, boy!" Tiyatti slapped hands with his little brother and hugged him hard before Devontay kissed Duchess on the cheek and headed out the door.

"Be careful, Devontay, and stay out of trouble," Duchess yelled from the kitchen before the door closed. "I'm really proud of him." Duchess sighed and murmured after Tiyatti walked up behind her and swallowed her up in a hug while she remained sitting. He helped her to her feet and took the plate from her hands.

"I'm proud of him, too. I can't wait to see the first time he steps foot on that college football field. It's all he ever talks about." Tiyatti cleared the table and helped her with the dishes. When they finished putting the dishes in the dishwasher, he dried his hands off and kissed her neck, pulling on her earlobe with his lips before stuffing his tongue in her ear.

"Don't start a fire that you ain't going to put out, Tiyatti." Duchess giggled and pushed her plump ass back against his growing hardness. His excitement pressed against her, and she leaned her head back until it rested on his chest, exposing her slender neck to the teasing titillations of his magical tongue. Tiyatti cupped her swollen, braless breasts with both hands and tenderly twisted her extra-sensitive engorged nipples through the black and gold embroidered T-shirt with his fingers. His mouth attacked her neck with affectionate licks and kisses followed by soft, succulent wet sucks.

"Ummmmhh," she moaned her approval and submitted to his oral manipulations. She felt his erection poke her ass cheek and the flood gates to her flower opened up. *Ooh, he finna twist my back out!* she thought lustfully and squeezed her pussy muscles in an attempt to contain her joy.

Tiyatti was a patient and considerate lover, always cognizant of her every sensuous want and whim. He knew what buttons to touch, when to touch those buttons, and exactly in which way those buttons needed to be touched.

"Let's take this to the bedroom, baby," he told her after releasing her nipples and scooping her up into his arms. Gently laying her on the king-sized bed, he went about setting the scene up to compliment the mood: a slow jam mix tape CD, vanilla scented candles that he knew she loved, following that up with a slow, deliberate strip tease he was sure would get her juices flowing. He removed every article of her clothing and stood naked at the foot of their bed with his dick on hard. His swollen manhood throbbed and pulsated with pleasure at the sight of her exquisite nakedness. Tiyatti tugged on his elongated love muscle and teased her until she was hot with lust and beside herself with desire.

"Make love to me, Ty!" she begged while covering her stomach with both hands.

Knowing she was self-conscious about her body while struggling to adjust to her baby bump and the newly added weight that came with pregnancy, Tiyatti made it a point to move her hands and show some love to the small swell of her stomach. He lovingly caressed the surface of her skin with the rims of his fingertips, tracing heart-shaped patterns around her belly-button. He climbed further up onto the bed and slowly lowered his head to her breast, taking her swollen right nipple into his mouth.

"Ooh yes, Tiyatti!" His tongue crisscrossed back and forth over her ultra-sensitive bud as he softly sucked on the tip of her titty. *Umm, she tastes so good!* he thought as he moved over to give her left titty some attention. His longest finger dipped into the hot, wet slit between her thighs, and he leisurely poked her passion pit as his thumb contacted her clit and tormented her freakiness. When she purred aloud, he stuck a second finger in her and slowly moved it in and out as his mouth performed magic tricks on her tit. Excited, Duchess exhaled and threw her head back onto the fluffy pillows behind her. She spread her legs wider and thrust her hips toward his fingers. After several minutes of his fingers playing in her pussy like a classical pianist, his weight shifted and he repositioned himself. Within seconds, Tiyatti's head was between her thighs tasting her wet joy and swallowing her creamy excitement. His tongue flickered wildly all over, in, and around her soaking wet flower as his fingers furiously stabbed in and out of her sweet spot. Her passion poured out profusely, and he eagerly lapped up every drop of her juice as he alternated his fingers and tongue.

"Do it to me, Tiyatti! Please, baby, make love to this pussy!" Duchess cried out as she busted her first nut, her tall luscious frame shaking as she erupted and exploded in ecstasy. R. Kelly's "Marry the Pussy" played as Tiyatti climbed higher and maneuvered his way between her legs. The swollen head of his full grown erection split her lips open and stretched her pink folds wide. Duchess loved how his long, thick dick curled slightly to the left. "Ungh!" she grunted loudly as he pushed it up in her hella slow, his dick head rubbing up against areas in her pussy that her fingers had never touched. When his curved dick hit rock bottom, she knew for a fact he had gone where no other man would ever go.

After making passionate love for the better part of the morning, they lay cuddling and conversing for a while, until Tiyatti extracted his body from her loving clutches and went to run some bath water. He washed every inch of her body with painstaking affection. When he finished with her, she lovingly returned the favor. Later, after drying off and retreating to the bedroom, he rubbed her feet and massaged her entire frame with Ambi Shea and Cocoa Butter the same way that he made love to her, slow, firm, and attentive to every inch of her womanly being.

Once fully dressed, he kissed her on the lips, checked his pistol one last time, and stuck the Ruger in his waistband.

"Be safe, baby," she whispered against his lips and hugged him tight.

"No doubt, ma." He kissed her again before heading out the door. *Another day in this wild ass world*, he thought after closing the front door behind him while looking up into the cloudless sky and squinting at the sun. "Please God, get me through today and bring me back home to my family," he prayed under his breath as he made his way toward the root beer brown Chrysler 300. He tucked the Ruger under the driver's seat and altered his state of mind, transforming from loving family man to hard-hearted thug. His foot pressed down on the gas, and he headed in the direction of one of Miko's dope spots. *I hope like hell I don't catch a case or have to take a life today.*

CHAPTER 6

Wahdatah

My heart beat faster when I thought of the beautiful woman I'd met on a fluke and fallen in love with as if it were destined. I remembered squeezing Tocarra's fingers eighteen months ago. I remembered the occasion well because it was the first time since I'd been shot by that bitch Miko that my body responded to a command from my brain.

A foreboding enveloped my essence when Tocarra stopped showing up at my bedside. I remembered having a premonition that something bad had happened to her. The feeling was so profound that it negatively impacted my recovery efforts. Once she stopped showing up, it's almost as if my body stopped fighting, and my will had vanished. Or at least that's how I felt inside. Mentally it took a lot out of me, and for a while I lost my resolve to fight. There were times when I begged death to come and claim my body. I welcomed the world of peace and tranquility that a comatose state offered. No stress, no fears, no worries. Just breathe and live until I died. But that mindset only lasted for a minute. It was only a matter of time before I reminded myself that I was a strong-hearted black man with a passionate desire to live. When it became clear to me that Tocarra wasn't coming back, I accepted that unfortunate fact and made up my mind to bounce back on my own, solo bolo. I soon discovered a strong will to recover and conquer my tragic circumstances. Killing Miko became my most deeply rooted motivating factor.

As I rewound my mental tape and pushed play on my past, images of that dirty bitch Miko busting shots at me angered my spirit. I thought about her words the day Tocarra played the

35

tape in my ear. That rotten-hearted 'ho had the nerve to brag about how she murdered my mama! How she had Drape killed! And then her punk ass boasted about framing my brother on a bogus double murder beef!

I'd been lying in this bed for the longest time feeling so many different things, suffering through many excruciating emotions. The most agonizing thing I'd been forced to endure, outside of missing Tocarra, was the helplessness that came in waves some days. To not have any control of what's going on in the world around me was beyond challenging.

Right now my body couldn't feel anything, but I was fully aware of the presence of people and their conversations, yet I couldn't do a damn thing about it. That's the worst kind of suffering. All day, every day, I lay not having a clue whether it's day or night until one of the nurses said something, revealing the mystery of time.

A big ass tube in my stomach fed my system and sustained me. And to add insult to injury, I was wearing a fucking diaper, man! I was shitting and pissing on myself on a daily basis because I didn't have control of my bowels. The nurses usually bathed me afterward, and then they repositioned me from time to time to keep me from developing bedores. I heard one of the nurses explaining that to one of the interns some time ago.

I didn't know if I should love Tocarra or hate her. *Did she abandon me and leave me for dead because she couldn't cope with my current circumstances? Or did something happen to her that prevented her from being by my bedside like she used to?* Before, her presence gave me a strength that I can't put into words. Now her absence had taken something out of me. *Is my condition that fucked up? Is my situation so bad that she can't see herself standing by my side and supporting me under these circumstances? What's going on with Shug? Is he* dead? Is he alive? Is he in the pen? I miss my brother hella bad!* The opportunity of getting to know him after all those years of beefing and being bitter enemies was stolen from us, taken away by that janky ass bitch, Miko. *Why the hell did my father ever have to steal that money in the first place? If he hadn't done that shit, my mother would still be alive! Shug's mother would still be alive! My granny would still be alive! We would've had a normal childhood and lived a regular fuckin' life like everybody else!*

For a minute I became angry at my father. But then I thought about it on a deeper level; just like I couldn't step away from the game when I knew better, he probably couldn't step away from it either. So I really couldn't blame him for doing what he felt like he had to do back in the day. I guess being a thug was in our DNA.

My thoughts kept flashing back to the world of 'what ifs,' and I wondered what if my father had never gone to prison? How different would my life have been? How different would Shug's life have been? What if my granny were still alive? She would've loved Shug! It would have been one of her greatest joys getting to know her only other grandchild. What if Tocarra and I had just bounced with my half of the five million and the briefcase full of bling? How different would our lives have turned out had we gotten out the game and gone legit? My 'what if' finally came to rest on Miko and conquering this coma.

After all the pain and death and suffering that led to this shit, would I be able to walk away from this thug life and let bygones be bygones? Would I be able to forgive that bitch Miko for everything she'd done to my family and me? Not a ma'fuckin' snowball's chance in hell! *If I ever come up out of this coma, and I get the chance to do something to you, Miko,*

I am going to harm you in the worst way possible and personally put a bullet in your head when I'm finished!

I don't know if people understand it, but being in this coma is like never falling asleep while living in an ongoing dream or nightmare, depending on my train of thought. It's like floating in a state of awareness that I am powerless over. My mind is awake every minute of every day, yet I dream and have nightmares that leave me hella thrilled or truly terrified. Dreams that are so vivid, I honestly think I ain't in a coma anymore, and my nightmares are so real they scare the shit out of me, literally.

Being comatose is like being a prisoner in a cruelly designed prism of pain; painful thoughts, painful memories, and pain at the possibility of never waking. Having to suffer like this is the worst type of misery imaginable, because even on my best day I still know that I am at my worst. Absolute helplessness. *Maybe if I find a way to hold my breath long enough, I will just fade away.* I tried to hold my breath to see if it would work.

CHAPTER 7

Baby Shug

The po-pos did what they normally did after an inmate was stabbed or killed. They questioned everybody who might've seen something or heard about it and attempted to elicit information out of them, but cats on the yard knew better than to answer any of those questions with anything other than: I didn't see nothing; I didn't hear nothing; or I don't know nothing. So that's exactly what the po-po came up with, nothing.

The institutional lockdown was lifted, and the prison's program went back to normal. I passed on chow when they called breakfast and climbed off my bunk. Then I stretched my frame with a long ass yawn before walking over to the toilet and pissing for damn near a full minute. After washing my hands and face and then brushing my teeth, I decided to start cleaning the cell. I rolled my mattress up and used a towel to sweep the floor, then soaped that same towel up and began washing the floor. I wiped the walls down until the entire concrete cage was spotless and as clean as I could get it. My cell was my sanctuary, and it was mandatory that the place where I rested my head was clean and sanitized; it didn't matter if I was on the streets or in prison.

Once I put everything back into place, I stood in front of the mirror and stared at the man looking back at me. After a few moments of contemplation, I decided I needed a fresh line to tighten up the edges around my waves. I made a mental note to holla at the building barber and set up an appointment. I set four chili-flavored Top Ramen noodles along with two brand new razors on the locker as a reminder, in case I got too busy during the day and forgot. Checking my watch and realizing I had another hour or so before morning yard opened, I put on my charcoal gray mesh basketball shorts and all-white Nikes and started knocking out sets of push-ups, sit-ups, and other exercises that kept my frame as solid as a rock.

Just because I was in the penitentiary didn't mean the world stopped spinning. Life went on; haters still hated and needed to get hands laid on them. The drama never stopped. In fact, it only got worse behind these walls where drugs flowed freely and the hatred ran deep. Cell phones were commonplace, and convicts gambled on everything from table games and sports to how long a suspect individual would last on the yard before somebody broke his ass off with the steel and poked him full of holes. Physically, I was solid. Mentally, I was forcing myself to endure my circumstance and handle it like a good soldier was supposed to. Having served time in prison before, I knew how vital it was to develop and maintain some sort of daily structure. It kept me from going off the deep end, or being forced to go upside another convict's head for violating my personal space. Having a day to day routine made my time go by faster. It also kept me away from most of the bullshit that jumped off in prison. I guess having something to do rather than looking for something to do made the time quicken its seconds. At least that's how it worked for me; the situation with the mean-mugger was an isolated incident.

I sat down on my rolled up mattress and leaned back against the back wall of the cell and cracked open the book I'd been reading to help the time pass during lockdown. *The Adventures of Ghetto Sam* by Kwame Teague was my preferred book of the week. Minutes later, I was in the middle of turning a page when the cell door popped open, and a warning flashed through my mind. *Get on yo' gangsta, Shug!* I was instantly on my feet, ready for whatever. The cell door slowly slid open, and a young, light-skinned dude stood on the other side of the doorway with a bedroll in the crook of his arm and a hesitant, somewhat uncertain expression.

A new arrival! I ain't finna have no bitch-made ma'fucka living up in the cell with me! This cat look lightweight spooked, I thought. *I need to see what he's built like, find out if he's gangsta or a pussy.* I put my mean-mug on, turning my thug up and turning my understanding down to zero. *If he a Blood he ain't coming up in this cell wit' me! We gon' resolve that on the spot!* I declared, before opening my mouth and finding out.

"What's up? Where you from, cuz?"

He dropped the bedroll and kicked it into the cell, then took a step forward and closed the door behind him. "I don't bang, bruh, and on some real shit, I ain't looking for no drama. But if you feel like you need that, then I ain't turnin' down no fades, homie."

I like that! He ain't scary, and he seems like he solid. I was impressed with the heart he showed. I liked the fact that he didn't buckle up and fall back in fear. His actions and his reaction told me for the moment that he wasn't a coward, and I respected that. But I still wasn't convinced about his overall get down. In due time, if there was something foul or faulty in him, it would definitely come up out of him. But until then, I decided to give the youngster the benefit of the doubt and let his true colors show through his conduct. I stuck my hand out and offered it to him.

"Calm down, killa. It's all good. If you ain't looking for any drama, then you ain't going to find none, at least not up in here. They call me Baby Shug. What they call you, bruh?"

He looked into my face, sizing me up. I could tell his mind

was racing, trying to figure out my level of sincerity, while assessing how much of a threat I posed. I understood exactly what he was going through because I went through that same kind of shit during my first bid in the joint. His body language calmed down a little bit, but his eyes continued to nervously try to read mine.

"Khory. They call me Khory." That was all he offered, so I went ahead and steered the conversation. It was my way of breaking the ice and helping the new kid relax a little more.

"As you can see, I got the bottom bunk, so the top bunk is all you, dawg. Go ahead and do your thang, Khory. I'ma get out your way and let you get your rack right." I pushed past him and posted up by the door, so he could have some space while he fixed his bunk up.

After making his bunk and jumping up on his rack, he put his tough face on and acted as if he was staring at the ceiling, minding his business.

"If we gon' be livin' up in this cell together, bruh, we need to establish an understanding out the gate. It's like this with me, Khory: you all good with me until your actions show that you ain't no good to me." I looked at his empty locker, then back into his eyes. "You ain't got no property or whatever, so until you get on your feet, feel free to watch my TV or bump the sounds, you feel me? Closed mouths don't get fed, so if you hungry speak on it, you dig? I got noodles and a gang of zoom-zooms and wham-whams, plus some other shit to snack on, so go ahead and help yourself, homie. All I ask is that you respect my shit and don't disrespect my shit and we good folks." I was about to turn away when a thought occurred. "Oh, and every other day it's your turn to clean the cell. I already cleaned it today. I'll hit it again tomorrow to show you how it go, and the next day it's your turn, you feel me?" Based on his expression, he hadn't expected me to show him that type of hospitality and structure. I guess all those scary ass prison stories he heard when he was in the county jail didn't prepare him for that. It was my way of teaching him how to do his time the right way, respect for self and others. For lack of a better description, he was speechless, so I kept talking. "It's nothin', my dude. Real talk, that's how real ma'fuckas get down. There ain't any strings attached to none of this shit." I assured him it wasn't a set-up, and then I sat back on my rolled up mattress and went back to reading *The Adventures of Ghetto Sam.*

"That's what's up. I appreciate it, bruh," he said in a low voice after a few seconds passed. I could tell he wasn't convinced that it wasn't some type of shady scam.

I marked my page and asked, "Do you read?"

After a brief pause he answered, "Yeah, I know how to read."

"Well, I got a few books down there in my locker if you wanna read something. Go ahead and get your read on, bruh." I sat on the hard, steel edge of my bunk and leaned over toward the locker and started fingering some of the books I'd managed to get hold of since hitting the yard. "I got books for the brain like *48 Laws of Power, The Art of War, The Art of Seduction, Malcolm X, Roots,* and *Think and Grow Rich.* But if you into the urban book thang, I got a few good reads: *White Lines* by Tracy Brown, *Justify My Thug* and *Thug Matrimony* by Wahida Clark, *The Coldest Winter Ever* by Sistah Souljah, and *Torn* by Keisha Ervin, that book go! Plus this book I'm reading now by Kwame Teague and a few other books I got out on the line so the homies can get they read on. This is my lil library down here, so whenever you want to feed your brain, it's good, bruh. Go ahead and do your thang."

A few minutes later, the cell door popped open again for

yard call. I grabbed my workout gloves and bounced outside to go do my thug thang: blow trees with the homies, bust down with my workout partner, and walk a few laps with my comrades and tell war stories, or listen to somebody else tell a gang of lies. As soon as the sally port door opened, and I stepped foot out on the yard, I got bum-rushed by a group of hard-faced, granite-jawed gangstas with mean mugs and angry dispositions.

"You did yo thang on that ma'fucka, Baby Shug!"

"You banged the fuck outta that fool, cuz!"

"You do know that they had to life-flight that bitch ass fool up outta the prison, right? That shit was hella savage, cuz!"

A clique of my closest Crip homies surrounded me and showed me love with celebratory handshakes and hugs. They were hella turnt up about the sticking that got the institution put on lock down. Since they lived in other buildings, we didn't get a chance to see each other, or holla while we were on lock down, so it was always a reunion after shit like that popped off.

We mobbed around the yard in a thick crowd like a pack of wolves. The other animals inside the steel and concrete jungle understood clearly that we weren't the ones to be fucked with, because fucking with one of us could get you flat-lined or flown up out the penitentiary on that life-flight chopper, a helicopter ride no convict wanted to take. While my wolf pack and I were spinning laps around the yard, I noticed a LA Crip called Droop Loc watching me a little too closely. It seemed he was studying me, or sizing me up. I returned his gaze and mugged him from a distance. *If you lookin' for some drama, I'ma give you more than you can handle, ma'fucka!* I thought, eyeing him from across the yard while mobbing in the midst of my crew of Crips.

CHAPTER 8

Tiyatti

"I don't feel too good, Ty. My stomach hurts, and I feel weak." Duchess clutched her belly with both hands and leaned into Tiyatti's body, her forehead lay against his chest as tears streamed down her face.

Oh shit! My baby! Please God, don't let anything happen to my baby! "I'm taking you to the doctor. Sit down, baby. I'll be right back." Inwardly, Tiyatti panicked, but outwardly, he exuded a picture of calm. Duchess was four months pregnant, and it was their first pregnancy. He wasn't taking any chances. He hurried off into their bedroom and grabbed her jacket, a blanket, a pillow, and her purse. He entered the living room and set the items on the sofa next to Duchess. "I'll be back in a minute, baby girl, okay? Just breathe easy and relax, ma." He lightly tapped the knuckle of his index finger against Devontay's bedroom door. Tiyatti twisted the knob and opened it before his little brother could respond. "Lil bruh, Duchess ain't feeling too good, so I'ma run her to the doctor real quick to see what's up? Are you straight?"

"Yeah, I'm straight. Is she a'ight, Ty?" Devontay asked with concern. He sat up and wiped the sleep from his eyes and tried to adjust to the sudden disruption of his peaceful slumber.

"She's crying and says that her stomach is hurting. Make sure you get to school on time, Devontay, a'ight? Here, take this and stay out of trouble, lil bruh. Hit me on the cell when you leave the house, okay?" Tiyatti peeled off a twenty dollar bill and tossed it on the nightstand next to Devontay's bed. "I love you, bruh." He roughly rubbed Devontay's uncombed head and turned to bounce.

45

"I love you too, Ty," Devontay told him and dove back under the blankets trying to catch up to the dream that had him going a few minutes ago.

Tiyatti ran the stuff he had gathered earlier out to the car, then came back and carefully escorted Duchess to the root beer brown Chrysler 300 sitting at the curb. He had one arm around her waist and the other one at her elbow holding her up for support. The weight of her body pressed against his.

"Aagghh!" she grunted in agony when a streak of pain shot through her abdomen.

Twenty minutes later they were sitting in the waiting room at the doctor's office. Twenty minutes after that, they were walking hand in hand out of the doctor's office.

"I am so sorry, baby. I didn't mean to scare you like that, Ty." Duchess buried her head under his arm and covered her face with her jacket, embarrassed.

"Don't trip, baby. It's a'ight, ma. The main thing is that you and our baby are okay." Tiyatti leaned down and kissed her on the top of her head, then pulled her closer.

"I'm so embarrassed though, babe. I had you all shook up over me having a bad case of some damn gas!" She said it in a way that let him know she was hella embarrassed.

It was serious, but he didn't want her to be too hard on herself and get to feeling like she couldn't open her mouth if something similar happened again.

"Better to be safe than sorry, ma. I'd do it again every time, Duchess." He opened the passenger side door and helped her into the Chrysler 300. He knew that humor was something that almost always eased the tension between them whenever it got thick. "Pppffffttt!" He made a farting sound with his mouth before slamming the car door shut. He burst into a fit of laughter.

"Forget you, Ty. That's not funny!" Duchess tried to poke her lips out and pout but couldn't hold back her laughter. She burst into a hard laugh that bent her in half and made her eyes tear up. "You ain't right, Tiyatti Jones. You ain't right at all! For real, you are so stupid for that one." She was barely able to get the words out.

He pushed the whip out of the medical complex and merged into traffic. When he got on the straightaway, he touched a button on the dash and Beyoncé's soulful voice filled the car up with a heart-stirring vocal.

Devontay hit him on his cell when he was ten minutes away from the house. They spoke for a minute and said their good-byes. Devontay was on his way to school, and Tiyatti had to go to work in an hour.

After he asked Duchess if she was okay for the umpteenth time, she damn near had to force him to leave the house. She assured him that she would be okay and insisted he take his ass to work. They had bills to pay, a baby on the way, and three hungry mouths to feed. Gas costs money, and the rent was $1,200 a month, and it seemed as if a new bill showed up in the mailbox every other day. They were trying to bank as much money as possible.

Duchess didn't necessarily like the fact that Tiyatti over extended himself for his little brother. It was something they had talked about before, but she resigned herself to the fact that he wasn't budging on his position. Tiyatti felt a huge sense of responsibility when it came to his brother. Devontay was his last living relative, and he felt it was his duty to protect and provide for him. After their mother died, Duchess was by Tiyatti's side every step of the way, so she witnessed his feelings of helplessness firsthand as he watched Devontay go through an agonizing emotional anguish that nearly broke his mental. Tiyatti watched his brother almost crack under the strain of losing their mother. They never knew their father growing up, so Tiyatti assumed that role early as a teenager and became the man of the house long before a young boy should have to take on a responsibility of that magnitude. But he did it and he did it well.

After being laid off, Tiyatti was left with either collecting an unemployment check that did nothing as far as bettering their circumstances, stealing for a meal in order to survive, or taking his chances in the streets. He chose the latter, and the latter currently had him posted up on the block with a Ruger on his hip, providing lookout/security for one of the smaller dope houses under the umbrella of Miko Dunbar's drug empire. He chewed on a Dorito tortilla chip with slow deliberation and sucked the salsa verde flavor off his fingertips. His light brown eyes critically scanned the entire vicinity around the dope spot. He squinted against the glare of the sun and zeroed in on the tall, skinny brotha half-staggering up the narrow walkway leading to the crack house's front door. The dude was about twenty yards away from the front door digging in his pockets when Tiyatti set the bag of Doritos down and reached for the Ruger. He took in the man's appearance and sized him up, evaluating the threat level he represented. *Raggedy ass mismatched clothes that's hella dirty and a full head of nappy ass hair. Beat up ass Adidas tennis shoes, worn on the sides with holes in 'em and no socks on. White lips hella parched, and his tongue keep darting out trying to keep 'em moist.* The tall, skinny dude's appearance screamed drug addict, but looks could be deceiving, so Tiyatti kept watching him. *The eyes tell the truth,* he thought and looked into the eyes of the approaching figure, at which point he made his final assessment. *Bloodshot eyes never seeming to focus on any one thing while constantly blinking for clarity; definitely a dope fiend.* He ain't no threat, Tiyatti concluded. He held the Ruger in his paw just in case. Even a desperate, unarmed dope fiend could find the courage to run up on a dope spot and chance stealing a sack rather than buying a rock.

The fiend purchased a ten dollar dose of death, then turned and scurried off in the direction of the nearest hiding spot, so he could go beam himself up, all the while never knowing that a Ruger with a full clip had been aimed at his back as he did his drug addict business.

The dope spot wasn't as congested with crackhead traffic like it normally was, but Tiyatti's eyes never stopped observing his surroundings. He stuffed another Dorito in his mouth, and inconspicuously patrolled the perimeter out of his peripheral. The Ruger under his hoodie was always at the ready.

A grimy cat named Nario approached from the same direction the crackhead had just left. Tiyatti shrugged and stuffed another tortilla chip in his mouth, chewing on it slowly as he watched the stocky built Nario walk toward him with an exaggerated limp and his arms swinging like George Jefferson's.

"What's hadnin' wit' it, Tiyatti?" he asked when he was within five feet of Tiyatti.

Corny ass clown! "Ain't nothin' hadnin' wit' it, Nario. Same shit different toilet, bruh. Why? Whatchu got goin' on?" He knew the only reason Nario was speaking to him was to feel him out and see what caliber of thug he was. He didn't like entertaining Nario, but in order to keep the hater shit to a minimum, he indulged the shady-type thug with the shifty eyes, intent on keeping the conversation short.

"Nothin', just finna go make this pickup and get this money ready for Cream and them before they show up and start stuntin'."

"Go 'head and handle your business then, bruh. Don't let me hold you up, playa," Tiyatti replied, wanting to shake the fake thug as fast as possible.

"A'ight then, I'll see you later. Stay up and keep it real, bruh," Nario told him, before heading to the dope house.

Nario made a similar trip to all of the other dope houses in the neighborhood, collecting money from each one before counting it, bagging it up, and having it ready for Miko's two cousins, Cream and Suspect, when they stopped by to pick it up. It was a weekly ritual.

If somebody ever wanted to stick Miko for a grip of cheese, it wouldn't be hard to do. They too confident in their gangsta . . . thinking won't nobody jack 'em 'cause they got the whole city shook up. Shit, if I ever needed to hit a lick and get major paid . . . Tiyatti forced the theory out of his mind before it became more than just a thought. He stuffed another chip into his mouth before turning the bag up and drinking the tortilla crumbs hiding in the corner of the bag. *On the real though, it would be easy as hell to jack her for a grip of cheese.* He couldn't help but finish the bold thought as he balled up the empty bag and tossed it on the ground near his feet.

CHAPTER 9

Young Glock Gang

♫ *Somebody gotta die, if I go, you gotta go, somebody gotta die, let the gunshots blow*

Somebody gotta die, nobody gotta know, that I killed yo' ass in the mix, bitch ♫

Biggie Smalls' "Somebody's Gotta Die" quietly beat through the Pathfinder's Bose sound system while the four goons sat behind the tinted windows and filled the car with kush smoke.

"Damn, homie, this shit smell like it's some crucial!" G-Mack announced from the backseat, as he clutched the freshly lit blunt and put it to his lips. Two tokes later, he was passing it to his left, squeezing his nostrils shut trying to hold the Granddaddy Kush in his chest as long as his lungs would allow. He blew a cloud of smoke into the air, then coughed the rest of it out into the top of his balled up fist.

"Man the fuck up back there!" Bony James clowned from behind the steering wheel.

"Fuck you, Bony! This shit is bomb, blood!" G-Mack shot back between coughs.

"He ain't lyin' 'bout that!" Jayquan agreed, before hitting the blunt and holding a chest full of the Granddaddy Kush smoke in. He too blew out a line of white smoke and succumbed to an uncontrollable fit of coughing.

"Bitch ass pussies! Y'all hella soft!" Bony James was on them with jokes.

When the blunt made its way around to Bony's hand, all eyes were on him. He took a deep puff and held it hostage in his chest for a few seconds before releasing it. His eyes gleamed wet with pride as he took another puff, this time a stronger and longer puff than the last one. He swelled his chest up and held the second puff captive in his chest cavity for as long as he could, then breathlessly blew out what remained. At the end of his exhale, he started coughing hard and the other goons in the Pathfinder erupted into a raucous bout of laughter.

"Bitch ass ma'fucka!" all three of them yelled in unison. Uncontrollable laughter filled the SUV, mixing with the thick fog of kush smoke swimming in the limited space around the four thugs. Biggie Smalls was still making death threats through the speakers as the Pathfinder pulled off and headed across town en route to one of Miko's more richly supplied stash houses.

Twenty minutes later, Bony James eased up to the curb half a block away from their intended target and shut the engine down, killing the music. Apprehensive silence filled the tight space, and the leather screamed out under the weight of the four heavily-armed restless gangstas.

Bony James put the headrest in a chokehold when he turned toward the backseat to look at G-Mack and Jayquan. Goldie turned sideways in the passenger seat and faced the others as well.

"Check it, y'all. This is the real deal now. It's do or die when we run up in this ma'fucka, so let's be the ones doin' the doin' and not the dyin'. We been over it a hundred times, but you can never be too careful, so let's run that shit again and go over our assignments." He made eye contact with his Glock Gang cohorts and spoke in a loud whisper. "My guy on the inside said there are four workers in the stash house. He said there are only two bedrooms, both of which are decoys; the rooms don't have any work in 'em. All the work is underground in a basement that can only be entered through a trapdoor in the kitchen. There are six concrete steps leading down to the basement where one of the workers always stays guarding the product. Based on what my guy said, he doesn't come up for food or water, but he does come up to use the bathroom. Is y'all wit' me so far?" Bony James asked the other three and stared intensely into each set of eyes.

"Yup," Goldie said, nodding and licking his dry lips.

"Yeah dat," Jayquan replied much the same, swallowing his nervousness and stilling himself for the murderous campaign.

G-Mack mumbled, "Fo' sho'," while cracking his knuckles and twisting the tension out of his neck.

Bony James pulled out his scribbled sketched version of the house's blueprints.

"Okay then, this is how we gon' enter. On the roof there's a boarded up window that leads to the attic upstairs. The attic opens near the end of the hallway before the two bedrooms and farthest away from the living room and kitchen area where the other three workers are likely to be. It ain't any guarantees though where those fools might be once we get up in there. One of 'em could be in the bathroom taking a dump. One of 'em could be in one of the bedrooms asleep. It ain't no tellin', so be ready for anything." Bony James stopped talking for a second and looked into each one of his homeboys' faces. He coughed in his hand and cleared his throat.

"We ain't takin' prisoners or holdin' no hostages. We killin' everybody in that ma'fucka, you feel me? Any ma'fucka in there who ain't one of us gots to get it, no exceptions! Are there any questions?" he asked.

"Yeah, I got a question, what if it's some 'hos up in there with them?" Jayquan posed a valid question.

"Then they gots to get it too. No exceptions mean no exceptions! 'Hos make good witnesses on the stand too!" Bony

James answered coldly, responding with what to him was an equally valid point. Everybody in the Pathfinder mumbled their understanding and donned grim expressions.

That's right, put ya murder masks on because we killin' some ma'fuckas tonight! Bony James thought.

"Once we smack everybody in the house, we gon' use the MP5s on the boy in the basement, then we gon' load up the duffle bags and get the fuck on." He looked at Goldie and said, "Goldie, stay out here in the Pathfinder until I call you. When I call I want you to bring the truck up to the house, that way we don't have to make a gang of trips back and forth." When Goldie nodded with understanding, Bony James went on. "Goldie, you also gotta stay in the truck in case the law shows up." Bony turned and faced forward in his seat, then made eye contact with his homies through the rearview mirror. "I'ma go in first. Mack, you follow me, and then Jayquan, you come in last. C'mon y'all, let's go do this damn thang!" All four goons pounded each other's fists and ski-masked up.

Bony James exited the vehicle first, followed by G-Mack, and then Jayquan. Goldie climbed across the console and got behind the steering wheel. He put his hand cannon in his lap, set the assault rifle down next to him in the passenger seat, and then rolled his ski-mask up like a beanie.

Ready for action, three of the four members of the Young Glock Gang were now on the roof of the two-bedroom house tiptoeing around quietly in all black jacker attire. It took Bony James ten minutes to remove the nails and wooden boards from the window with the hammer he'd brought with him. One by one, each man squeezed through the opening until all three were huddled in the attic on their stomachs, crawling toward the attic's trap door. After taking a deep breath, Bony James opened the trap door and boldly peeked down at the area below him. Nothing. Only white walls and a burnt orange shag carpet.

All those grueling sets of pull-ups in the penitentiary paid off as Bony hung from the attic door and slowly lowered himself to the ground below, his feet silently landing on the carpeted floor. The silencer-equipped pistol in his hand pointed straight ahead, ready to explode. He looked above him and motioned G-Mack to come down. G-Mack landed on the carpet with a soft thud. They all managed to quietly enter the stash house undetected. When they tiptoed to the corner of the hallway, shit got ugly.

Bony James peeped into the first bedroom he approached and saw a stocky, dark-skinned dude standing naked on the side of the bed with his dick stuffed deep inside a skinny, light-skinned chick's mouth. The woman was fiercely sucking on the stocky dude's dick with her eyes closed. Stocky dude was leaning back on his heels with his hands on his hips and his head back, thoroughly enjoying the woman's head game. He groaned his pleasure out loud, and his entire body tensed up like he was on the verge of busting a nut.

Pfftt! Pfftt!

The first shot hit stocky dude in the heart. The second shot hit him in the middle of his ribcage. Oblivious to the violence going on around her, the chick continued to hungrily suck. His body shook from the gunshots just after he started squirting his nut into the skinny chick's throat. She assumed his jerking gyrations were a result of his sexual gratification and her phenomenal head game.

Thoomph!

When his body fell back and hit the floor with a loud thump, the light-skinned chick realized something was seriously wrong. She saw blood seeping from the bullet wounds in his body, then turned her head toward the door and looked into Bony James' eyes with a mouth full of cum. Her eyes bugged wide, and she was about to scream out.

Pfftt! Pfftt!

A bullet hit her in the forehead above her right eye, another in her neck, and she choked and died on the edge of the bed with a jaw full of cum.

The three heavily-armed thugs tiptoed further down the hallway until they came up on the second bedroom; it was empty. When they reached the living room, they found two men seriously engrossed in a video game, their fingers furiously working the controllers in their hands. Bony James pointed his pistol at the man closest to him. Jayquan pointed his pistol at the other dude. G-Mack pointed the MP5 at both of them.

"If one of you makes a noise, I'ma air your asses out like it's nothin'! Now put your ma'fuckin' hands where my eyes can see!" Bony James ordered as he walked up to one of the workers with his gun aimed at his face. He stood him up with the tip of the barrel in his ear hole. "Get on your feet and turn around and face the wall!" He turned the shook thug away from him and whispered in his ear, "Now, call ol' boy in the basement and tell him to bring his ass up outta there. Tell him that your partner over here is having chest pains."

Pfftt!

A bullet hit the other stash house worker in the chest.

"That should help you to sound a little more convincing. If you can't convince him to come from down there, then I'm deflatin' your dome, bruh. You feel me?"

"Um hmm." The shook stash house worker nodded and mumbled.

Bony James walked him over to the basement and forced

him to his knees with the pistol on his head. Prodding from the end of the gun made the stash house worker very convincing.

"Ay, Tiny, come up top for a minute. I think Melvin's havin' a heart attack or something!" Shook dude was extremely believable. A rustle of muted noises could be heard below before the lock clicked and the trap door opened.

"What the fuck you say—"

Pffttt! Pffttt! Pffttt!

As soon as the trap door opened, three bullets hit the worker named Tiny in the face.

Pffttt!

Another bullet hit the shook worker in the ear and came out the other side of his head through his temple. He slumped to the floor and died after a violent convulsion racked his body.

Bony James and the others quickly searched the house to make sure there were no other occupants hiding out or laying in the cut. They met back in the living room three minutes later.

"I'm callin' Goldie. Go down there and start bagging all that work up, y'all."

Ring. Ring. Ring. Ring. Ring. Ring. Ring.

Goldie's cell phone rang incessantly. No answer.

What the fuck is going on with Goldie? Why the fuck he ain't answering his phone? Bony James snuck a peek out the window and tried to look down the block in the direction where the Pathfinder was parked. Nothing. *Damn it! Something ain't right!* He tried calling again. Still no answer.

"What's up, Bony?" G-Mack quizzed, after making his first run and seeing the perplexed look on Bony James' face.

"I don't know. Finish loading up those bricks while I check on something," Bony told him. He peeked out the window again with his gun in hand, finger lingering near the trigger.

CHAPTER 10

Goldie

Goldie saw the muzzled flashes light the house up several times and wondered if the neighbors or a passerby taking a late night stroll might've seen the same flashes of light. *If they did see it, will they recognize it for what it is and call the po-po?* Panic momentarily raced through his body as soon as the thought entered his mind.

"Come on! Come on! Come on, y'all! Hurry the fuck up, man!" he anxiously whispered while tapping the fingers of his left hand against the leather wrapped steering wheel. His right hand fondled the Glock in his lap impatiently. Suddenly he detected some movement up the street out the corner of his eye and to his left. A group of three hardheads were walking down the block in the direction of the parked Pathfinder. *Damn it, this ain't good!* He slowly screwed the silencer on, while his eyes stayed glued to the trio of hoods coming his way. He twisted the silencer on tightly and readied himself for a confrontation.

As the trio of young hoods neared the Pathfinder, all six eyes simultaneously looked over toward the truck, and the noisy chatter amongst them immediately died. Curious stares morphed into antagonistic mean mugs. A cricket chirped in the bushes several feet away. An alley cat meowed off in the distance, causing a dog to bark an angry response seconds later. When the three thugs were even with the Pathfinder, the tallest of the three spoke for the group.

"What's up, potna? Fuck is you lookin' at, chump!" His voice dripped with hostility, his body language wild with animated motions. "You got a problem, punk?" the tall thug posed the question, twisting his face up into an angry mask.

Goldie touched a button and powered the driver's side window down. He laughed before responding in a low, even tone. "I suggest you clowns keep pushin' and stay the fuck outta grown folk bizness 'fore you find yourself in a precarious predicament." He gripped the Glock tighter and collected his thoughts.

"Precarious predicament! Is you serious?" the youngster asked with incredulous disbelief. "You got me hella fucked up, fool! I'll come over there and fuck yo' bitch ass up, and then take yo' whip when I'm finished!" The young hood was turnt up at the prospect of showing out in front of his boys and ganking the man for his vehicle in the process.

With more important matters weighing heavy in the balance, Goldie searched for a possible solution as how to best go about resolving the unforeseen intrusion. The last thing he needed was a scene that brought attention to him and his crew and the dirty deed they were currently knee deep in. *Man, I'm straight up and down with my shit. I ain't got time to play with these bustas!* In one fluid motion, the truck's door flew open, and he was on the sidewalk with the Glock ready to explode. With the menacing silencer attached to the end of the gun it looked like a foot long instrument of death, terrifying as hell.

"Shut the fuck up and lay your bitch ass down!" He turned to the others. "You too, ma'fuckas! All y'all get flat or get clacked!" He waved the pistol back and forth until all three young hoods lay stretched out on the concrete shaking with fear. "The first one of you bustas to utter a word is gon' be the first one I put a bullet in!" he promised, with the pistol steady in his grip.

A rustle of noise in the bushes nearby made Goldie swing the Glock that way, and a cat jumped from its hiding spot and ran up a tree. Half a block away, a car horn honked. Goldie quickly went to work on the young street toughs.

Ten minutes later, they were connected at the wrists with zip- ties and wrapped around a tree with duct tape sealing their mouths shut. Goldie was settling back into the SUV when his phone started blowing up in the passenger seat. "Yeah dat," he answered the phone out of breath.

"Where the fuck you been, ma'fucka!" Bony James shouted.

"I had to handle some business out here. Calm the fuck down, bruh!"

"Hurry the fuck up, Goldie! We ready to roll and bounce the fuck up outta here!"

* * * * * *

"Yes sir!" Bony James held a kilo of dope in each hand, feeling himself in a major way. "This how real ma'fuckin' gangstas get it!" He tossed both heavily-wrapped kilos atop the pile of other bricks sitting in the open duffle bags at his feet. "Sixty-two bricks of top-shelf yay, y'all. I think it's safe to say that the Young Glock Gang is officially back in the ma'fuckin' game!" he exclaimed boisterously, then fired up a blunt. Kush smoke was thick in the room, and glasses clinked together amidst a roar of laughter as each thug celebrated the success of their come up.

"Man, that shit went hella smooth, bruh, no hiccups or nothin'!" Jayquan had a blunt in one hand and a brick in the other hand tucked in the crook of his arm like a football. "Take a flick of this shit, Goldie!" He parked the blunt between his lips and struck a Heisman pose.

Goldie grabbed Jayquan's phone and took a picture of him

clowning with the brick of dope. The four of them continued to celebrate the occasion, smoking trees and telling their version of how the robbery went down. Then Bony James fucked the mood up.

"I wanna know what the fuck happened to you?" He aimed the question at Goldie; the hostility in his tone was clear and palpable. The mood in the room instantly transformed from upbeat and celebratory to silent and somber.

"What the fuck is you talkin' 'bout, Bony? Don't be gettin' at me like I'm some kinda busta or somethin'! What the fuck wrong with you?" He set his glass down and pushed himself off the couch. Goldie was a whole lot of thangs, but a coward wasn't one of them.

Bony James was an aggressive alpha male with a deep seeded propensity to create conflict and confrontation. He couldn't help himself. Putting a ten on a two was as natural to him as picking his nose or passing gas in public. It wasn't cool, but when he felt the need to do so, he did it.

"You heard what the fuck I said. Where the fuck was you when I called you? We were up in that bitch with ma'fuckas whose guns were every bit as big as ours, and the plan was, when I called you, your ass was supposed to answer the phone. It took ten minutes for you to answer your phone, blood!" he growled and balled his fist, ready for a squabble with his homie.

Jayquan and G-Mack watched the exchange with mild interest. They too wanted to know why it took Goldie so long to respond and show up.

"Miss me with all that interrogation shit, Bony. Who the fuck is you?" Goldie's chest swelled and his face twisted ugly with anger.

"You ain't said shit, bruh. If you feelin' like you need that, then you can get it right here, right now!" Bony James challenged Goldie to a fight.

"You ain't said nothin', homie! Fuck yeah I want that!" Goldie was good with his hands too and didn't mind taking a fade. "As a matter of fact, I need that, bruh. You got me hella fucked up!" Goldie was up for the challenge. He pulled his pistol from his waistband and tossed it on the couch he had been sitting on. Goldie squared off with his fists balled up and positioned in front of his face.

G-Mack stood and got between his two homies while Jayquan helped him keep the two thugs separated.

"Both of y'all need to chill the fuck out on all that rah-rah shit! Real talk, homie. Let that shit go! We just came off the biggest lick of our lives, and y'all ready to chunk 'em over some shit that ain't had no effect on the outcome. How the fuck stupid is that!" G-Mack knew that if he didn't say the right thing to redirect the two thugs' attention, then it was going to get ugly fast.

Goldie wasn't budging or backing down none.

"Miss me with that shit, homie. Get at that ma'fucka with all that. He the one who out of pocket!"

"You coulda got us fucked off tonight! You had a job to do, and you almost didn't do it. You the one who was out of pocket, blood!" Bony James wasn't budging or backing down either.

"Man, turn that shit down, Bony. You don't know what the fuck was happenin' out there with me! You don't know why the fuck I didn't answer the phone!"

"Why didn't you answer your phone, Goldie? What the fuck did happen out there?" G-Mack hoped his question would steer the tension into a less volatile atmosphere.

Goldie mean-mugged Bony James before explaining how he

saw the muzzled flashes and wondered if others had as well. He then told them about the hardheads who walked up on the Pathfinder and forced his hand.

"When you were hittin' me on the cell, I was busy takin' them lil ma'fuckas down and tying their asses to a tree." Goldie finished telling his version of events. When he was done talking, the room fell silent for a moment.

"My bad then, homie. I didn't know it was like that. Why the fuck didn't you just say that from the get go?" Bony James reached his hand out toward Goldie in an attempt to squash the beef.

"Because you ain't ask, ma'fucka!" Goldie took his hand and the two goons briefly embraced. Easy laughter soon followed, and the celebratory mood immediately returned. The beef was squashed, and the thugs were back on good terms. It was the gangsta way. They went back to celebrating their come up, and then randomly throwing out thoughts of what they were going to do next.

CHAPTER 11

Miko

The hi-tech earpiece fit securely in Miko's ear while her right hand remained close to her clutch, near the nickel-plated .380. Her face distorted into an annoyed mask as her cousin filled her in on the latest developments. She was sitting in the back of a Cool Whip white Maybach with the dark velour curtains drawn shut. She interrupted Cream and coldly issued out instructions.

"I want all three of those sonofabitches strapped to chairs in the chamber when I get there. Don't let any of them communicate with each other, or anybody else for that matter. You understand me? Send somebody to sit outside the stash house and have them keep an eye on any traffic coming or going too. I want a detailed report on whoever stops by or rides by snooping around looking guilty. If the police show up, I want to know who and how many. Do you understand me, Cream?" She toyed with the .380 now resting next to her.

"Say no mo', Miko. I'm already on it. I took their phones as soon as we showed up. We took 'em from where we found 'em and brought 'em to the chamber. I got Suspect sittin' down there watchin' 'em with the Mac-10. That fifty-round clip with the suicide trigger got 'em shook the fuck up and marinating on nervous," the six-feet-four, LL Cool J look-alike responded.

"Perfect. That's good thinkin', cousin. What about Capone? Where's he at?"

Cream lowered his voice to a whisper. "He's standin' here with me. Why? What's up?"

"Keep him close to you, Cream. As much work as I lost last night, I don't trust anybody right about now." Miko popped the clip out of the .380 and turned it over in her hand, then inspected it before sticking it back into the pistol. "I should be there in about twenty minutes." She ended the call and pulled the earpiece from her ear.

* * * * * *

Cream stuffed the phone in his pocket and pulled the chrome Desert Eagle from his shoulder holster. "Walk with me, Capone. Let's go keep an eye on these fools in the chamber." Cream waited for Capone to lead the way. They joined Suspect in the room downstairs, and he brandished the hand canon with the intent of adding to the fear factor already present in the windowless concrete room. After whispering something in Suspect's ear, Cream looked into the eyes of all three youngsters and knew without a doubt that the huge .45 had achieved the desired effect.

* * * * * *

Miko leaned back in the luxury whip's soft leather and pushed buttons until some mind-calming murder music serenaded her mood. She closed her eyes and let the old school rapper Scarface's threats of unspeakable violence massage her mental. The lyrics guided her thoughts to the past, forcing her to go in reverse and flashback to when she was just a five-year-old girl sitting on her daddy's lap the night before he was murdered. His words embedded in her brain like a headshot. The fact that he had been murdered shortly thereafter, locked those words into her memory bank forever.

With her eyes already closed, she allowed herself to go there.

"What the fuck you mean Bojack dead and my money's

gone!" *Kiko Dunbar screamed into the phone after pushing little Miko off his lap. "How much of my money is missing?" Kiko stood up, livid. His face twisted as if he had just touched some dog shit with his eating hand. He was talking to Brodie, the head of his security team, a cold-blooded killer. Miko stood off to the side and stared up at her father's mean mug as he continued to cuss out and quiz his worker.*

"All of it! What the fuck you mean all of it? That's five million dollars! Who the fuck else got killed other than Bojack?" Kiko listened to the answer before quickly reaching a conclusion. "Get me Bad Boy's address! I want his location yesterday. Do you understand what the fuck I'm sayin', Brodie?" Her father slammed the phone down and continued talking shit, spitting out words that would forever be etched into her memory. He looked at her with uncut ruthless fervor in his eyes. "Never let a man check you, never let a man disrespect you, and don't you ever let a man threaten to wreck you, baby girl. You hear me?" he told Miko as she prepared to go to bed. She nodded up and down and waited for more game. "I'll die before I ever let a ma'fucka steal from me, because if a ma'fucka got it in him to take your money, then they also got it in 'em to take your life!" He walked her to her room and tucked her into bed, then lovingly stroked her face and kissed her good night.

It was the last time she'd ever see her father alive. His last words would haunt her heart for years. They were the words that would instill an unflinching fundamental belief in her, that to this day she was willing to fuck hers off for: "Never let a man check you, never let a man disrespect you, and don't you ever let a man threaten to wreck you, baby girl . . ."

Her father's words echoed in her head as she sat in the backseat fuming over the stash house robbery. Twenty minutes later, the Maybach eased into the driveway of the heavily reinforced nondescript house and came to a stop a few feet away from the curb. Miko text Cream and let him know she had arrived. Her driver got out and opened the rear door for her. The statuesque queenpin touched her Pucci pumps onto the rain dampened surface of the concrete and stepped out of the luxury whip with boss swag oozing from her aura. Hers was a regal gait as she navigated the cracked concrete like it was a runway in Milan, gliding with purposeful steps up the walkway toward the front door.

Anthony stood behind her guarding her back with his hand on the pistol inside his jacket. The heavily fortified door opened just as the knuckles on her balled up fist hit the hard outer surface. Miko followed Cream into the house, and Anthony closed the door behind them. She instructed Cream to go get Suspect and Capone and leave the three thugs alone in the chamber while she questioned him. Minutes after her arrival, she was grilling her worker Capone.

"A'ight, run that one more time, Capone, and don't leave out nare detail, you hear me?" Miko stood in front of the seated man with her arms folded across her chest and her eyes shrouded in mystery behind a pair of tinted Versace lenses. Her lips were poked out in anger, and the snarl on her face made it evident to all parties present that she was pissed off— nostril's flared, chest inflating and deflating with agitated disgust with every breath she took.

Cream stood near the door with his chrome on display, the built-like-a-tank thug was an imposing figure. The fact that he was rumored to have at least seven bodies under his belt gave credence to that. Suspect stood behind the seated Capone, adding a sense of unknown trepidation to the nervous worker.

"Like I told you before, Miko, I was making my rounds

same as I do every night, and when I rolled up to the stash spot I instantly knew that something was wrong."

"How the fuck did you instantly know that something was wrong, Capone?" Suspect posed the question with an accusatory inflection wrapped around it. He also stepped closer and chambered a round in his thumper.

"I knew something was wrong because the door was open, man!" the dark-skinned gangsta named Capone answered with a little more attitude than he should have. He pissed Miko's already angered cousin off with his condescending tone.

Bap! Bap!

"Bitch ass ma'fucka! Who the fuck you think you talkin' to like that! I. Will. Kill. You. For. Rais—ing. Your. Voice. At. Me. Punk!" Every word out of Suspect's mouth was followed by a blow with the butt of his pistol. He mounted the fallen Capone, who lay curled up in a fetal position trying to shield his head and face from the savage blows relentlessly raining down on him.

"That's enough, Suspect!" Miko called her bloodthirsty cousin off with the quick, direct order. "Help him back into his chair."

Capone put his hand to the side of his head and wiped the stream of blood running down his face with one hand. He stood up with a mean mug, shooting daggers in Suspect's direction before taking his seat again.

"Finish runnin' that, Capone." Miko offered no sympathy. She wanted answers and she wanted them now. If it took Capone getting pistol whipped to draw out those answers, then so be it.

He touched his face again and shook his head at the sight of blood on his fingers, then he grit his teeth and took a deep breath.

"The door was open, Miko, so off top I knew that something wasn't right. I called Cream right then and there and waited for him to show up." The hostility in Capone's voice had vanished. A tamer, more cooperative tone replaced it.

Miko silently stared at the man she entrusted to canvass all of her stash houses throughout the night and keep detailed notes and accounts on each house's condition. He'd been riding patrol for Miko since she first established herself in the dope game, and this was the first incident of any kind under his watch. His work record was spotless, but Miko didn't trust him as far as she could throw him. His words sounded convincing, but his eyes were dishonest as hell. His posture reeked of perfidiousness. *The tapes don't lie!* The thought suddenly crossed Miko's mind, and she decided to let the silence eat him up before leading him into a trap for her next question.

"Capone, you say you called Cream as soon as you saw the door to the stash house open, right?" she asked offhandedly, looking down at her top. Miko picked an imaginary piece of lint off her blouse.

"Yeah," he answered with conviction.

Miko held her hand out in front of her face admiring her manicure.

"At any time before Cream got there, did you or anybody else enter the house? Did you kill, or see anybody kill any of my workers, Capone?"

"Nope. Hell naw! Why would I kill your workers? It happened just like I said it did. I called Cream as soon as I peeped that the door was open, and then I waited outside until he showed up." Capone was confident in his answer.

Miko let the answer ride.

"Okay, what happened next?"

"Cream and Suspect showed up and called the cleaners to clean up whatever happened inside the house. Cream told me to post up and make a detailed report of everything I saw or knew, so I did, and he came and told me to follow him in my car, and now here we are." Capone gave his version of events as he knew them to be. Miko dismissed him after apologizing for her hotheaded cousin Suspect's violent actions.

As soon as Capone was gone, Miko turned to her cousin.

"Cream, I want you to pull up the surveillance footage from the stash house's basement and have it ready for me ASAP, a'ight?"

"I already handled that, Miko. I told Theo to take care of it and send me the footage as soon as he could." Cream looked down at the Rolex Miko had given him when he got out of prison. "As a matter of fact, he should have it ready any minute now." He made a mental note to call Theo, their IT guy, and press him about the video footage if he didn't call in the next ten minutes.

"Okay, good. Now, tell me about these three clowns in the chamber."

"When I showed up at the stash house after Capone hit me on the cell, I called the clean up crew to take care of the bodies that were still in the house before the police got up on it. Suspect searched the inside of the house while the others checked around outside. They found the youngsters halfway down the block zip-tied around a tree with duct tape around their mouths."

"What about the bitch that was in the house?" Miko asked.

"It looks like she was a whore. Melvin and those other fools were violating protocol."

"Was she involved in the robbery in any way?"

"If she was, she's dead now, but I don't think so."

"Have you spoken with any of the three downstairs yet?" Miko asked.

"Naw, not really. I thought you'd want the first crack at 'em."

"Let's go do this shit then." Miko had her bizness face on as she followed Cream and Suspect to the underground room she had built-in. She had the two-bedroom house remodeled and specially designed for this type of thing: violently eliciting vital information from uncooperative people.

She carefully tiptoed down the cracked concrete steps while Cream held the door open for her. The three young thugs were wrapped tight in wooden chairs with nylon rope, stewing in fear. Each of them sported terrified, desperate expressions. Side by side they sat, unable to move, duct tape sealing their mouths shut.

Miko walked in front of them and dramatically chambered a round in the .380. The metallic clicking sound had the desired effect as each of them started shifting about anxiously. An ominous silence filled the room. One of the three thugs audibly passed gas when fear punched him in the belly. Miko smiled with pleasure, knowing she had them shook like that. The pistol dangled precariously from her hand when she spoke.

"Last night one of my stash houses was robbed by someone, and something very valuable was taken from me, and the fact that the three of you were in the vicinity cuffed to one another around a tree tells me one of two things: either you were directly involved with the person, or persons responsible for robbing me, or you were indirectly involved. And be that as it may, I am convinced that you must know something about it one way or another."

"Mmmpphh uummpphh ummm." The tallest of the three tried to plead his case from behind the duct tape.

"Shhhhhh." Miko put an expensive manicured index finger against her full lips and silenced the frightened young, baby-faced thug. He swallowed a mouthful of fear and complied, sweat beading up on his forehead and rolling down his face.

Miko slowly walked around and squatted next to him, leaning back on her haunches, her chin resting on the heel of her left hand, and the .380 clutched firmly in the right one. With grim silence looming as a backdrop, Miko used the youngster's fear as a way of seducing the coward in him to the surface. She touched the tip of the nickel-plated pistol against his face and caressed his cheek with the murder weapon. Like an affectionate lover, she tenderly stroked his smooth dark-chocolate skin with the steel. Patient in matters concerning money and emotions, she felt that impeccable timing was everything. Her money, or the drugs that produced her money, had been stolen, and the three young teenagers emotions were frazzled and at their most vulnerable point.

Gradually she traced the .380 along the strip of duct tape on the terrified teenager's mouth and let the unsettling silence eat at him. He mumbled something, but she immediately shut him down again, placing the flat side of the barrel against his mouth and pressing it against his trembling duct taped lips. She wanted him to stew in trepidation. When she felt he was in the exact position she wanted him in, she spoke in a soft but serious tone.

"Fact one: sixty-two kilos of my dope are missing. Fact two: at least one of you guys know something about my dope being missing. Fact three: I can assure you with the utmost certainty that two out of the three of you are going to die in this room. I don't care if I kill an innocent man today. What I do know is that whichever one of you talks first and tells me where my dope is, he will be the only one leaving up outta here with his life today. First one to talk is the first one to walk." Miko stood up and took a step back. She put her weight on one hip and crossed her arms, the .380 dangling in her right hand like a menacingly motivational carrot. All three young thugs started shaking and sniveling through the duct tape. She slowly peeled the strip of duct tape from one of the thug's mouths and spoke quietly. "Talk to me. Where's my dope at, baby boy?" she asked the tallest youngster first.

"I swear. We didn't have nothin' to do with your drugs gettin' jacked, lady!" He was crying real tears and telling the real truth the instant the duct tape was removed from his lips. Miko didn't give a damn about his tears. Her only concern was the whereabouts of her sixty-two bricks.

"So, is that your final answer? You don't have any idea where my dope is?" Her questions were direct and to the point. The texture of her voice was void of emotion.

"I swear we didn't—"

Pop!

She interrupted his response with a shot from the .380. The bullet crashed through his front teeth and severed his uvula before lodging in the nape of his neck. His eyes widened with shock, and his body jerked up and got stiff for a split second before his muscles relaxed. He pooted and shit his pants before his head bobbled to the side and hung at an awkward angle. His final death pose was a shitty one indeed.

Miko stood and turned to speak to Cream while shrugging her shoulders. "All he had to do was tell me where my shit is. It ain't like I'm asking for anything crazy." She shrugged again. The sarcasm was thick in her voice as she walked over to the next young thug and presented him with the same offer she extended to his partner, ripping the tape off his mouth. It instantly became obvious to her that the second youngster was built a little stronger than the first. His mean mug twisted up and was aimed at her as their eyes locked in a battle of wills. She ignored his tough guy façade and asked, "Where's my dope?"

"I don't know what the fuck you talkin' 'bout. I ain't fuck with your dope!" He spit the words out like he was pissed off.

"Is that it? Is that all you gotta say to me?" she asked with a hand on one hip. He remained silent but his eyes screamed, *Fuck you, bitch!*

Pop!

"Who the fuck you think you lookin' at like that!" Miko exclaimed with a touch of anger in her tone after popping off a shot and hitting him in his right eye. The rebellious young thug leaned back in the chair with his mouth wide in death. His brains and blood-splatter eased down the wall behind him.

Seconds later, Miko was squatting next to the third young thug, giving him the same opportunity as the others. As soon as she peeled the duct tape off his mouth, the rough-looking, hard-faced street thug started telling her everything.

"I swear we didn't have anything to do with your stuff getting jacked, lady. I swear! Last night we were just walkin' down the street when my 'potna started fat-mouthin' to some dude in a Pathfinder. Then the dude in the Pathfinder jumped out on us with a banger. He cuffed all three of us to a tree with them plastic things and bounced. He left us like that until them other dudes found us wrapped around that tree. You gotta believe me, lady. I swear we ain't take nothin' of yours!"

A dude in a Pathfinder . . . now we're getting somewhere! Miko twisted her neck and turned her head toward Cream; her right eyebrow arched with interest. She felt like a crucially pertinent clue was right at her fingertips.

"What did this dude in the Pathfinder look like?" she coolly asked the frightened teenager, her hopes up.

"I couldn't see him all that good because it was dark, and the street light was busted out," he replied with wide eyes.

Miko exhaled her anger and placed the tip of the .380 to the edge of his tightly tapered line-up. The youngster felt the steel on his head and panic inflated his heart with fear. She bit her bottom lip, and her finger calmly stroked the surface of the trigger, about to squeeze.

"I didn't see his face all that good, but I know he had gold fronts in his mouth!" he blurted loudly in desperation.

Miko relaxed her trigger finger and leaned forward with curiosity.

"What was that you said? Did you say the dude driving the Pathfinder had a gold grill?"

"Yeah, his whole front grill was gold, the top and the bottom. I remember because it blinged in the dark when he drew down on us and made us get on the ground." The young teenage thug spoke with a rush of excitement, hoping his answer would persuade the trigger-happy queenpin to show him mercy.

Miko leaned closer and whispered softly into his right ear, "Is there anything else you can tell me that might help me find out who hit my stash house last night?" Miko felt optimistic she could squeeze another telling tidbit out of him.

"Naw, that's all I can think of. It all happened so fast. The dude jumped out the Pathfinder with his gun up and put us on the ground hella fast."

Miko gently caressed the youngster's face with the palm of her hand, nodding with understanding. She leaned in closer, her lips brushing his earlobe as she spoke in a barely audible whisper, "Thank you for keepin' it 100 with me. You've been a huge help, baby boy." His heart beat faster with a newfound sense of hope.

Pop!

When the .380 sounded off, Miko could feel the blood from the headshot spray her face with a fine mist; her lips were still touching his earlobe as the dying youngster struggled to take in his final breath. The last thing registering in his mind as he breathed in his last breath was the sweet smell of cinnamon on her breath. Miko stood and wiped the blood off her face, then calmly stuffed the .380 back inside her clutch bag.

"What! Why the fuck are you lookin' at me like that, Cream?" Miko asked, glaring at her cousin.

"Nothin', Miko. It is what it is," Cream responded.

"Naw, obviously something is on your mind, so speak on it, Cream!" Miko's feathers were ruffled. She was almost beside herself with indignation, growing irate at the notion that he questioned her get-down.

"Let it go, Miko. It's nothin'."

"Naw, it is something, because I'm makin' it somethin'!" Miko was up in his face.

Cream was kicking himself in the ass for making something out of nothing. He shrugged. *Fuck it,* he thought and spoke his mind. "I just don't see the point in killin' 'em like that, Miko. They were kids! Ain't nare one of them ma'fucka's remotely close to eighteen years old, and it's obvious they didn't have anything to do with the spot gettin' jacked, so killin' them was pointless as far as I'm concerned."

Miko threw her hands up and looked at him like he had just said the dumbest shit she'd ever heard.

"As far as *you're* concerned? Pointless! Cream, is you fuckin' serious! Are you not thinkin'?" She walked up on him and repeatedly poked him on his forehead with her index finger. "Do you not have a brain in this thick ass head of yours?"

Cream closed his eyes and chewed on his molars in an attempt to restrain himself. Suspect looked on with surprised interest. Miko continued to check her younger cousin.

"They may not have been the ones who jacked us, Cream, but it ain't any doubt about it that they know about the stash house getting jacked! And if they know about it, and are allowed to live to tell about it, then it's just a matter of time until the police know about the stash house and the dead bodies in it! And as far as how old they were? I don't give a fuck if they're fifteen or fifty! They gave us information that will hopefully lead us to one of the people responsible for robbing me, for robbing us! It is your job to find that ma'fucka, Cream! And if you do happen to find this fool with the gold grill . . . better yet, if you happen to kill this fool with the gold grill, then *as far as I'm concerned*, the only ma'fuckas who can tie *that* murder to you is one of those three dead ma'fuckas right here! So to say that what I did was pointless, I think not! My killing them wasn't pointless at all. I killed them so that when you finally do your fucking job, you won't have to worry about anybody testifying on your shallow-thinking ass!" Miko breathed hard as she stood in Cream's face and stared down her cousin.

Realizing that Miko had a valid point and was acting in his best interest, Cream turned his head and inhaled deeply, resigned to the fact that once again she had out thought him. He hated having to admit that she was right, but it was what it was.

She saw the realization register in his understanding.

"Exactly! That's why I'm the fuckin' boss, and you're the ma'fucka who works for the boss! I taught you everything that you know, Cream, but I didn't teach you everything I know!"

She intentionally rubbed it in. Miko couldn't help herself; it was something she'd done since they were kids. Not only was she older, in truth she was more intelligent and heartless than they were when it came to the game as well. She walked away and let her words marinate on his mental. Miko didn't feel when she killed. In her mind, killing was just another way of communicating, a way of shutting people up and silencing them forever. She loved and respected her cousins, despite the fact they weren't as savage-hearted as she was, and she didn't want Cream to leave feeling some kinda way.

"Cream, come here," she called out.

"What?" He was butt-hurt, but it wouldn't last long. He turned to face her.

"You know I love you, cousin. Right? All I'm saying is, if you're going to be involved in this shit, then I want you to be the best at it, you feel me?" She held her arms out and offered a hug. He hugged her briefly and tried to let her go, but she held him close to her. Miko cupped his ear and whispered, "First, I want you to clean this mess up. Then I want you to find me some new workers and another stash house to operate out of. This time though, make sure whoever you promote has some type of security background. I want somebody who knows how to handle a pistol and who can smell a stick up from a mile away."

"A'ight, consider it done, Miko," Cream responded begrudgingly.

"Oh, and one more thing, Cream."

"Whaddup?" He stopped and listened.

"I want you and Suspect to personally go see about this dude in the Pathfinder with the gold grill. If he exists, I want his head on a platter. Find out who he runs with, or who he hangs out with, and don't hesitate to bring all their asses down here to the chamber, you feel me? I don't give a fuck if we gotta kill a dozen people to get my product back, that'll just be twelve more ma'fuckas that died for a good cause."

"A'ight," Cream told her and walked out the room, seething with frustrated hostility. It was hard for him to accept being checked by a chick, even if she was right about everything she said, but still it was a hard to swallow. Cream fumed as he pulled his phone out and started calling shots and issuing instructions to his underlings while murderous thoughts bubbled in his heart.

CHAPTER 12

Cream & Suspect

Cream jumped out the black Denali truck, all business no bullshit. Still angered about being checked by Miko, today somebody was about to feel his wrath.

"Whaddup, Nario? You got that ready?" Cream skipped over the pleasantries and got straight to the point as he accosted the lower level worker who met him on the sidewalk in front of the house.

Along with a powerful presence, Cream's demeanor was all thug. He rocked a pair of black jeans and black boots with a wife beater under the bulletproof vest. The handle on his chrome poked out the holster and hung off his left shoulder. Members of his entourage spilled out of the trailing truck, eyes on the landscape and hands on pistols.

"Yup, it's in the house," Nario responded, before turning and walking toward the dilapidated house situated off Meadowbrook Drive.

"Post up, y'all. I'll be back in a minute," Cream instructed his crew of goons and fell in step behind Nario.

When he approached the porch, he yanked the .45 out while his eyes surveyed the front entrance to the house. *Can't ever be too careful; gotta make sure ain't nobody layin' in the cut waitin' to dome me!* He looked at the windows in an attempt to detect any type of movement, or out of place shadows. He studied Nario's back, trying to identify hints of shady signs in his body language. Nothing seemed out of order, but the .45 stayed swinging by his front right pocket anyway.

Nario twisted the doorknob and pushed the door open and walked into the house leaving the door wide open. Cream's ears perked up, and his eyes peered into the dimly lit living room, mug on mean and finger on the trigger.

"Are you the only one in here?" Cream posed the question to Nario's back.

"Yup, you said don't ever let nobody else step foot in this crib, so ain't nobody else been up in here but me." Nario turned and tried to maintain eye contact with Cream, but lost the eye-boxing battle when Cream's cold eyes stared through his without blinking. Nario broke eye contact and quickly recovered by changing the subject. "You want something to drink while I go get it?"

"Naw, Nario. I'm good."

"A'ight then, I'll be right back," Nario replied and turned toward the bedroom to go get the money.

As soon as Nario disappeared behind the door, Cream moved to the other side of the room out of habit. Thinking like that was the difference between a live gangsta and a dead one, as far as Cream was concerned. While he waited, Cream's ever observant eyes took in everything around him: the ashtray on the table with the half-smoked cigarette sitting in it, the ripped condom wrappers on the floor near the couch, the mountain of dirty dishes piled up in the sink.

Seconds later, Nario came out of the bedroom with a duffle bag in his right hand. His left hand was empty. "Here you go, Cream." He extended his left arm and handed the bag to Cream.

"Is it all here?" Cream asked, reaching for the bag of money with his left hand.

"Yup."

Cream swiftly raised the .45 in his right hand and touched the chrome against Nario's temple. Nario cringed in fear when the gun pressed against the side of his head.

"What the fuck are you trippin' on, Cream?"

"The next time you lie to me, Nario, I'ma blow yo' face up, boy. You hear me?" he threatened through clenched teeth and a steady gun hand.

"Whatchu talkin' 'bout, Cream? I ain't lie to you, man!" Nario squeezed his eyes shut and turned his head away from the pistol's tip, his body frozen with fright as he waited for an explosion or an explanation.

Bap!

Cream's fist caught Nario flush on the jaw and staggered him.

"Lie to me again, and I'ma slump yo' punk ass, bruh! You said ain't nobody else been up in this crib but you. Since when yo' bitch ass start wearin' lipstick, ma'fucka!" Cream banged on him, referring to the half-smoked Newport sitting in the ashtray with the red lipstick on the filter.

Nario paused with panic and a lie on the tip of his tongue. He carefully considered his response and weighed the consequence of a lie versus the punishment over the truth. On one hand, he now knew that Cream knew he'd brought a bitch to the spot. On the other hand, Cream just threatened to blow his face up if he ever lied to him again. He'd known Cream since middle school. He knew without a doubt the trigger-happy drug boss would carry out his threat without hesitation. The truth came pouring out of his mouth like a desperate plea.

"I only had her up in here for a few hours to serve me some brains. I swear, Cream. She doesn't know what type of spot this is, man! She don't know 'bout what I do for a living, man! My bad, bruh. It won't happen again. On er'thang, Cream, that's my word!" Nario pleaded his case while the chrome pressed up against his face.

Cream tapped the tip of the .45 against Nario's forehead with authority and issued a final warning.

"Disrespect me again, Nario. And on mommas, I'ma stuff this gun in yo' mouth and serve your brains wit' it. You understand me?" Cream reached back and smacked him in the back of the head with the butt of the gun, then watched him crumble to the floor in pain as the back of his dome opened up, bleeding from the inch-long gash in it.

Nario was on his knees holding his head trying to stop the blood from pouring out.

"I understand, Cream. I swear it won't happen again!" he promised, cowering at Cream's feet.

"It bet' not happen again! It's a reason why it's rules in this game, you hear me? If this money comes up funny 'cause you ain't on your shit, then it makes me look bad! It's a bad look for my reputation. Are you trying to shit on my reputation, Nario?"

"Naw, never that, Cream. It won't happen again, bruh. I swear. That's my word!"

The .45 pushed against his scalp. "If it does happen again I'ma blow yo' face up for real, Nario, that's *my* word!"

Nario kneeled in silence and held his hand to his honeycomb patterned waves, desperately trying to stop the bleeding.

"What's this right here?" Cream asked, shaking the duffle bag.

"That's twenty-four thousand," Nario painfully whimpered, pissed that his head was hurting, but he was relieved that it was still on his shoulders. This could have ended with an entirely different scenario—his death.

Cream ignored Nario's pain and asked how he was on product. "Y'all straight over here? Is everybody sack full?"

"Yup, we good. Catlow came through this morning and dropped off some work."

"Good, I'ma slide back through next week. You already know what it is," Cream told him and walked out the house with the duffle bag full of loot in his hand.

"A'ight," Nario said, thankful Cream was leaving.

Cream and his crew of goons had already made nineteen other stops similar in nature before stopping at Nario's spot. Every week they stopped by the many pickup spots Miko had throughout the city, picking up a duffle bag full of dough.

The drug houses in her budding drug empire were bringing in roughly half a million dollars a week. Once Cream collected the money from the pickup spots, it then went to one of two money houses Miko had, where the money was then separated by denomination, counted, and wrapped before being boxed up and transferred to a third money house, where Miko later personally picked it up and took it to a secret location known only to her. While the dope houses yielded big cheese, a good chunk of her profit came from the big order sales to the gangstas and hustlas who copped whole bricks through Cream and Suspect and her other thug lieutenants.

Minutes later, Cream was sitting back in the Yukon Denali with Suspect in the passenger seat and two gunners in the backseat holding big guns with long clips sticking out the bottoms. All twenty duffle bags were piled in the rear of the Denali. A Dodge Durango full of heavily armed shooters was parked a car length behind, providing additional security.

"What's good?" Suspect posed the question to Cream after several quiet moments.

"Nothin'. I was just trippin' off somethin'," Cream said, electing to keep his thoughts to himself. His ever observant eyes continued to scrutinize the urban landscape before him. The driver of the Durango behind them briefly leaned on the horn one time in an attempt to get his attention. Cream ignored the restless party behind him. The truck full of gunners got the message and followed his lead, waiting in silence as well.

"Ali? Vamp?" Cream addressed the two goons in the Denali.

"Whaddup?" they responded in unison.

"Pull them hoodies down low over y'all head and go beat on that fool Jrake's door."

"Huh?" the two confounded henchmen asked in unison again.

Cream's voice had an angry edge to it when he spoke. "You heard me, ma'fucka! Throw yo' hoodies up over yo' lids and go beat on Jrake's door! Keep your hands in your pockets close to your guns too while you do it!" The two hardheads obediently followed instructions like the good street soldiers they were, hands on the guns in their pockets and hoodies pulled low as they walked up the block and made their way to the spot Jrake slung dope out of.

"What's up with that?" Suspect quizzed his older brother, watching Ali and Vamp move in the direction of the dope house.

Cream leaned over and pointed his finger. "See ol' boy sittin' over there on the wall with that bag of chips in his hand, the fool with the gray fit on?"

"Yeah, I see him. What about him? His name Tiyatti, ain't it?" Suspect asked with interest. Cream grunted "yeah" and sat up in his seat. His eyes narrowed to slits as he watched with keen interest as Ali and Vamp made their way toward the front of the crack house.

"Yeah. Watch how on point this Tiyatti cat gets when Ali and Vamp walk up on the spot lookin' like they up to no good. I been watchin' this dude for a minute now, and I think he has what it takes to run security at the new money house Miko want us to open up." Cream's eyes locked in on the scene playing out up ahead.

Suspect laughed and said, "Wow, you sent Ali and Vamp over there like crash test dummies! What happens if the shit turns into some gunplay?"

"Then it turns into gunplay. Them ma'fuckas knew the gun was loaded when they got in the game. Matter of fact, I got a $100 say Vamp and Ali don't even get they straps out." Cream tried to bait Suspect into laying a wager.

"Bet that, bruh!" Suspect eagerly jumped at the opportunity to one up his brother and peeled a crisp hundred dollar bill from his knot and tossed it on the dash.

Vamp followed behind Ali as the two made their way up the narrow walkway, hoodies pulled low and their hands deep in their pockets. The look of suspicion shadowing them came naturally.

Tiyatti put the bag of Doritos up to his mouth, tilted his head back, and downed what remained in the bag. His eyes inconspicuously followed the two gangstas who'd just turned up the narrow walkway seconds ago. He discreetly reached for the steel in his waistband and made it unsafe with a flick of his finger.

Ali and Vamp moved with determined strides in the direction of the house with the slot in the front door at the end of the walkway. When they walked past the thug on the wall, both of their fingers fondled the pistols out of habit. Immediately, they scanned the area in front of them.

"I think Cream is testin' us, Vamp," Ali whispered over his shoulder.

"Yup, no doubt about it. Stay on your tiptoes, Ali," Vamp replied with caution in his tone.

"Oh shit! No, no, no, no, no! I'm finna have to use the

Ruger!" Tiyatti murmured, taking a deep breath, mentally and physically preparing to confront the suspicious duo.

Vamp thought this had to be some type of test as he eyeballed the curtains behind the dope house's window. *I'ma bust this thang 'til it's empty. Don't be testin' my gangsta!* He finished his foul thought and stroked his pistol's trigger with his index finger. They were ten yards away from the reasonably prosperous crack house.

Click!

The metallic sound echoed in Vamp's ear just as the Ruger touched the back of his hoodie. *Aw shit!* was Vamp's first thought. *This ain't good,* was his second thought.

"Let me get that strap before I bless the back of your head with a hollow tip," Tiyatti told him, relieving Vamp of his gun.

By the time Ali realized that something was going down behind him, Vamp was on his knees and a Ruger was pointing up at him.

"If you pull your shit out, I swear I'ma clap yo' ass, bruh," Tiyatti promised him with a fixed hand, the Ruger unmoving.

Ali did the math real quick. *This ma'fucka got the drop on me, and he look like he with the bizness. I ain't gotta chance. Shit!* He embarrassingly threw his hands up and surrendered, knowing Cream and Suspect were watching the scene unfold.

"Now get flat or get clacked!"

Ali had no choice. He joined his partner on the dirty cracked concrete.

"What the fuck I tell you!" Cream hollered victoriously, snatching the hundred dollar bill off the dashboard. "That lil ma'fucka is on his shit, lil bruh, huh?" After stuffing the big face in his pocket, Cream sent Suspect over to soothe the bruised egos of their two henchmen, instructing him to tell Tiyatti to come join him in the Yukon alone.

In mere minutes, Tiyatti gladly agreed to accept the promotion Cream offered. In doing so, he went from making $2,500 a month to making $4,000 a month. With a pregnant girlfriend and a younger brother to look after, the extra money would definitely come in handy and help ease the tension on his pockets.

Tiyatti was good with the idea of working security at one of Miko Dunbar's money houses. It would get him off the streets and out of harm's way; it would put a lot more money in his pockets, and it would definitely make life a lot easier for him, Duchess, and Devontay. In one way he was so right in his thinking, in another way he was so wrong . . .

CHAPTER 13

Baby Shug

"Ay, I been meaning to ask you something for a while now, Shug. Why you always fold your sheets and blanket and then roll your mattress up?" Khory asked, facing me as he began brushing his teeth.

I pulled my eyes away from the book I was reading, and let my eyes convey that I was dead serious.

"Unless you wanna get snuck, stuck, or caught slippin', then you better be on point at all times, because ma'fuckas be layin' in the cut to do ma'fuckas dirty. Long story short, it's a way of keeping you from lying down and falling asleep during the program hours and not getting stabbed the fuck up or beat the fuck down with a sock full of batteries."

Khory continued brushing his grill while mulling over what I'd just told him.

I looked at him and said, "Nowadays, in these crazy ass California prisons, you gotta stay on your toes, bruh. You gotta keep your head on a swivel, or you gon' fuck around and get got, you feel me?" Judging from his silence I think he got the message loud and clear. We chopped it up for a while and I cleaned up, and then decided to bounce to the yard on a mission.

A few hours later, I came back to the cell on deck. I was able to secure a cell phone with the charger from one of the homies in another building. Since Khory moved in my cell a few weeks ago, I'd taken a liking to the youngster. He was solid, and so far he was passing every test. He stood his ground like he was supposed to when other convicts on the yard hit him up, and the way he conducted himself on a daily met with my approval,

91

so I decided to take him up under my wing and welcome him into the fold.

"Ay bruh, I noticed you got a few letters since you been here, but you don't ever use the phone to call anybody." It wasn't really none of my business, but I was lightweight curious about it.

He finished wiping up the sink and said, "Shit, everybody I know either got blocks on their phones, or they don't have the Global Tel Link hook up. My sisters are waiting for me to send them the info on how to get the prepaid accounts on their cell phones." His voice had a trace of disappointment in it.

"Well, check this out. I got at one of the homies in 2-Building about lettin' me use his phone for a day or two, and he let me bump this one until yard call tomorrow." I pulled the black Samsung Galaxy S4 with the charger from the folds of my sweats and showed it to him. "We got twenty-four hours to do what we gon' do wit' it," I said and handed him the phone. "I ain't really got anybody to call, so I'll fuck with it after chow and see what's good on Instagram and YouTube, maybe watch a movie or two on Netflix. Go ahead and call your folks, so you can touch base with your loved ones, bruh."

"Aw man! Thanks, bruh. Good lookin' out, Shug. I been really wanting to holla at some people hella bad too. Real talk, dawg, this good lookin' out!" Judging from his response, he was ecstatic to say the least. He jumped up on his bunk and pulled the privacy curtain over a little, so that it shielded him from the line of vision in the event somebody happened to look inside the cell window.

After handing the phone off, I slid that B.o.B *Underground Luxury* in the CD player, put my headphones on, and gave him some privacy while he chopped it up with his folks.

He was an hour into his conversation when he finally leaned

over the end of the bunk, and then held the phone out toward me.

"Here ya go, Shug."

That was fast, I thought and said, "What, you finished already?"

"Naw, my sister Khadida wants to speak to you."

What the fuck does your sister want with me? The thought flew through my mind before I opened my mouth and asked, "Why she want to speak to me?" I ain't gon' lie, I was caught off guard.

"I don't know," he said, holding the phone out, waiting for me to take it. I took it from him and leaned back on my bunk into the corner where the walls met.

"Hello?" I said, not knowing what to expect.

"Hi, I'm Khadida, Khory's older sister." Her soft voice was melodious. It sounded beautiful, like a Lauryn Hill a cappella.

"Okay, what's up with it? They call me Baby Shug." The splendor of her voice had me lightweight stuck, but I was intrigued and wanted to hear her talk some more.

"I just wanted to thank you for looking out for my little brother since he's been at that prison. He's only nineteen and it's his first time being locked up and Khory really is a good kid. He's not a gangbanger or anything like that. I really mean it when I say thank you for having his back." The sincerity in her words and the emotion she expressed in her gratitude made me smile in my head. I could tell she was the overprotective type who really cared about her brother.

"It's nothing, ma. He's good people, so it's only right that I have his back like that. You feel me?"

"Yeah, I feel you." She said it like I could take that in more ways than one. "Do you have a girlfriend?" She came out of left field with that one.

I hesitated before answering. Images of Miko's punk ass flashed behind my eyelids and hatred made my heart swell up and throb violently. My response was curt. "Naw, I ain't got a girlfriend."

"You said that like it's coming from a place of pain." Her voice was a mixture of curiosity and concern.

If only you knew! I got unusually uncomfortable. I wasn't in the mood for any psychoanalytical bullshit. As far as I was concerned, it was trust no bitch on mines! "Look here, I'ma let you holla back at your brother, a'ight?"

"Shug, hold up." She called my name out with tenderness.

What the fuck you want! I thought irritably, ready to hand the phone off. My patience was running thin, but at the same time I didn't want to disrespect Khory's sister, so I acted like nothing was wrong.

"Yeah?"

"I don't know what she did to hurt your heart, but not all of us are like that. Call me if you just wanna talk, or kick it about whatever." She said it in a way that made me feel different about her.

I was about to give the phone back to Khory when I thought better of it. *Go 'head Shug, fuck with her. You never know what'll happen!* The voice in my head was very persuasive.

"Ay, look here, Khadida. I'ma let you chop it up with your brother for a while so y'all can catch up and whatnot, but later on tonight sometime I'll hit you back. If you're still awake, then we can talk some more, a'ight?"

"I'll be awake," she assured me.

Her soft, melodic tone seduced my intrigue. A warm sensation coursed through my body and instantly put me in a better mood.

"A'ight then," I told her with a smile.

"Bye, Baby Shug." Her voice was like a warm hug to a cold-blooded dude like me.

Khory used the cell phone for a couple more hours and got in touch with all the people he needed to get in touch with. Then he handed the phone back to me when he was finished. I hooked it up to the charger, and then called Khadida as soon as the po-po did their last headcount. *I ain't got anybody else to call. Wah in a coma; Camron is six-feet deep; and Monisha is resting-in-peace next to him. Everybody I ever loved is either dead or in a bad way. I'm lonely as fuck, man! I can't even lie about that.* A few hours ago, talking to Khadida didn't seem like such a good idea, because trusting a bitch and me weren't on the same page. But after giving it some more thought, I figured talking to a chick like Khadida was exactly what I needed to help my mind escape from prison and these two life sentences I was carrying on my shoulders.

"Hello?" That soft voice immediately set the mood.

"What's crackin'?" I replied, confident. She giggled girlishly at my response.

We ended up chopping it up all night, and some time in the wee hours of the morning we exchanged pictures. She texted me back after I sent her my picture: *Nice!* I texted her back when I saw her picture: *Impressive!*

When the CO woke the building up with that loud ass bell, we said our good-byes and made plans for her to visit in the near future.

That morning I walked to breakfast with a lil more pep in my step. *A chick like Khadida might be exactly what a thug like me needs in my life right now—somebody to help me do this time and keep me from losing my mind.*

My thoughts were interrupted when I saw the LA crip named Droop Loc clocking me from across the yard. *Once is a coincidence, two times is a ma'fuckin' problem!* I slid my hand down into my waistband and inconspicuously handled the tightly wrapped end of my knife. *First chance I get I'm finna nip this shit in the bud and see what's really good with this fool!*

CHAPTER 14

Miko

After killing the three teenage thugs, Miko sat in her study trying to fix what was broken. Her fingers danced across the keyboard as she entered her password, causing a row of monitors to appear on the screen in front of her. She swiped at the smart screen until the image she was looking for materialized in high-def. With fury in her eyes, she watched the video footage of Capone creeping through the basement of the stash house searching for stray bricks that might've been left behind after the jackers who robbed her stash house had already bounced. She coldly eyed the footage of him pulling out his cell phone and talking to somebody while in the empty basement. It was all the proof Miko needed. *That sonofabitch lied to me!* She fumed over Capone's definitive answer when she quizzed him about whether he had entered the stash house after the robbery. *That bitch stood in my face and told me a boldfaced lie!* It became painfully apparent that one of the few workers she trusted was up to no good. Her father's words echoed in the back of her brain and instigated her anger: *"I'll die before I ever let a ma'fucka steal from me, because if a ma'fucka got it in him to take your money, then they also got it in 'em to take your life!"* One of her father's last utterances aggravated the savage in her. Capone's shiesty ways certainly required her immediate attention.

I got somethin' for your scandalous ass, Capone. You don't know it yet, but you picked the wrong bitch to fuck with, 'ho! She shook her thoughts from that evil line of thinking and focused on another matter that needed addressing. Softly thumbing through her phone, Miko called her cousin.

Ring. Ring. Ring.

"What's good, Miko?"

She got straight to the point.

"Cream, I want you to find Capone's snake ass and bring him to me."

"Okay, what's up with him?"

"That ma'fucka lied to us. He went in that stash house and made a call while he was in there. He's playing both sides from the middle." An ominous silence filled the space. "Bring his bitch ass to me, you hear me? But first, I want you to bring this Tiyatti fellow by, so I can interview him before I officially assign him to that new position."

"Um okay, you want me to bring him to your crib?" Cream asked, wanting to be certain.

"Yeah, you can drop him off. I'll have Anthony take him home once I'm finished interviewing him."

"A'ight, I'll be through in about thirty minutes."

"Okay then, bye," Miko told him and reached for the dossier in front of her. Miko's head snapped back faintly with piqued intrigue when first glimpsing the photograph of the handsome, cocoa-brown complexioned brotha with the intense, intelligent eyes. The detailed dossier compiled by her private investigator was loaded with pertinent personal information that would, or could, come in handy for future endeavors if it ever became necessary. It was how the queenpin conducted her business and stayed two steps ahead of the people around her, an invaluable lesson of the game, compliments of Javier.

There was something magnetizing about Tiyatti. Carefully, she studied the picture for several more minutes before her eyes dipped down to the caption below it. She scanned the words with mild interest, her perfectly plucked eyebrows arching with curiosity on more than one occasion as she read every known tidbit of information that could be unearthed regarding the life of Tiyatti Jones. She noted the absence of a criminal record. *He's a square,* she thought, before subconsciously shaking her head at the mention of his mother's untimely death. As she read his file she made a mental note of his unblemished work history and found herself inwardly wondering what critical circumstances pulled him out of the work force only to push him into the unforgiving street life. *So sad, a gullible sheep playing in a world full of savage wolves,* she mused.

Who is this bitch? A twinge of envy pinched her heart when her eyes took in the exquisite beauty of the woman in the photograph on the subsequent page, or was it a twinge of jealousy? She checked herself and regrouped her ego. *So what! He got a bitch. That 'ho ain't on my level. That bitch ain't a boss like me!* Yet her curiosity grew stronger, and her desire to know more about Tiyatti became more intense with every excerpt she read. Something about him reminded Miko of her ex-fiancé. Not the part of Baby Shug she despised, but the aspect of him that had supplied her with the best of pleasures on so many occasions, the thuggish swag and the cocky sex appeal that he wore like a perfectly tailored suit. Her pussy moistened at the possibilities. *Umm yes, I gots to have me some of this!* she declared privately and squeezed her thighs in an effort to further arouse the fire down there.

Half an hour later, the phone on her desk sounded off with a soft ring.

"Yes, what is it?" she asked with a bit of impatience.

"Your guest has arrived, Ms. Dunbar," her maid dutifully informed her.

Ooh okay. Now let's see what he's like in real life, she thought before speaking.

"Show him in." Miko was short and to the point. She didn't believe in socializing with the help.

Tiyatti walked into the luxurious designed office, and the vague scent of Crystal Versace perfume toyed with his sense of smell, sensuously teasing his nostrils. He looked at Miko and stuck his hand out, trying his damndest not to recklessly eyeball her. Helplessly captivated by her beauty, try as he might, he was unable to fully maintain his composure. His awestruck eyes canvassed her curvaceous frame with a lusty gleam.

"Ay, uh, hello, it's a pleasure to meet you, um—" he stammered, at a loss as to how best to address her.

She gave a lighthearted laugh at his discomfiture while holding his eye contact. She too was sucked in by his sex appeal, struggling to maintain her own equanimity.

"Miko. Call me Miko. It's a pleasure to meet you as well, Tiyatti." Her gaze was bold and full of hidden messages. The handshake sent an electrical surge through her body before softly exploding like an erotic bomb in the center of her essence. Her heartbeat sped up and thumped harder. His powerful swag and sex appeal were overwhelming. *This man is fine, and he just looks like he can fuck!* It wasn't often that a man had that type of effect on her, but he was having it and she was feeling it.

"Please, sit down," she said politely and encouraged Tiyatti to take the seat across from her desk. Her normally hardened demeanor vanished, and the soft, sensuous woman beneath surfaced. She was convinced that sex with him would be amazing at the very least, worth adjusting her self-imposed sexual standards. *I don't give a damn that he ain't a boss. I'm fuckin' him!* Her sex sauce drenched her panties. Sitting down was a joy in and of itself, the petals of her flower blooming with pleasure under the weight of her frame. She looked at him again and squeezed her legs together while fictitiously browsing the already read papers in front of her. Her mind raced with scenarios of seducing the handsome, wannabe thug. Tiyatti sat across from her, silently waiting for her to initiate the discussion. She decided to withhold her revelation about his file, a file that no doubt invaded his privacy and revealed a lot more about his life than he'd probably care to disclose.

Miko was an overly sensuous woman with an insatiable, erotic appetite. The passionate, hot-blooded Puerto Rican side of her demanded that her ravenous sexual cup be filled constantly. The strong-willed Creole side of her was adamant that it stay full and be replenished properly. As soft and luscious as she was in the physical sense, she was conversely as hard and unrelenting in the mental sense. Miko felt as though she deserved the world and believed in taking what she wanted, whether by force or by leaving you with no other choice. Her ambitious, bold, take-no-prisoners attitude settled her mind on getting what she wanted *right now*—having the thuggishly handsome Tiyatti Jones on her terms.

Miko tilted her head downward and peered over the gold-wire Gucci framed reading glasses sitting atop her nose and glanced in his direction. His fingers were busy checking the messages on his phone. While he focused on his phone's screen, she let her lustful thoughts loose to run wild and provoke the freak deep within her. Her skin goose bumped up with pleasure.

She stood and ironed out her dress with her expensive manicured hands, knowing she had his undivided attention. After slowly removing the Gucci frames from her face, she delicately set the designer glasses on the desktop and picked up the dossier she'd been reading. Ignoring Tiyatti's presence, she made her way over to the file cabinet on the other side of the office, her ass cheeks rhythmically rotating under the body-clinging, high-priced wool fabric. Pausing near the cabinet for a few seconds, she bent forward slightly, arching her back and making her bubble ass poke out dramatically. Her eyes narrowed to mere slits as she stared at the priceless vase in her line of vision. Its glossy reflection gave her an advantageous peek at the unsuspecting Tiyatti. She watched as he slipped his cell phone into the right front pocket of his baggy sweat suit. She took her time placing the file in its appropriate place, and observed Tiyatti grab hold of his growing erection. In seconds he had a fistful of rock hard, grown man meat in his right hand, surreptitiously stroking it while eye-fucking her from the back. That was all the urging she needed, her pussy was on fire! *Yeah, you're just like any other man; can't resist the pussy once it's thrown in your face.* It was a struggle, but she managed to keep her cool and act completely unaware of the scene of seduction she so shrewdly orchestrated. She carefully stuck the dossier between two others, and after closing the file cabinet drawer, she rested her weight on one hip. Her ass formed the perfect cup and poked out beautifully. A quick peek at the vase confirmed he was still eye-fucking her frame.

Enamored with the lovely sight of Miko's slow moving ass, Tiyatti was so engrossed with readjusting his pipe through the sweats that he was caught off guard when she suddenly turned on her heels and caught him dead bang with his hand in the cookie jar, on the candy bar.

Ooh damn, he got big meat too! she concluded, upon seeing what he was gripping. Her eyes swept upward from the hard-on in his hand to his slightly embarrassed eyes.

"Oh my! I see you're very excited about this new job opportunity."

The conniving smile and knowing look in her eyes put him on the defensive. He offered a weak reply.

"Naw, naw, it ain't like that. I was just fixin' my clothes and shit, you feel me?"

Yeah right, who the hell you think I am? Miko took several measured steps in his direction until she stood within arm's reach. "Stand up, Tiyatti." The tenor in her voice was strong and seductive; it was more an order than a request.

Feeling like he had been caught in a compromising position, Tiyatti followed her instructions without question. He towered over her and looked down at her, standing inches away in an uncomfortable silence, breathing in the Crystal Versace fragrance. His dick involuntarily jumped as the powerful essence of her aura enveloped him, rendering him helpless. *Don't do it, Tiyatti!* He thought about Duchess and struggled mightily to summon the strength to resist the irresistible pull of Miko's alluring feminine charms. *This bitch is so wet it's crazy!*

She reached out and caressed his cheek, tracing the outline of his slightly parted lips with the tip of her finger. His dicked jumped again, and the full-grown erection energetically pressed against the baggy material. Miko stood so close to him that the end of his constrained erection brushed up against her midsection.

No! No! No! the voice in his head kept screaming. He wanted to slap her hand away and shove her onto her ass. Instead he succumbed completely to her seductive influence when she squatted low, resting her huge ass cheeks on the heels of her pumps and pulled at the front of his sweats. Uhhmm! An impious groan of satisfaction escaped his lips when she took his length into her warm, wet mouth. Hearing him groan only spurred her on. She placed the heel of her hand against his nuts and effortlessly swallowed him whole, slowly rotating her neck and enthusiastically sucking on his meaty thickness. His long dick curved left and hit the back of her throat off center every time she gulped his hard-on down.

"Uhnngghhh!" He pulled his dick out of her mouth with regret, then shoved it back in with renewed desire. *Damn it!* He became angry at himself for not being able to resist her head game.

Miko knew Tiyatti had gone further than he wanted. She also understood he was far beyond the point of resisting. The power in that knowledge made her pussy flood with pleasure. She tore her mouth away from his dick and let her tongue lick wildly all over his love muscle.

"You like that?" she asked coyly between wet licks and loud slurps.

"Uhmm-hmmm!" His knees buckled when her tongue licked from the nut sac to the swollen mushroomed head, and then took every inch in her mouth and swallowed him whole again. He was past the point of feeling anything other than the intense sexual pleasure all over his dick. For the next fifteen minutes, Miko served Tiyatti with the hottest head of his life. He tried to stop it but he couldn't. His brain refused to issue that command to his body. He put his hand on her forehead and tried to push her away. Miko refused to release him from her mouth and stayed attached to his dick like it was the lifeline to living.

"Uhnngghhh!" He grabbed a handful of her long hair and yanked it back with force, until his dick popped out of her hungry jaws. Her skirt was around her waist now, and her fat, swollen pussy print was pouting at him through her panties. "We can't do this. This shit ain't cool, Miko. I got a girl and she's pregnant and I ain't tryin' to clown her like that." Tiyatti tucked his dick back in and pulled his sweats back up. His eyes pleaded with her to understand.

Fuck what you talkin' 'bout, I need that up in me! Miko thought, ignoring him while pulling her panties down and stepping out of the expensive wet silk. She reached inside his sweats and grabbed his still hard meat, and then took it out and pulled him by the dick as she backed up until her luscious cheeks hit up against the edge of the desk. Using one hand, she climbed onto the desktop while her other hand held his manhood hostage. She spread her legs wide, rubbing the head of his hard-on against her wet lips. Resisting a slice of pussy that powerful was almost impossible. "You know you want this good-good. Stop playin' and come fuck this pussy up!" Miko thrust her hips forward and kidnapped the head of his dick with her coochie. He needed no further prodding.

Tiyatti snatched his dick out of her hot, wet, tight pussy and tore his clothes off, throwing them behind him onto the chair. Then he turned and pushed himself inside her until his nuts slapped her plump ass cheeks.

"Uhnngghhh!" she screamed out when his dick slid deep up in her.

No matter how hard he tried to fight his feelings, he was stuck in her sticky for good now. The thought of her bullying him out of his dick lightweight angered him. The thought of him pulling his dick out of her bomb ass pussy eluded him. Tiyatti's carnal nature kicked in and took over. He roughly snatched her by the ankles and spread her legs as wide as he could, holding them up and open as far apart as possible.

Her body relaxed completely when it became clear that his resolve had been conquered.

"Aaagghhhh!" she let out a loud, throaty groan when his long, thick dick hit the bottom of her wet pleasure-well a second time, rubbing the right wall of her pussy all the way down to the deepest part of her being. The pleasure from his left turn curve blew her mind, causing a strong orgasm to overpower her essence, exploding in her guts and setting every inch of her skin aflame with an intense, lustful fire. His dick sank to the bottom of her passion pit again and again, and again and again. His rock hard meat slammed into her soaking wet pussy repeatedly as his pace picked up, and he plunged deeper with more force. The rhythm in his hips was unbelievable. That left-turn curve drove her mad with lust.

"Oh yesss, muthafucka! Give it to me just like that!" she yelled and grunted with passion as he pounded her out with violent, deep strokes that slid her cum-slicked ass across the desktop every time he hit her depths.

Blam! Blam! Blam! Blam! Blam!

He beat up on the pussy like that for twenty minutes. She was delirious with the dick and kept cumming continually. His heavy nuts smacked against her cheeks with each thuggish thrust of his hips, causing her to wrap her arm around his neck and put a hand on the desktop for balance. She threw the pussy back at him, matching him hump for hump.

"Get it, Tiyatti! Get this pussy good, muthafucka!" Her next orgasm was so incredibly powerful and violent it shook her entire body. Her creamy juices flooded her pussy and washed over his hard dick in waves.

Blam! Blam! Blam! Blam! Blam!

He kept digging deep into her guts and beating on her pussy walls with uncompromising consistency.

"Yes! Yes! Yes! Oh fuck yeah!" Every time his dick head hit the back of her pussy, an intense tingling sensation shot down her spine and exploded in the center of her hot, wet core. Tiyatti kept banging between her widespread thighs as he pried her arm from around his neck and pushed her back down onto the desktop. He put his hand around her slender throat and stepped in closer for better footing. Her ass and pussy were hanging off the edge of the expensive African wood. She was even with his waist, presenting him with the perfect position to poke and plunge without hindrance. Miko lay on her back, beside herself, her hands roaming all over her body as she frantically searched for ways to add to the intense pleasure that had every inch of her skin hot and horny with freaky desire. She pinched and pulled on her erect nipples through the silk blouse with one of her hands and repeatedly slapped her fingers against her swollen clitoris with the other hand. She dug the heels of her feet into his fast moving ass and tried to speed up his hip action. Miko was wild with want.

Tiyatti reached back and grabbed both of her ankles again, then put them together and held them high in front of him. Her legs were closed, thighs pressed together while her pussy poked out playing peek-a-boo with him. When he slid his hard curved dick between her puffy lips and hit the bottom of her wet delight, Miko slammed her hands onto the tabletop and tightly clutched the edge of the desk as he rammed her repeatedly, his rigid dick slamming inside of her harder and faster and deeper than before. He jackhammered her pussy for fifteen minutes straight without slowing as sweat coated his skin and dripped from his brow. Furiously, he fucked her guts while her hands held onto the rim of the desk for dear life. Then he suddenly slowed his pace, fucking up in her hella slow, his dick going all the way in as far as it could go and then coming back out until he left it sitting an inch-deep in her wet folds. Slowly, he stroked and poked her pussy that way.

"Uhhmm! Uhhmm! Uhhmm!" Her grunts and groans of gratification soon turned into pants and purrs of pleasure.

The tables had turned. Tiyatti had fucked the fight out of her. Miko's body shook with pleasure as another orgasm rocked her world. He knew he had conquered her coochie when he felt another wave of her cum wash over his dick. *This bitch got the wettest pussy I ever fucked in!* He couldn't believe how good her pussy felt. *So wet! So tight! So bomb!* He slowed his deep stroke down to the point he was pounding her slow motion, dipping his dick in from a different angle on every down stroke.

"Uhnngghhh! Uhnngghhh! Uhnngghhh!" Miko continued to purr and enjoy the best dick she ever recalled having.

An hour after sticking his dick in her, Tiyatti leaned forward and pushed his meat in to the hilt and bucked hard as he bust a nut and released himself somewhere deep inside of her hot hole. He pulled out of her pussy, and his wet fuck-stick glistened with their juices.

Oh my fucking goodness! That's the best dick I ever had in my life! Miko thought breathlessly while lying across the desk on her back trying to catch her breath. Her pussy throbbed hard from his relentless pounding, matching the violent beating of her heart.

Minutes later after catching her breath, she scooted off the desk and walked up to him, touching the side of his face with her hand and zigzagging her fingers along his jawline. Her fingers traced his lips, his chin, and then she traced the cursive Duchess tattoo decorating the left side of his neck.

"I think this is going to be a perfect working relationship, Tiyatti. Maybe one day I'll consider introducing you to boss status, so you can cut this bitch loose and upgrade to a real boss bitch." The inflection of her tone was sinister mixed with sexy.

Tiyatti grabbed her wrist and twisted it with force before

snatching her hand away from his neck. The look in her eyes was teasing and taunting with a victorious gleam that shone bright when she smiled. *She got me fucked up! Think because I hit the pussy she can get at me any ol' way. I won't be making this mistake again,* he vowed as he picked through his pile of clothes. A discomfited silence hung in the air as they dressed and composed themselves.

She looked across the room and addressed Tiyatti in a condescending tone.

"Report to work in the morning. Cream will be in touch with you with the details. That's all, you can go now." She turned her back on him, ignoring the sideways look he gave her.

Thoughts of the traitorous Capone filled Miko's mind and occupied the space in her head. *You can run but you can't hide, Capone. When I find your punk ass it's a wrap, ma'fucka!*

CHAPTER 15

Young Glock Gang

"I just got off the phone with my man on the inside, and he confirmed that tomorrow is pick-up day." Bony James returned to the living room holding a banana and a cell phone that he stuffed in his pocket.

"So our next lick is a go, y'all," he said, peeling the banana that he'd already retrieved from the fridge. He walked up on the group of gangstas sitting around the coffee table and joined them.

On top of the coffee table sat a Monopoly board game.

"I drove through with him the other day to get a feel for what we'd be up against, and after he broke the entire operation down to me, I put a plan together. This is what I came up with." Bony James grabbed a handful of red motels, diagramming a scene. "When Cream, Suspect, and their crew show up, they always arrive in a two-truck caravan and park right about here to pick up the last bag of money on the route." He put three red motels in a row to signify the arrangement of houses and apartments on the block. Then he took the little silver car and the wheel barrow and carefully placed them in front of the red motels. "The wheel barrow represents the truck with all the money in it—the truck that Cream, Suspect, and the two other shooters will be in. The car represents the security vehicle; it's the truck filled with at least six heavily-armed cats who either ride escort, or provide the protection while they make the money runs." Bony James grabbed the dog and the hat and continued to map out his plan. "We're gonna hit them when they least expect it, when they're at their most vulnerable point." He continued to break the job down

111

step by step, going over it again and again until every thug in the room understood their individual roles.

* * * * * *

The next day . . .

The Yukon Denali rolled up the block and slowed before coming to a stop in front of the house Nario occupied. The truck full of gunners eased up behind the Denali and parked several feet behind it. Cream and Suspect jumped out the black Denali like the streets owed them something. Ali and Vamp followed close behind. Nineteen duffle bags carrying the week's take sat in the back on the floor of the SUV. The Durango behind the Denali remained motionless. In all, six stone-faced thugs sat piled in the Dodge Durango guarding the Yukon Denali with big guns that had a gang of bullets in them.

"Why they ain't gettin' out, Bony? I thought your boy said that the fools in the other truck were supposed to get out too!" Jayquan said, louder than necessary, from the passenger seat of the stolen Chevy Blazer.

"Chill out, 'Quan."

Bony James wiped his brow with a balled up green bandana, erasing the fine film of perspiration that formed when the two trucks showed up and broke protocol. He thumbed his phone and put it to his ear and waited for the person on the other end to pick up.

"What's good?" Goldie answered.

"It looks like there might have to be a change of plans," Bony James spoke calmly into the phone.

"What are you talkin' 'bout? Why? What's up?" Goldie asked.

Bony James ground his teeth and told him, "Because the

truck full of shooters behind the Denali with all the money in it ain't following the script. I count six heads in the Durango. All of 'em strapped and ain't none of 'em budgin', homie."

"This shit don't sound right, Bony. You think your man is puttin' some shit in the game?" A touch of worry laced his voice.

"Nah, I don't think so." Bony James defended his guy.

"Is we gon' call it off then, or what? We can always hit 'em up next week when they make their next run."

"Fuck nah, homie. We ain't callin' shit off. We finna make this pop today!" Bony James concocted a quick remix to the plot they had tirelessly gone over yesterday.

"Talk to me then. Tell me what it do?" Goldie was on his gangsta.

Bony James' mind raced with scenarios before he finally trusted his instincts and settled on a game plan. "I'm sending Jayquan over there with you and G-Mack. I want y'all to stick to the script and do what we already planned yesterday."

Jayquan turned in the passenger seat and looked at the side of his head like he was crazy. "Whatchu gon' be doin' then?" Jayquan interjected when he heard his name mentioned. Goldie asked the same question on the other end of the line.

Bony James answered them both. "I'ma take the Durango out by myself."

"What!" Jayquan asked, full of disbelief.

"How?" Goldie exclaimed loudly at the same time.

Bony remained poised and patiently explained. "I look at it like this, y'all. I can take out all six fools in the Durango with one move by crashin' into 'em with this big body Blazer. They not gon' be expectin' no shit like that, and it's gonna take all they asses out the equation when I plow into 'em. After I ram the Durango, I want you, Jayquan, and G-Mack to roll up in the 4-Runner and do your thang just like we planned; only difference now is Jayquan will be jumping from the bed of the 4-Runner and bustin' on Cream, Suspect, and the two clowns with them." He paused for a second. "G-Mack is still hoppin' out the passenger side and snatching up the duffle bags in the Denali and tossin' 'em into the 4-Runner. After I crash into the Durango, I'ma jump out and light that bitch up. Once I body them fools, I'ma start bustin' on the other mafuckas with Jayquan. Goldie, you stay in the truck, because as soon as G-Mack got all the duffle bags, we gettin' up outta here with the quickness. G-Mack is gonna ride in the front with you while me and Jayquan hop in the back. Throw your guns in the back too, because if we fuck around and run out of ammo while we gettin' on 'em, we gon' need those extra straps."

Sounds good to me! "Fuck it! Let's do the damn thang then!" Goldie's mind was made up.

"Let's go!" Jayquan was with it too.

Bony James looked over at Jayquan, and the two gangstas exchanged a hard handshake. "Go with Goldie and G-Mack, homie."

"Be careful, Bony." Jayquan had a lot of emotion in his words.

"Hurry up, 'Quan, before them other fools come back!" Bony James wasn't trying to get emotional with it.

Jayquan did as he was told. After switching spots, he lay flat on his back in the bed of the Toyota 4-Runner with the MP5 across his chest. Seconds seemed to go by like minutes. The sound of a big body truck grew louder as the Blazer accelerated to a high rate of speed and came barreling down on the Durango doing eighty miles per hour.

BLLAAAAAAAMMMMM!

The front end of the Blazer smashed into the side of the

truck, bending the driver's side of the Durango in half. It pushed the driver's door all the way into the passenger side of the SUV, crushing the Durango and instantly killing three of the thugs. The airbag in the Blazer deployed and softened the blow of the violent collision. Bony James' neck and head snapped back with incredible force. Car alarms sounded off and pierced the hot sunny day. Seconds after the Blazer banged into the Durango, Cream, Suspect, Ali, Vamp, and Nario ran out of Nario's house with their guns drawn.

Doom! Doom! Doom!

Cream let off shots with the .45.

Pop! Pop! Pop! Pop! Pop! Pop! Pop!

Suspect bust his thumper in the direction of the car crash.

In the midst of the gunfire, the Toyota 4-Runner came to a screeching stop on the driver's side of the Yukon Denali. Jayquan jumped from the bed of the truck with the MP5 waist high and let it go.

Kak! Kak! Kak! Kak! Kak! Kak! Kak! Kak! Kak!

Whizzing, hot bullets destroyed the front side of the house behind Cream and his crew.

Doom! Doom! Doom!

Pop! Pop! Pop! Pop! Pop! Pop! Pop!

Cream and Suspect returned fire from behind their hiding places.

Bony James shook off his discombobulation and desperately tried to regain his equability. He pushed the damaged door open, staggering onto the street with the nylon strap of the MP5 gripped tightly in his hand. Bullets whizzed past his head, shattering windows and slamming into the metal behind him. Flying glass sprayed his face and arms, cutting him in several areas. He rose up and sprayed the MP5 from right to left.

Kak! Kak! Kak! Kak! Kak! Kak! Kak! Kak! Kak!

Then he swung it back from left to right.

Kak! Kak! Kak! Kak! Kak! Kak! Kak! Kak! Kak!

Out of his peripheral he saw movement in the Durango. A thug with a mean mug had a Mac-10 in his right hand, poised to pop off.

Kak! Kak! Kak! Kak! Kak! Kak! Kak! Kak! Kak!

Bullets from Bony James' gun poked holes in him.

Bbbtttaaattt! Bbbtttaaattt!

The Mac-10 spit erratically inside the Durango and tore holes in the already dead driver's neck and back before ripping the dashboard to shreds.

G-Mack was busy grabbing two duffle bags at a time and throwing them into the back of the 4-Runner as guns bust all around him. He wanted to look around and see what was going on, but his role was to secure the money bags, and he was sticking to the script.

Kak! Kak! Kak! Kak! Kak! Kak! Kak! Kak! Kak!

Jayquan sprayed the entire area in front of Nario's house.

Kak! Kak! Kak! Kak! Kak! Kak! Kak! Kak! Kak!

Bony James was doing the same, keeping Cream and his crew flat on their stomachs and frozen behind whatever they could hide behind.

"Let's go! Let's go! Let's go!" G-Mack yelled, after tossing the last set of duffle bags into the bed of the 4-Runner.

Kak! Kak! Kak! Kak! Kak! Kak! Kak! Kak! Kak!

Jayquan jumped into the open bed of the Toyota and immediately switched out MP5s, letting the fully automatic weapon run wild with gunfire in the direction of Cream and Suspect. Bony James dived into the back and landed next to Jayquan. When he came up, he had a freshly loaded fully automatic MP5 in his hands as well and began firing furiously in the direction of Miko's two cousins. The Toyota punched it down the street and bent the corner at the end of the block doing sixty miles per hour. All four Young Glock Gang members in the Toyota 4-Runner were healthy with no new holes in them.

Cream and Suspect stood in front of the bullet riddled house and watched with anger as Miko's money disappeared around the corner. Nario, Ali, and Vamp lay stretched out on the ground slumped, bullet holes polka-dotting their head, chest, and stomach. Bullet holes also swiss-cheesed the Denali. The two brothers turned and disappeared into the apartment complex, fleeing the gruesome murder scene on foot as the sounds of approaching sirens got louder and louder.

As he hopped a fence and sprinted ahead of his younger brother with his pistol in his left hand, Cream swore on everything he loved that he would kill every one of the jackers and their families. He wondered how they knew their routine. Capone came to mind immediately.

CHAPTER 16

Baby Shug

It had been a little over two weeks since I'd first met Khadida over the phone, and since then we'd written a few letters and talked on the phone whenever I was able to get one from one of the homies. I told her a bit about me, but not too much. A chick gotta earn the right to learn about me. But the rapport we developed was strong, and things between us were heating up. Khadida was hella cool. Every time I looked at one of the pictures she'd sent, I couldn't help but think how much she resembled the singer Keyshia Cole, only Khadida was a little taller and a little thicker. Her visiting form had just been approved, and I was expecting her to call me out for a visit today when her sister Khassandra called Khory out. Khory went out first. Five minutes later, they called my name over the loudspeaker and told me I had a visit.

I pulled the door open and stepped into the visiting room with my swag turnt all the way up, overdosing on confidence. Taking a deep breath, I wiped myself down and coolly surveyed the visiting room. My eyes canvassed the sea of black and brown faces in search of Khadida. When I spotted her, the smile came easily. *Damn, she hella wet!* I thought, eye-fucking her curvy frame. She was sporting a pair of pink Capri pants that smothered her monkey and choked her ass cheeks out. The tight-fitting, sexy shirt did little to restrain the 36D's prominently standing up on her chest, poking out proudly. Long, honey blonde curls danced on her shoulders when she stood up. Our smiles widened as we approached one another. *The pictures don't do her justice.* Her light brown skin was flawless, and her face was painted model perfect. She had light brown eyes with hazel specks, and her full lips pouted naturally.

"What's up, beautiful?" I greeted her warmly with a hug.

"I'm fine. How are you doing, handsome?"

"I'm good now." She blushed and her eyes twinkled.

"Our first hug and kiss, huh?" I said and stepped closer.

"Yup." Her smile showed a set of perfect white teeth. I pulled her close, and my hands automatically cupped her well-developed derriere. Her slender arms wrapped around my neck, and her softness pressed against my hard frame like she was happy to be here. Our lips touched for the first time, and I immediately hoped I would have the pleasure of tasting her tongue many more times in the future.

"You smell nice." She complimented my cologne.

"Thank you, ma, but you smell better. You look gorgeous too, stunning!" I told her and our lips touched again. She sensuously sucked on my bottom lip while I squeezed on her back pockets. After sharing a second passionate kiss, we separated and she hollered at Khory for a few minutes. Then we sat at one of the empty tables near the back. The conversation came easy between us, the dialogue both interesting and intelligent. For the next five hours we chopped it up and enjoyed each other's company. She talked freely about her past and her future aspirations. In return I told her my story, my history, and the events that led up to my being in the penitentiary with a pair of twenty-five-to-life sentences. When I finished talking, she shook her head in disbelief and looked at me with eyes full of compassion. "Wow, that's crazy!"

"Yeah, I know, huh?" She leaned across the table and reached for my hands. *She got the softest hands! Damn, it feels good holding something so soft again!*

She looked into my eyes with genuine concern and asked,

"Have you heard anything as far as your brother's condition?"

I dropped my head with regret as a feeling of helplessness washed over me.

"Naw, I ain't heard nothin' regarding him in eighteen months. The last news I had concerning Wah was that he squeezed his girl Tocarra's fingers with his hand. I don't know if he's still alive or what." A moment of saddened silence hovered around us and darkened the mood for a minute.

She sat up straight, squeezed my hands, and broke the silence.

"Would you like me to drive down to San Diego and check up on him, see about his current status?" That was the first time in a long time that my heart was moved with any meaningful emotion. *Wow, she willing to go that far out of her way for me.* The idea impressed me. *She is earning hers now.*

"That's asking a lot of you, Khadida. I mean, I don't want to put that responsibility on you like that."

"A few hours of driving to find out how your brother is doing so that you can have a peace of mind wouldn't be asking too much, Shug. Trust me, it's not asking too much. Besides, you're not asking, I'm volunteering." Her smile was amazing. I liked how the mole above the right side of her lip accentuated her beauty. I was digging the fact that she was putting herself out there like that, offering to see how my brother was doing. This early in the game, to be willing to go to those lengths on my account spoke volumes about how she was built. It hinted at her having real *ride or die* potential.

"In that case, I would definitely appreciate it if you checked up on my brother for me, Khadida. On the real, it would mean a lot to me. How are you sittin' on finances?"

"I'm straight, why?" she asked with a perplexed expression.

"Because, if money was an issue I was gonna put a proposition on the table. I mean, with the cost of gas and the economy the way it is, people are holding onto their bankrolls a little tighter nowadays, you feel me?" I smiled at her, but my tone was serious. *I guess we'll see how ride or die she really is.*

She scrunched her nose up in a cute kinda way and looked at me like: *I bet you do have a proposition.* "A proposition, huh?"

"Yeah, if you're that type of chick. And for the record, Khadida, I do sense that you're that type." My smile was wider now, my tone cool. I was feeling how she met my flirtatious eye contact with some flirtation of her own.

"And what *type of chick* do you sense that I am, Baby Shug?" she asked, peering over the can of Pepsi that was about to touch her lips.

Those lips are sexy as hell! I thought and inconspicuously squeezed my half-hard dick. "Well . . ." I stared intently into her eyes after letting go of my piece. "My gut tells me that you're a ride or die type of chick. Like you might just know a thing or two about the streets . . . 'bout that life." I was reading her facial expressions and gauging her response. I wanted to know if she was really with the business, or if she was just fronting like she was. It didn't matter how she responded to my questions. I was going to fuck with her anyway. But the manner in which I was going to fuck with her hinged on her response to my question. If she wanted to chase paper with me, then I was gonna let her run like an Olympic track star. Have her on some Carmelita Jeter shit. If she wasn't the paper chasing type, then I was gonna proceed with that in mind and let it be what it was going to be.

She smiled slyly and set her soda down. "Your gut is very perceptive, Shug, and you're right. I do know a thing or two about the streets, or *that life*, as you call it." Her eyes met mine and screamed, *You better ask somebody!* Her feminine swag was the ultimate turn-on.

"Tell me more about the *thing or two* you're supposed to know 'bout that life. I mean, what makes a beautiful sistah such as yourself street certified and game approved?" I asked, my eyes locking onto hers.

"Well, if it's any of your business—"

"I'm tryin' to make it my business," I interrupted, letting her know that I was all alpha male. We were back to eye boxing again and flirting.

"Anyway, like I was saying, if you must know, my last boyfriend was in the life. He was doing his thug thang real tough before . . ." Her voice trailed off, and she looked down at the soda can and started playing with it. Her eyes welled up, and she bit her bottom lip.

It was obvious her last boyfriend was a touchy subject. I reached over and caressed her arm to let her know I was there for her.

"It's okay . . . Before what?" My tone softened with genuine concern.

She shook her head slowly, sadly. "He got shot and died last year." Her words were full of pain. The fact that she was still so emotional about it after a year had passed spoke volumes. It was proof that she invested her heart for real when she gave it to her man. I stroked the back of her hand with my thumb.

"I'm sorry to hear that, Khadida. I'm sorry you had to endure that type of pain. I'm sure your ex was a good dude." I squeezed her hand and confirmed my sincerity.

Her eyes were full of tears, but they refused to fall over the rim of her eyelids.

"He was a good dude, he really was." She looked off into

wherever her thoughts were taking her at that moment. Sometimes not saying anything was the best thing to say, so I let her familiarize herself with whatever emotion she was revisiting and comforted her with my presence. My hands let her know that I was there for her on an emotional level.

"If Trey Songz was a gang banger doing time in prison he would look just like this dude!" Khassandra, her loud, brash sister approached our table with Khory. She was definitely the boisterous one of the family. When it dawned on her that she had interrupted a heavy moment, she stopped and looked back and forth between me and Khadida, trying to determine if I was the one at fault for her sister's sadness.

"You okay, 'Dida?" Khassandra put her hands on her sister's shoulders and looked at me like I was guilty.

"Um hm. I'm good. It's all good. We were just having a moment." For a couple of seconds an uncomfortable silence lingered around us like a cloud. Khory's always inquisitive ass finally took care of that.

"Ay Shug, what's up with that room over there where the CO is posted up at? I keep seeing inmates give him something and go in there with their visitors." Khory was observant, if nothing else.

I looked over at the room he was referring to and smiled.

"That's the 50-15 room, bruh. That's the room you wanna be in if it's gucci like that, you feel me?" I looked at Khadida and discreetly winked.

"The 50-15 room? What the fuck is that?" Khory asked.

My eyes lingered on Khadida's for a few more seconds before I spoke.

"You give the CO fifty dollars, and he let you and your visitor rent the room for fifteen minutes. It's the only blind spot in the visiting room, and he hustlin' the hell out of it." I only told him what I'd heard from the homies on the yard.

Khadida used the interruption as an opportunity to shake off her sadness and asked the question, "Fifty dollars for fifteen minutes?" The look on her face was confused interest.

I looked directly in her eyes this time.

"Yup, and it's standing room only, so you gotta bend that ass in half and beat it up good to really get your money's worth," I responded, playfully squeezing Khadida's hand.

"Unghh, that's hecka nasty!" Khassandra let her feelings be known.

Khadida remained silent and stared thoughtfully off into space. Her mind was somewhere else. We took pictures and went back to our separate tables again. Way too soon visiting hours were over, and we were saying our good-byes. I squeezed on her back pockets again, and our lips locked with one final kiss before we parted ways; it was a hard, wet, passionate tongue kiss that was full of urgency. I watched her walk out the door and couldn't remember the last time I'd smiled so much. *Yeah, I got a feeling we gon' be seeing about that 50-15 room in the near future!* I walked away with a bulging dick pushing against my prison-issued pants.

CHAPTER 17

Miko

"What's the latest on Capone?" Miko asked when Cream returned from the kitchen with refreshments.

"Ain't nobody heard from him in weeks. I think he knows we're on him, and he in the wind," Cream volunteered his opinion.

"Stay on that, cousin. I want that bastard as badly as I want the ma'fuckas who been hitting our spots!" the anger in Miko's tone was unmistakable.

"Okay, we'll find his bitch ass eventually. He can't hide forever," Cream said.

"We need to go harder about finding out who keeps hittin' our pockets! Ma'fuckas is startin' to think we're soft and vulnerable because we gettin' touched and we ain't touchin' anybody back. I don't give a fuck if we gotta kill innocent people in the process; we need to start makin' examples out of ma'fuckas!" Miko wasn't used to being on the losing side of an ass whooping. She understood all too well that the streets didn't play fair, but usually she was the one not playing fair.

After pulling on his blunt and blowing a gang of smoke out his mouth, Cream spoke up.

"I got a team of our best soldiers scouring the streets right now trying to find out anything they can about anybody who weight suddenly got heavier, or somebody stuntin' with something new that suggest they might've came into a grip of money all of a sudden. We also got a squad of hardheads in the streets trying to find out anything they can about a cat with a gold grill pushin' a Pathfinder, or a crew who got big enough nuts to even try some shit like that."

Miko nodded in approval and pulled deep on the blunt. *Damn this shit is strong!* She reacted to the Platinum Cookie kush, coughing a couple of times before telling them, "The video from the basement shows three men taking the dope before Capone's bitch ass showed up on the scene. So right now we know for sure that it's at least a four-man crew, countin' the driver in the Pathfinder. Also, when they hit my money truck it was at least four people involved in that as well. Y'all wasn't able to get a good look at whoever hit the money truck, but I'm willing to bet my left titty that it's the same crew who hit the stash house." Miko made the observation in hopes that some missing piece to the puzzle would reveal itself and fall into place. *I know Capone is playing both sides from the middle; my gut don't lie to me. When I get my hands on him, I'ma do his sorry ass so bad he's gonna wish he was dead!* Miko's mind drifted off into a foul place, and she let the evil thoughts provoke her wickedness.

Another thought occurred, and a devilish smile crept onto her lips.

"It ain't no secret, y'all. Capone is the ma'fuckin' traitor. When we find him I know exactly how we can put an end to all of this shit!" Miko said, looking up at Cream. "Cream, I want you to—"

Ring . . . Ring . . . Ring . . .

The cell phone ringing in Cream's pocket cut short whatever Miko was about to say. *Who the fuck is this?* he thought while reaching for the phone. When he looked down at the screen, he held his hand up, indicating that it was a call important enough to interrupt their meeting.

"What's up wit' it, Hound?" he answered in a composed tone.

"What's good, Cream? Ay, check it out. I think we just got a hit, boss!" Dough Hound was one of his most thorough soldiers.

"Talk to me." Cream leaned forward after hearing the excitement in Dough Hound's voice.

"I think I found ol' boy with the gold grill who was pushin' the Pathfinder the night the stash house got jacked."

"What makes you think that?" A rush of excitement coursed through Cream's body.

"Because, I'm following a ma'fuckin' fool who got a gold grill as we speak. He's pushin' a white Glasshouse with a gold-metal flake paint job."

The rush of excitement Cream experienced a few seconds ago all but disappeared. "He got gold teeth, and he pushin' a white Glasshouse? What the fuck makes you so sure that potna you followin' is the dude we're lookin' for?" Disappointment shrouded his question.

"Because," Dough Hound said, pausing a couple of seconds, "before he got into the Glasshouse he pulled up in a black-on-black Pathfinder and jumped out of it, then switched keys with some cat who looked like he wit' the bizness. The dude he switched keys with handed him a backpack that looks like it could be full of work."

That rush of excitement was back. Cream optimistically hoped that Dough Hound had found the right man.

"You said you following him right now?" Cream asked anxiously.

"Yup, he's about half a block ahead of me."

"Where y'all at?"

"I just turned down Logan Ave, headed toward the South."

"Stay on him! Don't let that ma'fucka out your sight, Hound. You hear me!" Cream barked out the command while reaching across the couch, grabbing his thumper.

"Gotcha boss! Don't trip. I ain't gon' lose him."

"I'll hit you back in a few minutes when I get in traffic."

"A'ight." Dough Hound ended the call.

Cream stood up and smiled at Miko, who was waiting to hear what the call was about.

"I think Dough Hound found the driver of the Pathfinder." He told her about the exchange with Dough Hound, and then turned to Suspect.

"C'mon, let's go, bruh. We got work to do." He stuffed his phone in his pocket, then snatched his jacket off the coatrack. They were on their way out of Miko's office when Suspect stopped at the door.

"Are you comin'?" He turned and asked Miko.

"Hell nah, that's what I got y'all for. Go find that ma'fucka and bring his ass to me alive and in one piece," Miko told him and waved him off.

"Let's go see about this gold-toothed pussy in the white Glasshouse," Cream said to Suspect.

"I betchu money it's him. I bet you the price of his gold grill that it's him," Suspect said, donning an angry mug.

"Well, let's find out then. And if it is, you can keep the gold grill. Right after I shoot it out of his mouth."

CHAPTER 18

Cream & Suspect

Cream and Suspect simultaneously jumped out the beige Cadillac CTS with guns in hand and murder on their minds. They trotted across the street with the thumpers flat against their legs, crouching as they approached Dough Hound's car.

Tap. Tap. Tap.

Suspect hit the window with the back of his knuckle three times.

"What it look like?" he asked, after sliding into the passenger seat.

"He's definitely our guy. The dude's name is Goldie. He's upstairs in apartment 2-B with at least two other cats. I think they up in there conducting business." Dough Hound briefed the two brothers as he pulled a Newport out and lit it.

"What makes you say that, and how you know his name is Goldie?" Cream asked from the backseat while handling his chrome piece, checking the clip.

"Because, when I pulled up I flossed like I was using that pay phone over there." Dough Hound nodded in the direction of the pay phone outside the liquor store next to the rundown row of apartments to their left. "While I was flossin' on the phone, two wild lookin' cats came from that apartment up there, the second apartment from the right. When they came downstairs, some chick across the street hollered out to the dude in the white Glasshouse. She called him Goldie, and he responded like he knew the bitch. After that, he snatched the backpack from the backseat and followed the two wild lookin' cats upstairs. They been up there ever since." Dough Hound kept his eyes on the apartment door, staring through a cloud of smoke at the 2-B stenciled just above the brass- colored peephole.

"Whatchu wanna do, Cream? I think we should run up in that bitch and bust on every ma'fucka in there and take what's ours!" Suspect was turnt up and ready to kill.

"Naw, we ain't gon' do it like that, bruh. You trippin', Suspect." Cream checked his trigger-happy brother from the backseat.

"Whatchu mean I'm trippin'! That fool's up in that apartment with a bag full of our work! He's one of the ma'fuckas who murked our workers and jacked us for sixty-two bricks and half a million. You damn right I'm trippin'!" Suspect beat his fist on the console when he spoke to emphasize his points.

"Calm the fuck down, lil bruh!" Cream asserted himself while Dough Hound stared straight ahead at the apartment marked 2-B. "You ain't thinkin' right, Suspect! We over here deep in the South in the heart of Brim hood, and it's three of us and a thousand of them. Just because you don't see 'em that don't mean they ain't there! If we run up in there bustin', it's gon' be a street full of flamed up gun-totin' Brims playin' real life laser tag wit' our asses!" Cream could see the realization of his argument registering in his brother's brain.

Suspect's body language quieted. He relaxed and turned in his seat. "You're right, bruh. My bad . . . I'm so geeked on smackin' ol' boy's noodles, I ain't think about all that other shit. They'll be in the streets thick as shit when they hear them gunshots go off." He leaned back and spoke calmly. "How you wanna go about it then, Cream?" Suspect asked humbly, listening to his brother's response.

"For starters, we takin' a loss on that work he got up in that backpack. The way I figure it, if he sellin' some product, then that means he's finna come up outta there with a bag full of money. I say we let him bounce with the money, then hit his ass around the corner at the first stop sign he pauses at. I'll get in front of him in the 'Lac, while you and Dough Hound follow him. After I get in front, when I stop he's gonna have to stop too. That's when you get out and smack his noodles. After you plug him full of holes, grab the money and we out!" Cream slapped his hands, then rubbed them together triumphantly.

* * * * * *

Fifteen minutes later, the Cadillac eased to a stop two blocks away from the apartment that had 2-B on it. The white Glasshouse slowed as well, only feet behind the Cadillac's bumper. Goldie sat behind the steering wheel with his Glock in his grip and a bag full of big faces in the seat next to him. He impatiently leaned on the horn a few times when the Cadillac in front of him didn't move.

Bomp! Bomp! Ba-Ba Bomp! Bomp! Bomp!

Goldie's street senses kicked in, and he realized something wasn't right. This look like a fuckin' setup! His grip on the Glock tightened. He saw a flash of movement in his rearview. It is a setup!

Doom! Doom! Doom! Doom! Doom!

Suspect ran up on the right side of Goldie's whip with his arm outstretched busting shots through the back window of the Glasshouse.

Pap! Pap! Pap! Pap! Pap! Pap! Pap!

Goldie's Glock erupted like a small explosion. He was half turned to his right in the driver's seat busting shots back at the approaching figure. Bullets whizzed by Suspect's head, but that didn't deter him, he ducked low and kept coming, kept firing.

Doom! Doom! Doom!

His sixth shot hit Goldie behind the ear, slumping him over in the front seat, his body hugging the steering wheel as the seventh and eight shots hit him in the top of his back. The gunfire ceased as suddenly as it had started; an inauspicious silence filled the streets.

"They over there shootin'!" a woman screamed somewhere in the distance.

"Shut up, bitch, and get down!" a man yelled in response.

Suspect kept his thumper up and aimed at the motionless outline in the Glasshouse as he cautiously stepped toward the driver's side door.

Doom! Doom!

Two shots smacked into the back of Goldie's head and his body tipped over, falling limp on the floor under the dash. *Make sure he dead!* Suspect thought and smiled before reaching into the Glasshouse and snatching the backpack full of money from the passenger seat. He calmly walked toward the CTS and opened the passenger side door. He tossed the bag of money onto the backseat before fixing himself in the front seat as Cream revved the powerful engine.

The Cadillac pulled off leaving the Glasshouse frozen in traffic, Goldie's corpse stiffening under the sound system. Suspect turned and looked back at the murder scene. *I wonder if that bitch who hollered saw my face. I oughta go back and dome her ass!*

"I think that bitch saw my face, Cream!" he told his brother.

"What bitch are you talkin' about?"

"That bitch back there! We need to go back so I can handle that 'ho!" Suspect glanced in the rearview, anxious.

"Man, we ain't going back nowhere. It's a dead body back there, bruh. Is you crazy!"

Suspect mean-mugged his older brother and said in a huff, "A'ight, but if I fuck around and catch a case because that bitch saw me, that's on you, Cream!"

"Relax, bruh. Ain't nothin' gon' happen to you. We good."

That's easy for you to say. You wasn't the one whose face that bitch saw! Suspect thought angrily and mugged the side of Cream's face. He reached into the backseat for the backpack and pulled it into his lap.

"Nothin' bet' not happen to me!"

CHAPTER 19

Tiyatti

This is your last chance to back out, Tiyatti. You don't have to tell her if you don't want to, man! Yes you do. You do have to tell her! It's only right you keep it one hundred with her. Tiyatti wrestled with his morals. On one hand, he wanted to keep his dirty deed a secret, knowing it would keep the peace in his relationship. On the other hand, he felt an overpowering need to keep it real with the love of his life because the guilt was too heavy a burden to carry. He turned onto his back, opening his mouth wide with a yawn while twisting and stretching his body to its limits. The intoxicating smell of French toast, eggs, and turkey bacon had him ready to get up and start the day, but the thought of him breaking Duchess' heart made him want to cover back up and sleep his slip-up away. *Why did your dumbass have to fuck that bitch Miko? It doesn't matter why. What's done is done! Now you gotta live with the results of your actions!*

After several more minutes of grappling with right versus wrong, he finally made his mind up that confessing his infidelity to Duchess would be the right thing to do. At the end of the day, he knew that he could keep the act of betrayal to himself and get away with it, but he wasn't built like that. Tiyatti strongly believed in truthfulness as it pertained to honesty in a relationship. He was far from perfect, but he was as close to real as one could get.

"I fucked up. Now I have to man up and face the consequences," he whispered to himself as he sat up in the bed and slipped his size twelve's into the black corduroy house shoes. He crossed a line he vowed he'd never cross; the fact that he had done so without putting up much of a fight only made him that much more disappointed in himself.

Tiyatti knew how painful it was going to be for Duchess. He knew how deep the sword of betrayal would cut into her soul when he stabbed her heart with it. He knew exactly what it would feel like, because years ago Duchess had cut deep into his soul and stabbed his heart in much the same way. It had been early on in their relationship during their only break. After moving back in with her parents, while she was at her most vulnerable, a neighbor she'd grown up with sweet-talked her out of her panties after being the shoulder she needed to cry on. Duchess kept it one hundred and confessed her infidelity to Tiyatti after moving back in with him, but her confession didn't do anything to lessen the heart-wrenching pain he felt over her unfaithfulness. It was only a month long break up, and the fact that she sought comfort in the arms of another man not only pierced his heart with pain, it punctured his pride as well and mentally stayed with him a lot longer than she knew. It affected him in a much deeper manner than he let on.

After using the bathroom and washing up, he entered the kitchen with a picture of trepidation painted all over his face.

"Hey boo. Good morning, sleepy head," Duchess joyfully chimed over her shoulder as she multi-tasked around the small space. When she got no response, she stopped what she was doing and turned around. "What's wrong, baby? Are you okay?" She wiped her hands on her apron and went over to her man.

Tiyatti plopped down with a pained expression on his mug. He was searching for the right way to tell her, the proper string of words that might lessen her anguish.

Duchess lowered herself to her knees in front of him and

cupped his face with both of her hands. When their eyes met and she saw the troubled gaze in his eyes, she knew her heart was about to be broken. When he cast his eyes down in shame, her intuition told her that her heartbreak was at the hands of another woman.

A single tear rolled down his cheek, the pain of his shame was profound. Knowing he was about to break her heart was excruciating to his emotion.

"I fucked up, Duchess. I'm sorry, baby, but I fucked up. I cheated on you, ma."

The first slap stung his face harshly. The second slap numbed the skin on his jaw. He reached out and restrained her flailing hands as she silently lashed out at him, physically expressing her agony. The pained portrait on her face was heartbreaking.

"Why Ty? Why would you do me like that? I'm pregnant, Ty! What the fuck were you thinking? Who is she, Ty?" She struggled to free her hands in an attempt to continue her openhanded assault on his face.

"I'm sorry, baby. It just . . . happened."

She broke down in his lap and cried with so much sorrow, he knew at that moment he would never break her heart like that again. *I'd rather die than to see her this way again!* It didn't matter that she had done the same to him, or that his reaction to her infidelity was the complete opposite of hers. Whereas hers was violent and verbal, his had been silent and distant. Bringing up the past and reminding her that she had cheated on him wouldn't change the fact that he messed up. *Two wrongs don't make a right,* he thought as he picked her up and carried her to their bedroom. After closing the door, he came clean to her about sexing Miko, telling her everything.

She attacked him again, hurling harsh words at him and

saying hurtful things that could never be unsaid. Tiyatti took it. As far as he was concerned, he deserved every bit of her disrespect. They stayed behind the closed door of their bedroom all morning fighting over his infidelity.

"You need to find your ass somewhere else to work, Tiyatti!" Those were Duchess' last words to him before he left to go work at the money house.

Tiyatti drove toward his destination slower than normal, allowing his thoughts to connect like dots as an exit plan formulated in his head.

"Thirty days." He said the words aloud as if they would resonate more firmly in his determination. His mind was made up and his decision was final. Within the next thirty days he planned on stepping away from the game and out of the street life for good. It wasn't worth it. He had a pregnant girlfriend with a child on the way, and they needed him to be available at all times. He had a little brother who was on his way to a big-time college program with an extremely strong possibility of becoming a professional athlete, barring any serious injuries. His little brother looked up to him and deserved a better role model to pattern himself after. The money he was making was more than good, but the danger that went hand in hand with his current line of work, along with the risks he faced on a daily basis, wasn't worth his not being there to watch his seed grow up, or to see his brother shine and realize his full potential of joining the professional ranks. It damn sure wasn't worth jeopardizing the relationship he had with the woman he considered the love of his life, the woman he wanted to spend the rest of his life with.

Tiyatti eased up to the curb and checked his Ruger after putting security on the Chrysler 300. He headed into the money house for his twelve-hour shift.

When he entered the house, Miko was standing next to her bodyguard/driver, Anthony, who had a huge chrome canon tucked in his shoulder holster and a look about him that said: *I will break every bone in your body if you think about testing my gangsta!* "I'm glad to see that my workers are prompt and reliable when it comes to protecting my money."

Tiyatti's initial reaction was a rush of nervous uncertainty. It was the first time Miko had shown her face at the money house, and the black hulk next to her looked like he wanted to body someone in a bad way. Tiyatti shook off the uneasiness and managed to find his composure.

"That's what you pay me for, right?" he replied.

Don't fuck around and get hurt, smart ass! Miko thought angrily. She didn't like his smart-aleck response, but she let it slide for the time being. Her pussy was wet at the sight of him and the memory of their last meeting.

Tiyatti wanted to get far away from her and the big goon with the chrome canon.

"I got work to do," he said plainly and went to do his job. It was obvious the big dude's presence served the purpose of intimidation, and so far it was working. Tiyatti was far from a coward, but the black hulk standing next to Miko made him very uncomfortable. His posture made it evident that he was built to hurt people, or destroy them with his bare hands if need be. He looked like he got off on hurting humans.

Tiyatti had never killed a man, and he wasn't trying to start any new habits today, so he went about performing his daily duties as security of the most lucrative money house under Miko's umbrella. He went room to room double-checking the deadbolt locks and steel iron beams lying across the face of the heavily fortified doors. He double-checked the boarded windows and made sure that none of the two by fours had been loosened or tampered with.

"So, this is what I'm paying you top dollar for, huh?" Miko's voice dripped with sarcasm. She had managed to quietly creep into the room and surprise him. "I like a thorough man though, Tiyatti. It's a turn-on when a man knows how to protect the house, you know what I mean?"

Is this bitch for real? he thought, unsure if she was clowning or being serious.

"What do you want from me, Miko?"

The queenpin smiled and took five sensuous long-legged steps in his direction. She found herself inches from his face and cupped his chin, then ran the surface of her thumb across the outline of his lips.

"I want you. I want to have my way with you. You really do need to upgrade and shake the bitch that obviously got your nose so wide open." He could smell the cherry flavor emanating from her mouth, seductively jumping off her tongue and air kissing his slightly parted lips. Tiyatti slowly removed her hand from his face. She let her hand drop to her side and waited breathlessly for his response, confident that her irresistible charms and the memories of their last lustful encounter would be enough to lure him in again.

"With all due respect, Miko, if I left Duchess for you, I'd be downgrading. What we did was a mistake, a mistake I'll never make again. So don't get it twisted, Miko. I just work for you, that's it. That's all." Tiyatti brushed past her and left her standing there stewing in the heat of his shameful snubbing.

Click!

The sound of the round chambering stopped him dead in his tracks. He stood in silence facing the door, wondering if she was going to pull the trigger while thoughts of reaching for the

Ruger ran through his mind. He thought better of it; he'd heard the rumors of her ruthless reputation.

Miko walked his way until the end of the .380 pressed against the back of his head. She leaned close to his ear and whispered softly, "If you ever put your hands on me again, I will kill you, ma'fucka! I swear on my dead daddy's grave. If you *ever* disrespect me again, it will be the worst mistake you ever made in your life. I will murk your sorry ass like it was nothing. Do you understand me, bitch?"

Tiyatti remained silent, shaking fearfully within when he felt the pressure of the .380 pushing against his head.

"I said do you understand me, *bitch!*" Her voice, laced with murderous inflections, raised a few octaves. The .380 poked him near his line-up.

"Yeah, I hear you, Miko," he responded in a voice that had foul inflections in it too. The pistol to the back of his head had him feeling something he had never felt before—severe fear mixed with a hateful rage. *I need to get the fuck outta this game before I end up killing this nutty ass bitch!* Tiyatti felt the sting of humiliation for the second time that day, and both times Miko Dunbar had been smack dab in the middle of that crushing feeling.

She leaned closer to his ear, pressing her soft, voluptuous body against his. "Consider this your final warning!" She shoved the gun into the back of his head, forcing him off his square and making him stumble forward against the door. "Now, open the door for a boss, bitch!" she said coldly, then walked past him like he didn't exist. Vile visions began running through her mind. Visions so vile, her veins froze with cruel, icy cold vindictiveness.

CHAPTER 20

Young Glock Gang

Bony James sat in the darkened room with his face buried in his hands as the 50 Cent track serenaded his sadness.

♫ *Many men, many many many many men, wish death 'pon me. Man I don't cry no mo' don't look to the sky no mo', have mercy on me, have mercy on my soul, somewhere my heart turned cold.* ♫

G-Mack and Jayquan stood over the coffee table stuffing bullets into the clips in front of them. Two high capacity magazines were taped together, each capable of carrying fifty hollow tip rounds.

"I'm ready to go get on them ma'fuckas!" A trail of dried tears ran down Jayquan's angry face as he pushed a clip into the MP5 and walked over to where Bony James sat brooding.

"Yeah dat. I'm witchu all the way, homie. They knocked Goldie down. Now it's they turn to get clacked out the fuckin' game!" G-Mack said, feeling the same depth of pain the other thugs in the room felt.

One-fourth of the Young Glock Gang was dead and gone. It was a kind of pain the thugs had experienced before, only this time it was deeper, more profound. It was much more intimate and personal.

As the music played on, a somber silence filled the room and brought each thug closer to his own private grief. Tears of rage streamed down the fuming faces of the savage-hearted gangstas. Men who had taken lives without so much as batting an eye, who had killed in cold blood without feeling an iota of emotion, now sat amongst one another shedding tears for their fallen comrade with no shame. They had grown up together, and their bond was a familial connection that hurt just the same as if a sibling had been murdered.

"We finna do some shit that's gon' shut all they shit down!" Bony James interrupted the teary-eyed silence with those words.

"Whatchu say, homie?" Jayquan wiped the tears that had fallen again with the back of his hand. He was closest to Goldie.

G-Mack put his painful thoughts on pause to listen to what Bony James was about to say. Bony James stood and turned the music down wearing an evil sneer.

"I said we finna do some shit that's gon' shut all they shit down! We gon' shut that bitch Miko Dunbar's whole organization down, blood! It ain't a secret that it was her and her people who murked Goldie. It ain't no doubt in my mind that it was them bitch ass ma'fuckas who killed the homie. Now they hidin' like 'hos scared to show they coward ass faces." He eyed each of his comrades intently. "Since they scared to show they faces, we gon' shut down every spot they got and make business so bad for 'em that they gon' have to step out of the shadows!" He picked a half-smoked cigarette out of the ashtray and fired it up.

Jayquan cleared his throat and said, "I don't give a fuck how we do it, or who we do it to. On the set, I'm ready to get on a ma'fucka's head and get some getback for the homie!" Jayquan just wanted to kill somebody in the name of revenge. He needed to kill somebody in the name of revenge.

Bony James spoke with the cigarette parked between his lips.

"This ain't gon' be no regular ass hoo-ride, y'all. We finna put it on they asses and shut 'em down fo' reals, blood!" He reached for the automatic assault rifle and hit the cancer stick one last time before violently stubbing it out in the ashtray. "C'mon, y'all, let's go bang on them bitches!"

The three remaining members of the Young Glock Gang piled in the Pathfinder, ready to commit the most heinous of crimes. Within an hour, Bony James looked down at his phone and re-read the text message, confirming the address to the location. He pushed the Pathfinder around the corner and killed the engine.

"This is one of that bitch Miko's most profitable dope spots." He stuffed the cell phone in his pocket and took the MP5 off safety. He turned in the driver's seat and asked Jayquan, "You got the gas cans, bruh?"

"Yup, let's fire some shit up!" Jayquan responded a little too joyfully.

Bony James' bloodshot eyes shifted over to G-Mack, who was sitting in the passenger seat on hype. "You ready, Mack?"

"Fuck yeah, I'm ready. Let's make it happen!" He opened the door on his side and stepped out into the cold night air. He pulled the black Philadelphia Eagles beanie low over his ears and tugged on his leather gloves to tighten the fit.

Aawwckk twooo!

He snorted up a mouthful of mucus and spit a thick glob of snot onto the asphalt off to his right. They walked slowly in the shadows of the adjoining houses until they were close enough. Bony James pointed to a cluster of bushes twenty feet away and said, "Go post up behind those bushes over there and wait for my signal, G-Mack." He turned to Jayquan.

"Go ahead and get that side of the house. I'll get this side over here." The two thugs headed off in different directions.

Pffftt!

A silent shot from Jayquan's Glock smacked the lookout in the head. He had been sitting on the green meter box acting inconspicuous, trying to blend in with the surroundings. The point man fell dead in the dirt next to the meter box. Jayquan stepped over his lifeless body and proceeded to complete the task at hand. He poured gasoline all over and around the side of the house before making his way back to the front of the house where he took up his position.

Bony James met up with Jayquan with an empty gas can in his hand. He took both empty cans and returned to the Pathfinder and put them in the backseat before making his way back to the front of the dope spot. He made eye contact with Jayquan and G-Mack and nodded, letting them know that it was about to be on. Then he took the lighter from his pocket and set fire to the wet grass at his feet. Immediately, a crooked trail leading up to the front of the house lit up with fire. In a matter of minutes the entire shell of the house was ablaze.

Somebody from inside the stash house hollered, "Run! Get the fuck out!"

"Somebody call the fire department!" a lady yelled from somewhere down the street.

The front door of the stash house flung wide and gangstas ran out fleeing for their lives.

Kak! Kak! Kak! Kak! Kak! Kak! Kak! Kak! Kak! Kak! Kak! Kak! Kak! Kak! Kak! Kak! Kak! Kak!

Every gangsta who ran out of the stash house was blessed with a body full of bullets. One hundred fifty hollow tips and four dead bodies later, the three Young Glock Gangstas broke into an all out sprint until they were at the Pathfinder. The SUV jumped off the curb and pushed down the block and around the corner. Bony James wasn't content with them murking only a handful of Miko's people and leaving behind a house full of dope for the police to confiscate, if the fire didn't claim it first. It was just the beginning. In the span of three hours they managed to set fire to two more of Miko's establishments, killing a grip of her workers and burning down several more profitable spots. In essence, they'd lit a fire to her empire that would eventually smoke the bosses out and make Miko, Cream, and Suspect step from the shadows and into the streets to show their faces. They didn't have a choice. Failure to respond to the blatant declaration of war was an open invitation to all savages who roamed the streets of the Southeast Planet to pillage and plunder everything associated with the Miko Dunbar drug empire.

CHAPTER 21

Wah

I can hear, but I can't see. Vaguely I can smell, but I can't taste. My heart is beating and I'm breathing, but I don't feel alive. I've learned to play these mind games in my head in order to endure my condition; to reflect on my past and relive experiences and insert different outcomes to past scenarios, things that I wished would've happened instead of what actually did happen. I'd recreate different fantasy outcomes to the reality of my past. Sometimes I visualized myself sitting under the lemon tree chopping it up with my father and my brother. Other times I'd be pushing the Charger with Tocarra riding shotgun and Trey Songz beating out the speakers. Tocarra would be singing along to every song, word for word, hitting every lyric like she used to, only now it would be with our first son or daughter in the backseat laughing at our silliness.

On this particular day I was recreating the day I got shot, imagining Tocarra and me calling the movers and helping them load our property into a moving truck and driving over to our new home. My thoughts were interrupted when I felt another presence in the room. I stilled my thoughts and tried to focus on the person invading my space. The faint scent of Christian Dior Light Blue perfume contacted my weakened sense of smell and registered in my brain. *I remember that smell. It's Tocarra's favorite fragrance.* I heard a soft, feminine whimper, someone sobbing. *That's definitely a woman crying! Tocarra! Tocarra, is that you?* My mind was screaming the words. Hope had my heart beating fast and hard with wishful thinking. I felt what seemed like a warm breath blowing gently on the surface of the skin on my forearm. The warm sensation against my flesh grew more intense, the fragrance grew stronger as it invaded the walls of my sinuses.

Tocarra, is that you, baby?

CHAPTER 22

Khadida

Khadida tentatively stepped into the hospital room, and her heart immediately broke for Wahdatah. She was saddened by the visual in front of her. It pained her to see another human being in such a helpless state.

Her heart broke for Shug, the man she was growing closer to and developing stronger feelings for. She thought about the love she saw in his eyes whenever he talked about his brother, Wah. She felt the pain in his words whenever he spoke about Wah being in a coma and the events that led up to it. Khadida could only idly sit by and be a silent spectator when Shug dove deep into his pool of pain and swam soundlessly in his sufferance, floating heavily in his forlorn. A tear fell over both eyelids and rolled down her face. A small whimper jumped out of her chest, escaping from between her slightly parted lips. The tears began flowing freely, streaming down both cheeks, before falling and splashing noiselessly onto the cold, white linoleum floor. Her weeping grew noticeably louder; she made no attempt to wipe at her tears or dab at the dampness under her eyes.

Her eyes meticulously took in Wahdatah's situation. She wanted to commit every detail possible to her memory bank, so she could provide an accurate and in depth account of his condition when she took it all back to Shug on their next visit— the tall machine with the constant beeping keeping track of his vital signs, the pristine room with the white tiled floors and the white and green cotton bedding on the empty bed next to the window, the clear tube inserted into his stomach, feeding him and sustaining his existence.

Khadida timidly took small steps with one of her hands near her mouth, her fingertips pressed gently against her lips. Her head shook slowly with sadness, knowing that this could have just as easily been Baby Shug lying in that hospital bed in a coma. At that moment she was so much more thankful to have met Shug, despite his circumstances. Her mind drifted off as thoughts of Shug clouded her thinking. *To be able to communicate with him is a blessing. Being able to spend quality time with him in a visiting room is a blessing. To be able to touch him and hold him, and to have him do all of those things to me is a blessing.* In that instance she clearly understood that it could have been so much worse; life could have been so much worse than it was, for anyone.

Standing at Wahdatah's bedside, she wondered whether he knew that she was even there. When her tears stopped flowing and her vision cleared, the strong resemblance Wahdatah bore to Shug immediately became apparent to her. *They look so much alike!*

She reached out and touched his arm with her fingertips. Taking a deep breath, she closed her eyes and said a prayer for him. After praying, she put the palm of her hand against his skin and softly rubbed his warm forearm with heartfelt compassion, the gesture moved her deeply. After fully composing herself, she decided to talk to him, or at him. She didn't know if he could actually hear her or not, but if he could, she wanted him to know that there were people out here rooting him on, people who still cared.

"Hello, Wahdatah, my name is Khadida, and I am a friend of your brother's. Actually, Baby Shug and I are in a relationship. It's recent, but it's so real. He talks about you a lot, and it is killing him that he can't be here for you. So for what it's worth, I offered to step in and be here in his place until you come out this coma, or he gets out of prison, whichever comes first. It's tearing him up inside that no one is here to support you." Once Khadida opened her mouth and started talking, she couldn't close it. She didn't stop talking until the hospital staff informed her that visiting hours were over.

CHAPTER 23

Wah

It took the wind out of my sails and knocked the happiness from my heart when it became clear that it wasn't Tocarra returning to my bedside. But when she mentioned my brother's name and told me how they'd met and how he was doing, I relaxed my mental and took her words in like a movie, trying to visualize everything she was telling me.

When the nurse stuck her head in the door and told her visiting hours were over, she got up and bounced. I felt her breathe against my ear. Her whisper rang loud in my eardrum like an echo in a wide, deep canyon.

"You are going to come out of this coma, Wahdatah. Shug is going to get out of prison. And at the end of the day that bitch Miko will get everything she has coming to her." She squeezed my hand twice and then said, "I feel it in my bones, and I believe it in my heart. You have to believe it though, Wah. You have to fight like you ain't ever fought in your life to make that happen!"

It seemed as if she had been there for a few hours. Oddly though, when she got up and left, my spirit felt reinvigorated. The fight in me had renewed strength and determination. Based on the detailed information she provided, I could tell my brother must've really been feeling her. She knew too much, and she was doing more than enough, so I was convinced of that. Based on what this chick Khadida said, my gut was telling me that she was a good fit for my brother. Hell, the fact that she was at my bedside on my brother's behalf backed that theory up. It was proof enough for me.

CHAPTER 24

Miko

"I don't give a fuck about no police asking questions, or the detectives sticking their noses in my business. That ain't on my plate at the moment, Cream. What's most important to me right now is minimizing the damage that these punk ass ma'fuckas are inflicting on us!" Miko fluffed her hair and turned from the mirror. "It boggles my mind that a group of rag tag clowns with gas and guns have somehow managed to take out two dozen of my workers, rob me for sixty-two bricks of dope, and strong arm y'all for half a million of my dollars! All this in addition to burning down three of my most lucrative spots, and yet, we've only managed to kill one of them?" She evilly looked Cream in his eyes and said, "Please, explain to me why we are getting our asses whooped all over the Southeast streets by a group of unspectacular ma'fuckas! Better yet, Cream, explain to me what the fuck I am paying the two of you for!" Miko was livid at being awakened with the latest news that three of her drug houses had been burned down, and the San Diego Police Department was out shaking up the streets asking questions about the drug war being waged in the ghettos of Southeast San Diego.

"We're as frustrated as you are, Miko." Cream pointed to Suspect and included him. "But you gotta understand the makeup and mentality of some of these sets out here. The fools behind all this supposedly call themselves the Glock Gang or some shit, and they from Lincoln Park, and the only way we can—"

She interrupted him with a hand in the air and fire in her eyes.

"I don't need a ma'fuckin' history lesson, Cream. I don't give a fuck who is doing what, or when and how they're doing it to whoever they're doing it to! I want answers, Cream, or I want the fuckin' solutions to my problems in a body bag! Tell me what the fuck the two of you are doing about the ma'fuckas that are making me look bad. Correction, that are makin' you look bad, in my eyes!"

Cream and Suspect remained silent, marinating on angry, not knowing what to say.

"That's what the fuck I thought! You're good with a gun or beating somebody's ass when it comes time to getting on somebody's head, but when it comes to the most essential element of the art of war, y'all leave a lot to be desired!" Miko stopped her angry rant and picked up her laptop and started taking corrective action. *If you want something done, do it your fucking self! I can't keep waiting for those two bobbleheads to figure this shit out. I'll be broke and out of business by the time they get to the bottom of it.*

Too many losses were being suffered on her end. Entirely too much collateral damage had already been inflicted. She brought up the video of the first stash house robbery and meticulously studied the footage, rewinding and fast forwarding at some points, and pausing on others. Her eyes narrowed when she watched the image of Capone walking down into the basement and making a phone call. *You can run but you can't hide, bitch!* she thought as she replayed the scene over and over again, hoping something would click.

Then it did. *Bingo!*

Her fingers worked the smart screen as she attempted to clarify the grainy image, but no matter what she did, the picture remained too gritty to discern clearly. She reached for her phone and made a call.

"Hello. What's up, Miko?" Theo, her IT guy answered.

"Theo, I need you to work your magic"

"Talk to me, what is it that you need?"

"I need you to clear up the picture on the video from the stash house robbery. Actually, what I need is for you to enhance the video, so I can see who it is that Capone called from the basement. Can you do that?"

"Give me a minute, and I'll send it to you once I have something." She waited on the line while Theo did his thing.

Minutes later he told her, "You should have a picture with clearer quality on your computer now."

"I got it, and I see exactly what I need to see. Thank you, Theo. You're a genius!" Miko exclaimed, and then ended the call. She blew the image up until it was big enough to clearly show the screen on the phone in Capone's hand. The name and phone number were unmistakable. *You shiesty, no-good, backstabbing sonofabitch!* she thought hatefully and looked up at her cousins.

"C'mere y'all, look at this." She turned her laptop to the side. "Are you seeing this shit?" She pointed to the name and number on the frozen frame.

"That's who Capone's bitch ass called?" Suspect asked angrily.

"I'ma go snatch his punk ass up!" Cream declared, cracking his knuckles.

"Nah, don't do that, leave him alone."

"What! Why?" Cream's puzzled retort was full of hostility.

Miko gave him a look that warned him not to test the waters. "Because, he doesn't know that we're on to him, and I want it to stay that way."

Miko picked her phone up off the table and called Anthony.

"Yeah," he answered dutifully.

"I need you to have the car ready in five minutes."

"A'ight."

She looked at her cousins and said, "Let's go. We need to hurry the fuck up and make some big moves."

They strapped up and exited the office. Cream and Suspect trailed behind the queenpin, who slung her ass hard and strut with determined purpose in every step, as she made her way toward the front of her mansion, anxiously wanting to protect her financial assets.

CHAPTER 25

Young Glock Gang

"Bony James, I think we might've just hit the mother lode, bruh!" Capone yelled into his cell phone as soon as his whip jumped off the curb and merged into traffic.

"What the fuck is you talkin' 'bout, man?" Bony James was in the middle of pouring himself a stiff one. He twisted his neck halfway and hollered, "Y'all want somethin' to drink?" he asked Jayquan and G-Mack, sucking the remnant of Hennessy off his thumb.

"Naw, I'm good," Jayquan told him.

"Let me get one of what you drinkin' on, homie," G-Mack hollered back at him.

"Are you hearing me, Bony?" Capone asked with a hint of impatience in his voice.

"Yeah, I'm listenin' to you, man. You said some shit about hittin' the mother lode. What's crackin'? Whatchu got goin' on?" Bony James put his index finger to his lips, signaling to Jayquan and G-Mack to chill on the chit chat. He sipped from his glass and listened to Capone talk. G-Mack swallowed a mouthful of Henny and shook his head as the potent brown liquid burned a wet trail down his esophagus. Jayquan put fire to the tip of his blunt and pulled on it until it had a fiery red charred end. A thick cloud of smoke hovered around his face as the pungent kush aroma floated around the room, filling everybody's nostrils.

"The shit y'all been doin' is workin'! Half the people in her crew are shook up and ready for a mutiny! They graspin' at straws and runnin' around like chickens with they heads cut off. I just got word from a very reliable source that Miko is

163

about to move her re-up money to one money house. We talkin' anywhere between two to three million dollars!"

Bony James almost spit the mouthful of Henny out. "Don't play with me like that, Capone! Don't bullshit with me about that kind of money!" he said, wiping the little bit of liquor that had seeped from his mouth.

"I ain't bullshittin', Bony! On mommas, they shook the fuck up for real! She shuttin' most of her spots down and movin' her dough to one house. Word has it that she's spooked about losing product because of the fires y'all set. Plus the police are combing the streets asking a lot of questions. The way it was told to me, she figures her workers will be a lot less exposed while her small army of soldiers is out hunting for you guys. From what I hear, it's supposed to be a crew of young East Side Pirus huntin' for y'all on some shoot-on- sight shit."

"I don't care about all that. I don't give a fuck about them East Side Piru ma'fuckas. Tell me more about these millions of dollars you talkin' about, Capone. Where's the money supposed to be picked up at? And where is it supposed to be taken to? I want all the details, bruh: who, when, where, and how many of her people are going to be involved—all the details, you feel me?"

"Don't trip. I'm already on it, Bony. Miko's dumb ass don't know that I got two of her workers on my payroll, and one of them is providin' me the latest inside information on what's good in her camp. He been rockin' with me from day one, and I trust him. Trust me, my boy Nick is reliable," Capone assured him, before they went over the details of the massive money transfer.

They went over it until Bony knew as much about the money transfer as Capone did. *Just like I thought she would! That bitch's cage is rattled. Now she makin' moves out of desperation!* Bony thought and smiled inwardly. Miko was panicking, and the stranglehold she once had on the dope game in Southeast San Diego was slowly slipping away. A few chinks in her armor had somehow managed to expose the weaknesses of her kingdom. *Capone's ass better not be lying. If I find out that he's on some bullshit, I'ma personally flatten his helmet!*

The following day, Bony James and the rest of the Young Glock Gang sat inside a stolen Navigator armed to the teeth— MP5s and Glocks with lots of shots clutched tight in their grip.

"I say we run up in that bitch on some do or die gangsta shit! I'm countin' five heads outside, and your man said that it's supposed to be ten of 'em transportin' the money, which means it's five more of 'em inside! We can take half of 'em out right here right now. Call Capone and tell him to have his boy draw down on everybody inside the house as soon as we start bustin' on the fools outside," G-Mack said, facing the back of Bony James' head.

"Yeah, he right, Bony. I'm wit' Mack on this one. It don't make no sense for us to let them fools get out in the open, because we'll be exposing ourselves and losing the element of surprise. It's too many possibilities that can pop off once we're out in the open. I say we twist these silencers on and bust on every ma'fucka in that front yard." Jayquan wanted to get his hands on those millions bad!

Bony James sat behind the steering wheel chewing on his bottom lip, weighing his options, debating the pros and cons to the ideas his crew presented. The plush leather in the Lincoln Navigator whined under his weight as he leaned back and reached into his pocket to retrieve his cell phone. He started thumbing the keypad furiously:

Change of plans. We gonna kill all the workers outside.

Call your boy and tell him to hem up everybody in the house once he hears us out here, a'ight?

He pushed send and waited for a response to his text.

The three heavily-armed thugs waited anxiously for Capone to hit Bony James back with a reply. It was paramount that Capone agreed to the last minute change of plans, otherwise, they'd have to stick to the original script and risk exposing themselves to a lot of unnecessary gunplay out in the open; a lot of people shooting at each other in broad daylight was never a good thing.

The seconds ticked by like minutes, the minutes ticked by like hours. A thick cloud of apprehension filled the cockpit of the Navigator, smothering the patience of the pistol packing gangstas.

"What the fuck is takin' his ass so long?" G-Mack complained after five minutes passed.

"I don't know about this shit, Bony. Something ain't right. I got a bad feelin' about this shit, blood!" Jayquan grumbled his opinion.

Bleep.

Bony James' cell phone finally sounded off, alerting him of an incoming text message. All three members of the Young Glock Gang tensed and sat up erect in their seats, hearts pounding like a Mobb Deep beat as each one sucked in his breath anxiously.

Okay. Nick said as soon as he hears the gunfire he's drawing down on everybody inside. Take off!

A smile spread across Bony James' face when he read Capone's text. He stuffed the phone in his pocket and picked the Glock up from his lap, slowly twisting the silencer onto the end of it.

"Let's go do the damn thang, y'all!" Bony James was first to exit the Navigator. G-Mack and Jayquan quickly caught up to him, and together they marched up the block with the Glocks locked and loaded. The MP5s were hanging from the nylon straps draped around their necks and off their shoulders. When they were within shooting range, the five goons milling around the front yard stopped what they were doing and looked up at the approaching men. Bony James' left arm came up hella fast with his Glock pointing straight ahead spitting silent death.

Pfftt! Pfftt! Pfftt! Pfftt! Pfftt! Pfftt! Pfftt! Pfftt!

Miko's workers made a mad dash for cover and hid behind something in the front yard that the bullets couldn't penetrate.

G-Mack and Jayquan's arms rose up and they let their Glock's go as well.

Pfftt! Pfftt! Pfftt! Pfftt! Pfftt! Pfftt! Pfftt! Pfftt! Pfftt! Pfftt! Pfftt!

The Young Glock Gang continued to march forward and empty their guns in the direction of Miko's workers.

This shit is too fuckin' easy! Bony James thought, firing off several more shots.

Doom! Doom! Doom!

The thunderous roar from behind them shook all three Young Glock Gang thugs up.

Thoomp! Thoomp! Thoomp!

G-Mack took a bullet in the back near his left shoulder blade, and then another in the middle of his lower back, and a third bullet hit him in the back of his head on his way down to the ground. His dead frame twisted grotesquely in the middle of the street.

Oh shit! It's a set up! Bony James thought when he saw G-Mack go down out of his peripheral. His head was on a swivel as he frantically grabbed for the assault rifle. He yelled a warning to Jayquan as he turned and let the MP5 rip in the direction behind them.

"Watch out, 'Quan! They behind us!"

Kak! Kak! Kak! Kak! Kak! Kak! Kak! Kak! Kak!

Jayquan recognized the ambush and followed suit, squeezing the trigger on his MP5 too.

Kak! Kak! Kak! Kak! Kak! Kak! Kak! Kak! Kak!

Doom! Doom! Doom! Doom! Doom!

The street was an explosion of automatic gunfire and loud thunderous bangs from the hand canons that seemingly came out of nowhere. Suspect's chrome barked the loudest. His first bullet narrowly missed Jayquan, the next four didn't; his second shot hit Jayquan in the back of his ribcage and spun him around. The next three shots peppered Jayquan's chest and half spun him again, slumping him by the curb in front of the money house. His forehead cracked open when the front of his skull crashed against the unforgiving concrete edge.

Bony's eyes widened when Jayquan fell hard to the ground. Aw shit, they got the homies! Bony James broke into a full sprint, away from the deadly ambush, blindly aiming the MP5 behind him and squeezing off a couple quick bursts.

Kak! Kak! Kak! Kak! Kak! Kak! Kak! Kak! Kak! Kak! Kak! Kak! Kak! Kak! Kak! Kak!

Suspect stood in the middle of the sidewalk with his pistol turned sideways in his hand, his arm fully extended while he patiently popped off shots.

Doom! Doom! Doom!

"Aaagghhhh!" A bullet ripped into Bony James' back and tore through the tissue within, before settling near the front of his stomach. He stumbled and lost his balance, then staggered and crashed to the ground. Blood poured profusely from his gunshot wound as he struggled to stand back up. *I can't let 'em get up on me!* He got to his feet before stumbling and falling into some bushes. *Get the fuck up, Bony, 'fore they murk yo' ass!*

Sirens sounded off in the distance. Tires burned rubber in the street as most of Miko's workers fled the scene of the shootout. Suspect and Cream dashed full speed in the direction of the spot where Bony James had fallen into the bushes, guns up and filled with fresh clips. When they ambled up on the last spot they had seen him, they warily searched for the wounded thug.

"A puddle of blood! He can't be too far," Cream said after spotting the small pool of red fluid on the ground. He squatted low to look under the nearby cars. Nothing. "I know yo bitch ass over here somewhere! Where the fuck you at, ma'fucka?" Cream called out as he poked the bushes with his pistol, ready to pump rounds if a leaf so much as wiggled the wrong way. Nothing. The shrill piercing scream of the sirens nearing grew louder. The police were getting closer; they didn't have much time. The brothers stood near the puddle of blood on the sidewalk with their thumpers ready, wondering how the badly wounded Bony James managed to get away.

"It's like he disappeared into thin air, Cream. His bitch ass got away, dawg!" Suspect stated the obvious.

"I know, but he's bleedin' like a stuck pig, and he on his own now," Cream replied with a satisfied smile. There was no doubt about it that the other two Glock Gang members were as dead as dead got. "Let's bounce before the po-po show up," Cream told him after one last scan of the area. They trotted back to their car and jumped into their whip, heading across town in the opposite direction of the oncoming sirens. They figured they'd catch up to Bony James in due time and when they did they'd finish the job.

CHAPTER 26

Miko

Miko's torture chamber . . .

"UUUMMMMMMMPPPPPPPHHHHH!"

"Yeah, I know. It hurts, don't it? You backstabbin' ma'fucka!" Miko raised her voice to talk over the muffled screams of the cuffed and duct taped Capone. A sadistic smile plastered her face as the traitorous worker writhed wildly in pain against the handcuffs and chains that bound his wrists and stretched his arms out wide. His entire torso was taped heavily to the chair, as were his lower extremities, making it impossible for him to do anything. His boy Nick lay on the ground next to him with half his head missing, thanks to half a clip from Miko's .380 being emptied into his dome.

A dropper trickling drops of sulfuric acid onto each of Capone's eyeballs left the traitorous turncoat with melted holes of pink flesh for eye sockets. For the rest of his days on earth he would never again see the beauty of life.

"Pull his tongue out for me, Anthony!" Miko ordered the obedient hulk, after carefully sitting the dropper down on the table next to her. Anthony dutifully picked up a pair of pliers and pulled the duct tape away from Capone's screaming mouth.

"Aaaagggghhhhh, aaaagggghhhhh!" Capone's helpless horrifying screams filled the windowless room.

"You shoulda thought about that when you decided to put shit in the game. You disrespected me in the worst way, Capone. So now your snake ass is going to live the rest of your life suffering in the worst way. As far as I'm concerned, killing you would be showing you love, you sorry piece of shit! I want you to suffer every second of every minute, of every hour, every day for the rest of your pathetic existence on this planet. Do you hear me, you punk bitch!"

"Aaagghhhh, aaagghhhh!" Capone cried out something no one would ever understand.

"Yeah, yeah, yeah, whatever, you backstabbing ma'fucka!" Miko dismissively waved his plea aside as she grabbed the gardening shears and gave them a practice run. The huge scissors chopped at the air in front of her. After a short struggle with the thrashing Capone, Anthony had his tongue pulled out to its longest length between the biting grips of the iron pliers. The gardening shears snipped and clipped rather easily. When Capone's tongue hit the blood-stained floor, it wiggled about wildly for a few seconds before finally lying still.

"Aaagghhhh, aaagghhhh! Ummmppphhh, ummmpphhh!"

Capone's muted cries gave her tremendous pleasure. She looked him in his unseeing eyes and told him, "Oh, don't worry, boo. I ain't finished with your bitch ass yet!" Miko had to yell over his terrifying screams as she reached for his zipper and pulled his limp penis out, stretching it to its limits. "I told you I wasn't the one to fuck with, ma'fucka." Again, the garden shears snipped and clipped without difficulty. Miko held his severed, bloody dick between her thumb and index finger, smiling at the wicked thought that crossed her mind while Capone cried his agony out. She moved toward him with his dripping penis in her hand, stuffed it into his opened mouth, and then used both of her hands to close it.

"Umph!" Capone gulped loudly when he swallowed his own dick.

The cold-blooded queenpin turned to Anthony and issued out instructions.

"Get him to a hospital before he bleeds to death. I want them to save his sorry bitch ass, so he can suffer for the rest of his life since he thinks it's cute to steal from me."

"Done," Anthony responded, not the least bit disturbed by the gruesome shit that was going on.

Miko poured the rest of the acid onto Capone's phone, the same phone she had used to text Bony James back, after luring the Young Glock Gang into the deadly trap at the empty money house. There never was a plan to move all her money to one stash house. After discovering that Nick was in cahoots with Capone, she devised the devious plot to trap her enemies and eliminate them once and for all. Poor Nick never saw it coming, but that was the price one paid when playing both sides from the middle.

Her mind floated off to another place as she looked around at the bloody mess she'd made. The thought of sex and violence made her pussy grow super moist. *Tiyatti, Tiyatti, Tiyatti, what am I going to do with your fine, sexy, disrespectful ass? I'm not sure if I should fuck you, or just fuck you over!*

CHAPTER 27

Baby Shug

"What's good, beautiful? Did you have a safe trip?" I asked, bending slightly and having my way with her soft, full lips. "Mmm, you smell good and you taste delicious, baby," I told her the truth after our lips parted.

"Thank you, and yes, we had a safe trip. It was good actually. Khassandra, with her crazy ass self, was trying to give Beyoncé a run for her money all the way up the Pacific Coast Highway. Let me go say hi to my brother before we get settled in at our table. Come on." Her lips touched mine again, and we enjoyed another kiss, this one a little more passionate than the first. She took my hand and practically dragged me behind her as she quick-stepped over to Khory and Khassandra. The four of us mingled for a few minutes before they went outside to the patio. Khadida and I sat down at a table near the back of the visiting room, our normal spot.

"I got a surprise for you. Actually, I have a couple of surprises for you." Her brown eyes smoldered with flirtation, and her pretty smile made me grin. A good feeling swept over me, carrying me up to cloud nine. She wore a black tube dress that sensuously squeezed her frame and a pair of sexy black, peep-toe Louboutin booties that wrapped around her ankles. Her titties were pushed up proudly, ass poking out prominently, and her face was perfectly painted with makeup. The gloss on her lips made me wanna suck on them like a chocolate covered strawberry.

"Is that right? Well, you know I'ma sucker for surprises, ma. What's good?" I asked and waited to be wowed.

The smile vanished from her face and she got serious.

"Before we get to the surprises, baby, let me tell you how my visit with your brother went."

"Fo' sho', tell me everything, ma. How's he doing? What's he lookin' like?" At the mention of my brother's name, my curiosity was hella aroused.

For the next hour she told me everything she could recall about her visit with Wah. I asked a gang of questions, and she provided me with a gang of answers. She didn't know it, but at that very moment in time Khadida was winning my heart over and gaining my utmost respect. The fact that she took time out to check on my brother like she did and spent some time with him on top of that, simply to help provide me with a peace of mind, pointed to the true beauty and depth of her character. Having been in love with a scandalous bitch like Miko for so long and given her the best of me, only to discover she was as bogus as they came, made my standards unbending in my expectations of the next chick. It was a must the next woman in my life be a stand-up chick, and her stand-up characteristics would have to be evident in her every action. I was paying attention to everything this go around. So dealing with a woman who had solid character traits was a plus in my book, and Khadida had a gang of stand-up qualities.

"Why you lookin' at me like that?" She wore a coy smile, knowing that whatever I was thinking had to be something good.

"No reason, just taking in all this beauty in front of me."

"Like that?"

"Yeah, like that."

Our eyes were past the point of flirting. We were eye fucking each other and it was feeling good.

She sat up straight in her chair, the tip of her tongue snaking out as boldness oozed from her aura. Her eyes discreetly stole peeks over my shoulder, and then quickly over hers.

"Are you ready for your first surprise?"

"Yup, what's my first surprise?" I asked, trying to read her facial features for clues. I saw an ardent type of lust in her look. She leaned closer to whisper something in my ear, pulling on my hands while she did so, until my fingers were brushing against the hot skin of her soft inner thigh. I felt her breath on my ear as my fingers traveled up her smooth thigh until I touched her moist split. *No panties!* My heart beat fast. I hadn't touched on a pussy in damn near two years. I couldn't resist the urge to slide my longest finger all the way inside her. When she moaned I slid it out, then I stuck my next longest finger inside her tight wetness. I swear it felt like my fingers were playing in a bowl of warm molasses.

Her breath was soft against my earlobe.

"Fifty-fifteen, are you ready to bang this shit out, boo, because I really do need to have my pussy beat up!" she said, sliding back in her chair, causing my fingers to slip out of her warm wet-wet.

Am I ready to beat it up? Is you serious! My dick was harder than pistol steel! We casually made our way over to the room where the CO was standing posted by the door marked 'Supply Room.' Then it dawned on me that Khadida planned the whole thing out: tight ass tube dress, no panties, and a fifty-dollar bill at the ready, cuffed in her hand.

Although our first sexual encounter was taking place in a supply closet half the size of a bathroom, I felt she deserved as dignified a dick down as I could possibly provide. I didn't want her memory of our first intimate experience to be without a face, so I turned her around and we stood facing each other. Our lips touched and our tongues tussled with fervent lust as I pulled the black tube dress up until it was bunched around her narrow waist.

"Wrap your arms around my neck," I told her, pulling on my pants until they were in a pile around my ankles. Out of my peripheral, I noticed the clock on the wall: 11:05 a.m. Our lips lustfully reattached, and I palmed each of her soft, round, fleshy globes with my mitts, picking up every one of her luscious 135 pounds, and then sitting her on the tip of my tool. Her arms wrapped around my neck while her legs locked behind my back.

The hot, wet petals of her love flower blossomed, then swallowed the swollen head of my dick and gripped it like a gloved fist.

"Uhhmm!" she moaned into my mouth as she slid down the length of my thug muscle. She pulled away from the kiss and threw her head back, groaning loudly when she slid all the way down on my dick. It was in her to the hilt. She tight as fuck! I squeezed her healthy ass cheeks harder and pushed her down on the dick as far as she could fit on it, mashing her down on it harder, before moving my hips back and pulling the dick out slow, then shoving my long, thick meat back up in her hard until it couldn't go any farther. I sped my hip action up a little faster.

"Unghh! Unghh! Unghh! Unghh!" Every plunge had her grunting her pleasure in my ear. She hugged me hard as her body began to shake uncontrollably against mine.

"Oooohhhhhhhhh!" She came powerfully all over my hard-on. Wave after wave of her creamy juices drowned my dick.

Our tongues frantically begin wrestling again as I continued to pick her up and drop her down on my dick. When the clock read 11:10 a.m., I pulled the dick out and turned her back to me.

"Grab your ankles," I told her, bending her at the waist. She spread her legs wider and grabbed hold of her ankles as I stood behind her rubbing the fat head of my dick inside her soaking wet hole, pulling it out and slapping it against her swollen, sensitive clit. She was going wild with lust. I put my left hand on her hip and pushed every inch of my pipe up in her until my cum-heavy balls slapped her clit.

"Nngghhh, nngghhh, nngghhh!" I slow poked and deep-stroked the pussy, grunting every time my dick hit the bottom. It was feeling good, but it wasn't completely satisfying the animal lust in me. I needed to twist her back out and bust a hard nut deep in her gushy! I grabbed onto both hips and slung the dick in her as hard as I could.

"Aagghh, aagghh, aagghh!" she grunted.

My pelvis hit her cheeks, making that wet and loud slapping sound. This pussy is bomb! I kept looking up at the clock trying to distract myself. As good as her pussy was feeling I wasn't trying to bust a nut yet. The clock on the wall read 11:12 a.m. *I still got three minutes left! I want every one of my fifteen minutes of fame!* My grip on her hips was good while I beat it up from the back, so she let go of one of her ankles, swatting her fingers against her clit while I plunged deep.

"Unghh, unghh, unghh!" I grunted, banging the fuck out of her tightness!

As soon as the clock read 11:15 a.m., I pulled her ass against my body and buried my bone as deep as possible, shooting my nut deep inside her guts. She had both hands on her knees shaking and bucking hard with orgasm as we came together. Our first fuck was hard, fast, and furious—the bomb!

Knock! Knock! Knock!

The CO was serious about his hustle, fifteen minutes meant fifteen minutes. After adjusting our attire and making ourselves presentable, we stepped back into the visiting room like all was well in the world, because it was!

After fucking like that, we were famished. It was something about a good hard quickie that made a ma'fucka hungry as hell! We hit the vending machines and used every dollar they permitted the visitors to bring with them—hamburgers, French fries, chicken wings, candy bars, sunflower seeds, sodas, and a Snapple. After heating the food in the microwaves, we situated ourselves at our table.

"Are you ready for your next surprise?" The way her eyes twinkled with joy turned me on for real! It was like she was getting off on pleasing me.

I looked deep into her eyes and winked.

"Like I said before, I'ma sucka for surprises, ma."

She giggled girlishly and blushed before her eyes darted around the visiting room to ensure that no prying eyes were paying attention to whatever she was doing. Her hand came from up under the table, and she put her hand to her mouth and bit the top off something.

"Here, take this." With her back to the camera, she pressed a balloon about the size of a handball in my hand. I closed my fist around the balloon and looked at her with a questioning gaze. "I told you during our first visit that I knew a thing or two about the game. You asked if I was a ride or die chick. Well, this should answer your question. Besides, you're going to need some investment capital if you ever want to retain the services of a good legal team. You work on that while I run for you, and we'll both win in the end."

Now wasn't the time to play 21 Questions, but I needed to know the answer to one.

"Did you bag this shit up properly? I mean, I don't have to worry about this balloon busting in my stomach, do I?"

"Of course not. I told you I used to be with a D-boy, baby. This ain't my first time taking a penitentiary chance for my dude. Yes, I bagged it up right; I cellophane wrapped each sack first and tripled the balloon up, so you don't have to worry about anything busting. That's one big balloon holding forty-five smaller balloons. Fifteen street grams of meth, fifteen street grams of heroin, and fifteen balloons of the best Cali kush you'll ever have the pleasure of blowing. The weed is for your own personal use, baby. It's called *Goldie Locks*, because it's slightly gold in color, and it locks you up and keeps you stuck for hours!"

"You tryna make me fall in love, huh?" I smiled at her, and we both laughed.

"Some bitches say that they are ride or die chicks. I believe actions speak louder than words, so I'ma *show you* that I'ma ride or die chick, Shug."

"That's what's up, ma. I ain't mad atcha about that either." I was beyond impressed. Khadida was my kinda girl.

"When I was down in San Diego visiting your brother, I looked into the prospects of getting a good legal team to pick up your case and seeing if they would look into yours. Getting them to even accept and look at your transcripts is gonna cost $2,500. Afterward, if they accept your case, it's gonna cost a lot more. So I figured we can get a head start on the financial side of things right now."

We kicked it and conversed about our future plans for the rest of the visit. I swallowed several balloons at a time while eating the food and washing it down with soda.

The day after the visit, I started making verbal connections with potential clientele on the yard. In order to keep the prison-politics to a minimum, I wasn't selling shit to anybody who wasn't black. Khory stood at the door with his headphones on, keeping point for me as I threw fifty dollar papers into the pile of heroin sacks next to the mound of already bagged up meth bundles. *Now that you finna be the man on the yard, the haters is finna come out of the woodwork and put a gang of shit in the game, Shug. Be careful who you fuck with and how you fuck with 'em,* I reminded myself as I prepared to enter into the fray, the penitentiary drug trade.

CHAPTER 28

The Detectives

Detective's Joshua Ronan and Carl Braxton exited the elevator on the third floor and walked briskly down the linoleum tiled floor until they reached the nurse's station. Detective Braxton, an eleven-year veteran of the force, flashed the gold shield hanging from his neck and addressed the nurse on watch.

"Good day, ma'am. I'm Detective Braxton, and this is my partner, Detective Ronan."

"Hello, Detectives. How are you doing today?" the bubbly blonde nurse asked with a smile.

"We're good, thank you," Braxton replied cordially.

"How may I be of service, Detective?"

"We're with Homicide Division, ma'am, and our office received notification of a reported gunshot victim with suspicious overtones to it."

"Oh yes, let's see here." The bubbly blonde shuffled through the papers scattered around her desk until she located what they were looking for. "Try room 3351. He's an African American John Doe believed to be in his early twenties. He refused to give a name, or provide us with any information concerning his gunshot wound. He has numerous gang tattoos, and two other African American males around the same age with similar tattoos arrived DOA before his arrival."

Detective Ronan was busy scribbling in his notepad.

"Thank you, ma'am," Detective Braxton said and gave the bubbly blonde a curt nod before heading in the direction of room 3351.

When the two detectives stepped into the room, Bony James was lying in the hospital bed with his eyes fluttering heavy with sedation. Detective Braxton walked up to Bony James' bedside with a smug smirk splashed across his face. "Well, well, well. Look who we have here, partner."

Detective Ronan was a man of few words. He nodded, acknowledging that he knew who it was. The twenty-one year veteran of the force wasn't much on talking. He was into producing results, the kind of results that ended with felony convictions and long prison sentences. Detective Braxton addressed Bony James by his given name.

"Ebony James, I didn't expect to see you lying up in the bed when they told us there was a gunshot victim here. Normally you're on the other end of the pistol, the one doing the shooting." The smug smirk on Detective Braxton's face morphed into a wide, triumphant smile. "I've been trying to put your young punk ass away since you were in middle school."

"Fuck you, you bitch ass ma'fucka!" Bony James' head was foggy with sedation, but his mind was clear enough to recognize that the po-po were present, and it wasn't just any po-po, they were Homicide.

"I don't know if you had anything to do with the two dead bodies they brought in earlier today; maybe they died by your gun hand, Ebony James. Maybe not. But what I do know is that you're still on parole, and you've been shot, which is a violation of your parole. So, if you haven't killed anyone, and you want to avoid going back to prison, I suggest you start talking now." Detective Braxton had been putting gang bangers like Bony James away since his days as a rookie uniformed cop. His history with Bony James and many of the other gang members in Southeast San Diego area went way back.

"Fuck you in the ass, Braxton. I ain't got shit to say to you other than I want a lawyer!"

Click! Clack!

"Have it your way, James," Detective Braxton said, slapping a handcuff around Bony James' wrist, then slapping the other end of the cuff to the bedrail. Detective Braxton turned and spoke to his partner before leaving the room. "I'm gonna have a uniform come down and sit on this piece of crap. I'll be back in a minute."

"All right." Ronan's reply was short and simple.

Twenty minutes later, Detective Braxton returned to the room rubbing his palms together with zeal as if he had just discovered a juicy revelation. His body language caused his partner to perk up with mild interest. It was obvious he had uncovered something pertinent to the case they were working on. Detective Braxton winked at his partner and turned to Bony James. He looked at the bedridden thug with an expression exuding victory and said, "When you have that talk with your lawyer, Mr. James, make sure you let him know that the charges will include murder, at least two counts."

"Like I said . . . fuck you. I want a lawyer." Bony James adjusted the handcuff around his wrist and fought to keep his heavy eyelids open.

Detective Braxton was peeved that he didn't get the desired response he sought. It irked him that the arrogant gangster, who had managed to navigate his way through the judicial system, only receiving soft slap-on-the-hand jail stints when it was a known fact to the law enforcement community that Bony James and his Young Glock Gang cohorts were responsible for a number of cold cases and other unsolved violent crimes committed over the years. *Let's see if you still have that arrogant look on your face after this*, Detective Braxton thought and turned to his partner.

"Hey partner, you know those two DOAs they brought in

earlier? Well, coincidentally they've been identified as Jayquan Thomas and Jimmy "G-Mack" Lawson. If you add to the equation the now deceased Phillip "Goldie" Ranson, who was murdered a couple of weeks ago, that brings the total to three-fourths of the notorious Young Glock Gang who've been killed in the past two weeks." Detective Braxton smiled evilly and walked up on Bony James' bedside. "And judging from the looks of it, Ebony James, you came very close to being the fourth and final member of the Young Glock Gang to be murdered."

"Shut yo' bitch ass up, and get the fuck out my face, cracker! We done talking," Bony James told him and mean-mugged the detectives.

Detective Braxton's face turned red with rage. He reached out, pushed Bony James over onto his side, and pressed his finger down hard on the bandage covering his gunshot wound. He put his other hand over Bony James' mouth and muffled his painful cries.

"You cocky sonofabitch! Don't you dare disrespect me like that! Do you hear me!" Bony James grunted and looked at the detective with murder in his pupils. After one final push of his finger against the bandage, Detective Braxton moved back and turned to his partner.

"Gang Detail is downstairs filling out paperwork. When they're finished, they'll be up here to question this asshole." He turned back to Bony James.

"You do know that a death occurring during the commission of a crime are murders that will be tied to you, right?"

"Fuck what you talkin' about, bitch! I want my lawyer!" Bony James knew the routine. All the bullshit Braxton was doing and talking about didn't faze him in the least. He closed his eyes and tried to let sleep take him under.

"You're going to need a lawyer on this one, James, because something tells me the blood they found down the street from that double murder will come back a match to you. I'm also thinking the fingerprints and DNA found at a couple of other crime scenes will come back a match to you as well. It's not looking good for you, you slimy cocksucker. It's not looking good for you at all." Braxton was hoping that something he said would elicit a response from the street-hardened thug lying in the bed. He was disappointed when no response was forthcoming. Detective Braxton made eye contact with Detective Ronan and tilted his head toward the door, indicating to his partner that he was ready to leave. Detective Ronan pushed the plunger down on his ink pen, slapped his notebook closed, and headed into the hallway leaving Bony James alone in the room.

One of these days I'ma kill your punk ass, Braxton! On mommas, ma'fucka. I'ma slump your bitch ass and leave you lying in the gutter where your dirty pig-ass belong! The wicked thought was the last thing Bony James remembered before falling into a deep sleep as the sedation medications overwhelmed him.

CHAPTER 29

Tiyatti

"Whaddup, Jarvis? What's haddnin', Rooster?" Tiyatti slapped hands and dapped his two coworkers on his way inside the stash house.

"What's good?" the short, stocky thug named Jarvis replied.

"What it do, playboy?" Rooster respectfully responded as well.

"Is it anything new poppin'?" Tiyatti asked the same question he asked every day, wanting to be in the know in the event there were any changes.

"Nah, it's the same ol' shit, bruh," Rooster said.

"A'ight then. I'ma go 'head and make my rounds. Y'all good out here?"

"Yup."

"Yeah."

Tiyatti stuffed the Ruger in his waistband and armed himself with the sawed off 12-gauge that Cream supplied him with when he promoted him to his new security post. He had been working at the money house for a few weeks now, and the money was good. He held the heavy murder weapon in his hand and thought about Cream's words when he gave it to him. *Up close, in one of these rooms inside this house, this pistol-grip pump will serve you better than any pistol or rifle ever will. At this range, it will blow a hole in a man the size of a grapefruit!*

I'm thirsty! Tiyatti thought as he went to do his room-to-room inspection checking the windows and doors. *I'm hella thirsty!* he thought again moments later. The dryness in his mouth altered his course. Instead of finishing his rounds, he

189

headed off in the direction of the kitchen in search of something to sip on. As he neared the kitchen, he heard voices talking in hushed tones. His inner voice alerted him that Rooster and Jarvis were up to no good, prompting him to freeze and ear-hustle their conversation. Tiyatti paused in the hallway on the other side of the doorway and listened while the two thugs spoke to each other in a conspiratorial whisper.

"Man, I'm tellin' you, bruh, this is the perfect time to clip that bitch! It's two million dollars sittin' in this stash house, and that bitch back is against the wall right now. She been takin' heavy losses, Jarvis, and I don't see why we can't be the ones who benefit from it." Rooster sensed that he was close to convincing Jarvis to join him in his devious plot, so he took advantage of the momentary silence and pressed the issue.

"Why is you hesitating, Jarvis? It's nothin'! We bag that shit up and bounce wit' it, simple as that!" Rooster said, attempting to win Jarvis over.

Aw shit! Aw shit! If it wasn't for bad luck I wouldn't have any luck at all! Tiyatti panicked and almost lost his composure. The thought of Rooster and Jarvis trying to jack Miko's stash house while he was in charge of security put him dead bang between the proverbial crosshairs. *Hell ma'fuckin' naw!* He decided right then that he wasn't about to be in cahoots with Rooster and Jarvis, or have anything to do with crossing Miko and her goon cousins. Then a thought occurred and made him panic even more. *If they take the money and run, she gon' swear up and down that I had something to do with it!* He knew if he allowed Rooster and Jarvis to get away with their scandalous scheme, then the wrath of Miko and her cousins would come down on his head hard and without mercy. He was stuck between a rock and a hard place. Letting Rooster and Jarvis get away with the money guaranteed an ugly ending. His mind ran wild with what-the-fuck-to-do's. *I could call Miko and let her know what's about to go down. But after the last conversation we had, that crazy bitch might think I'm knee deep in the shit Rooster and Jarvis got going on.* He put his thoughts on pause and listened closely as the two thugs continued to lay out their plan.

"All we gotta do is bag the dough up, and when Tiyatti ain't suspectin' nothin', we gun his ass down and get the fuck outta town two million dollars richer." Rooster was cold and calculating with his thought process.

"Why we gotta kill him? We could just bust him upside the head and knock him out cold, then tie him up and get the fuck up outta here," Jarvis said, sounding a little more compassionate with his thought process.

"Because, if we don't kill him, that leaves a witness behind to point the finger at us if it goes all bad, bruh," Rooster replied.

"Yeah, you're right, Rooster. Fuck it. I never liked that pretty boy ma'fucka anyway." Jarvis' mind was made up.

They're plotting to kill me! I oughta kill both they asses right now! Tiyatti thought angrily. What he was hearing had him shaking with rage. He had never killed a man before, but it didn't look like they were leaving him any other choice. *Run Tiyatti! Get the hell outta here before the shit hits the fan!* the voice in his head yelled to him. *No, if you run now and they get away with the money, you'll look guilty as hell. Call Miko and tell her what the deal is!* He held the sawed-off in both hands, weighing his options. *I could run up in there and blast they asses, but if I did that, I would have to explain why I killed two of her workers without any evidence to support my claim of what they were up to.* He dismissed that option. *I could call Miko and tell her what they're up to. Fuck it, that's exactly what I'ma do!* He settled on the latter. Slowly, he started retracing his steps, tiptoeing backward toward one of the rooms.

Squeak!

His foot stepped on a weak floorboard, and his weight made the floor underneath him squeal loud enough to draw the attention of one of the plotting thugs in the kitchen.

* * * * * *

"Shhhh, did you hear that?" Rooster reached for his gun and stood up. Jarvis palmed his pistol and stood up as well. Both gangstas crept toward the doorway of the kitchen with paranoid caution. Rooster looked at Jarvis and put a finger to his lips and tiptoed toward the hallway where Tiyatti stood, his .40 caliber pointing straight ahead, ready to explode. Jarvis had his .357 Python up and aimed ready to do the same. Rooster touched the trigger with his index finger and prepared to squeeze off a shot as soon as he reached the doorway separating the hallway from the kitchen. Before he got there, he stopped and stood as still as a statue, taking a deep breath and letting it go before quickly spinning to his right with the .40 caliber on the cusp of blasting. The hallway was empty; there was no sign of Tiyatti. *Man, I'm trippin'!*

"Ain't nobody out here, Rooster. You hella 'noid, bruh," Jarvis told him after joining him in the hallway.

* * * * * *

Nervous energy flooded his senses as Tiyatti stood in one of the bedrooms with the Ruger in one hand and his cell phone in the other, his thumb accessing his call log as he attempted to contact Miko. The shotty was resting next to him. He also had a pocket full of shotgun shells, in the event he had to make his last stand.

Ring. Ring. Ring. Ring. Ring. Ring.

Miko's phone rang continuously. *Answer the fuckin' phone, Miko!* Tiyatti silently screamed in his head as he held the phone to his ear, focusing the Ruger at the center of the closed door.

Miko answered the phone in a confident tone.

"Something told me you'd have a change of heart. I guess it took a boss bitch like me putting a pistol in your face to bring out the—"

"Shut the fuck up and listen!" Tiyatti abruptly cut her off with urgency in his whispering voice.

When he cut her off, she looked at the phone like it was a piece of shit in her hand.

"Bitch, who the fuck do you think you talkin' to like that!"

Tiyatti ignored her indignant tone and whispered frantically into the phone.

"Rooster and Jarvis are about to rob the stashhouse! I overheard 'em plottin' to jack you for the two million dollars in the house and kill me in the process! They on some foul shit, Miko, and I don't have anything to do with it! I'm in one of the bedrooms and it—"

Blam!

The bedroom door flew open, nearly coming off the hinges as all hell broke out.

CHAPTER 30

Tiyatti

Pop! Pop! Pop! Pop! Pop!

Bullets whizzed above Tiyatti's head, penetrating the wall and the heavy wooden dresser in the area where he was cowering in the cut.

Pap! Pap!

The Ruger busted off two shots, splintering the wood on the door that was hanging on a hinge at an awkward angle. *Save your ammo. Use the shotty. It covers more space!* he reminded himself of Cream's words.

Bloooom! Bloooom!

After dropping the Ruger, the sawed-off shotty exploded in Tiyatti's hands. The shotgun blast tore a huge chunk out of the wall near the doorway.

Miko listened with rapt interest while fuming over Tiyatti's disrespect.

"Anthony, call Cream and Suspect and tell them to get their asses over to the money house! Rooster and Jarvis are trying to steal my money!" Miko barked out orders to her trusted driver/bodyguard.

She entered her password on the laptop's keypad, and a panel slid back on the desk in front of her. A fifty-eight-inch flat-screen appeared out of the opening, revealing a row of monitors. Her fingers furiously swiped at the screen. In seconds, the stash house came up on all of the monitors. Every room inside the money house was on display. She put the phone to her mouth and told Tiyatti, "Don't let them get away with my money! Do you hear me, Tiyatti! I pay you to guard my money. You bet not let those ma'fuckas steal what's mine.

Guard my money with your life!" Miko yelled angrily into the phone as she watched Rooster and Jarvis throw shots at Tiyatti, who was in the corner of the bedroom wedged between the wall and a dresser.

Tiyatti didn't hear anything she said. His phone was on the floor next to him. The Ruger was back in his right hand pointing at the door while his left hand dug deep in his pocket in search of shotgun shells.

Pop! Pop! Pop! Pop! Pop!

Rooster threw more shots at Tiyatti.

Boom! Boom!

Jarvis dumped his thumper in Tiyatti's direction as well.

Pap! Pap! Pap!

Tiyatti bust back at them with the Ruger.

Rooster cupped his hands over his lips and whispered in Jarvis' ear, "Go get the money together and put it in the bags! I'ma keep him pent down in here, then we gon' get the fuck outta here while we still got a chance!" He got off several more shots.

Pop! Pop! Pop!

Rooster dropped the clip out the .40 cal's ass and quickly reloaded, talking to Tiyatti in the process. "Tiyatti, this shit is gon' end real ugly for you, bruh, you hear me?"

Pop! Pop! Pop! Pop! Pop!

He threw shots at Tiyatti, knowing he had the upper hand.

"I can do this shit all day long, bruh. I got clips for days, Tiyatti!"

Miko irately watched as the scene played out on the screen in front of her.

Pap! Pap! Pap!

Tiyatti bust shots back at Rooster's voice, hitting the door inches away from his mouth with all three shots.

"If it ends ugly for me, Rooster, then it's gon' end ugly for you too!" Tiyatti told him. Thoughts of Devontay and Duchess flashed in his mind. He looked up at the wall above his head and stared at the bullet holes that dotted the area above him.

"It's just a matter of time before you run out of shots though, bruh, and when you do, I'm comin' in that bitch and filling you full of holes, boy!"

"If you bring your ass up in here, Rooster, this shotgun gon' tear your ass in half! So go ahead, bring your bad ass up in here if you want to!" Tiyatti threatened in response. *What the fuck is taking 'em so long?* He was hoping like hell Miko had already sent somebody. *I hope the police don't fuck around and show up. I ain't trying to go to jail; my family needs me!*

Miko listened to the exchange and watched the ordeal play out like a Netflix movie, only now she was watching it play out while sitting in the back of the Maybach speeding toward her stash house.

Minutes later, Jarvis crept down the hallway and knelt next to Rooster. He leaned in and whispered through his reddish brown dreadlocks, "The money is bagged up by the door ready to go!"

Pop! Pop! Pop!

Rooster decorated the dresser and wall next to Tiyatti with a few more bullets for good measure.

Boom! Boom!

Jarvis threw two shots that penetrated the wall inches above Tiyatti's head.

Tiyatti crouched low and bided his time in the corner with the shotty in both hands pointed upward. His brow sweat profusely as fear and apprehension choked his composure, his breathing was quick and shallow. He lost track of time as he waited to kill or be killed.

After some time had passed, he heard the faint sound of tires screeching. *I hope that's Miko's people!* he thought hopefully. *Oh shit, what if that's Rooster and Jarvis bouncin' with the money?* Panic gripped his heart and squeezed on it. *What if it's the police coming to gaffel us all up?*

"Please God, don't let it be the police. I ain't trying to die or go to jail!" He thought about Devontay and Duchess and vowed that today was his last day in the street life. *I'm done with these streets! Fuck this shit!* He'd had enough of the game. He had to get out before the game got him. Some people were built for the thug life. Tiyatti had come to realize in a live life and death experience that he wasn't one of those people. *I ain't built for this shit!*

* * * * * *

Miko powered the window down in the back of the Cool Whip white Maybach and looked over to the truck Cream and Suspect were sitting in when she pulled up. Cream was hanging halfway out the window waiting to hear what she was about to say.

"Take both of those ma'fuckas to the chamber, then go handle that other shit just like I told you to. Now ain't the time for none of that compassionate shit either, Cream. You hear me? I'm about to send a message to the streets: if a ma'fucka even think about steppin' to me, it's gonna be the worst mistake they ever made!"

"Done deal, cousin." He assured Miko her instructions would be followed to a tee.

Anthony got out of the front seat and transferred the bags of money from the truck to the Maybach's trunk. Miko stared hard at the two men sitting tied up and duct taped in the

Deeply Rooted 2

backseat of the SUV. Rooster looked back at her with a face void of expression. Jarvis nervously chewed on his bottom lip before bowing his head and burying his face in his lap. Cream pulled off and headed toward the house with the torture chamber in it.

The queenpin smiled sinisterly at the two traitorous workers, and then looked down at her laptop before closing it slowly. When Anthony opened the rear door, she stepped from the back of the luxury car and looked at the gritty dilapidated neighborhood around her. She wasn't worried about the police showing up anytime soon. Cops rarely made timely appearances in hoods like this one. Anthony followed her into the stash house as she took long-legged steps up the ragged walkway like royalty was in her bloodline.

"Tiyatti, it's Miko," she announced loudly from the living room.

After several seconds of silent uncertainty, Tiyatti appeared in the doorway of the living room, Ruger in his right hand, the shotty dangling dangerously from his left paw.

Miko stood stoic and bossy with her arms folded across her chest, her left foot tapping lightly on the wooden floor. Dressed in all black, the expression on her beautiful face was controlled and unruffled. Boss confidence shone bright in her eyes. Anthony stood off to the side with a grim look on his face, jawline as solid as Mount Rushmore. He was hugging his chest, muscles bulging on top of muscles while his hand inconspicuously rested near the huge chrome canon in the shoulder holster. The mood in the room was serious. It made Tiyatti 'plex up and feel the need to explain himself.

"They had me pinned down in the bedroom while they busted shots at me, Miko. There wasn't anything else I could do." He had no idea that Rooster and Jarvis had been captured

199

by Cream and Suspect as they attempted to flee the money house with their hands filled with duffle bags.

You should've never got into this game if you weren't ready to play with the big dogs, she thought, calling to mind his earlier disrespect on the phone.

"I told you not to let them steal my money, Tiyatti." Miko's voice was icy.

What the fuck are you talkin' about! He looked at her as if she was crazy.

"I ain't let 'em steal shit! I almost lost my life today!" Tiyatti almost yelled.

"And I almost lost two million dollars today!"

"Whatchu mean almost?" he asked with a voice full of skepticism, hope in his tone. *Maybe they never took the money!*

"Cream and Suspect caught Rooster and Jarvis running out the house with the money."

He let out a loud sigh of relief.

"Good, I thought they got away! Them ma'fuckas tried to kill me, man! I literally heard 'em plottin' to murder me like it wasn't nothin'! I'm done with this life. I can't do this shit no more, Miko. Fuck that, I'm good. Here." Tiyatti handed her the sawed-off and tucked the Ruger in the back of his waistband, walking past her and Anthony on his way out the door.

Click!

The hammer on Anthony's hand canon cocked loud enough to stop Tiyatti in his tracks.

"It ain't gon' be that easy, Tiyatti," Miko stated. "You know too much about my business, and your hands ain't dirty enough for my liking. As far as I'm concerned, the only way that you're going to step away from this life is if your hands got some blood on them too."

"Whatchu talkin' 'bout?" he asked, mortified.

"Rooster and Jarvis tried to kill you, right?" She posed the question.

"Yup."

"I told you not to let them steal my money, right?" she asked a follow up question.

No answer.

"That's what I thought. The way I see it, Tiyatti, you owe me two bodies, one for each million that you did not properly defend."

"You got your money back though! What the fuck are you talking about?"

"No thanks to you! You were cowering in a corner when they ran off with my money! Cream and Suspect are the ones who actually stopped them from getting away with my money, not you!" The boss bitch was freezing in her ruthless way of thinking.

Anthony relieved Tiyatti of his Ruger and escorted him to the Maybach.

Tiyatti walked with his head down wondering what was next. *Is she gonna make me murk Rooster and Jarvis? If she do, will I be able to kill them? What the fuck did I do to deserve this?* A pool of helpless tears filled his eyes as he fretted about the pitiful prospects that lie ahead. *If I have to kill them, then fuck it. They were dead set on killing me!*

CHAPTER 31

Baby Shug

I strolled around the track in the middle of a small mob of thuggish goons, knowing I stood out amongst them, the alpha male in the pack of hood wolves. All of them Crips, all of them killas, all of them devoted to me when it came to doing this thug thang. When I stopped and posted up, my pack of wolves stopped and posted up too. All my goons knew their roles, and every one of them played their positions without resentment. I was paying them well and providing them with a sense of economical security that helped relieve a heavy burden, one of the most troubling issues a convict would ever be faced with while doing a bid, financial stability.

Weeks passed since the visit with Khadida. The dope allowed me to carve out a nice niche in the illicit contraband market on the prison yard, a nice niche I was currently taking full advantage of. Instead of small balloons being secretly smuggled in through the visiting room, now it was ounces of hard and soft, black and white that I was bagging up and supplying the majority of the population with. I was serving huge amounts of kush to the masses: $400 ounce-sized bundles only. With the money from my first run of balloons, I was able to pay my way to a pipeline that flowed freely with any and every type of drug imaginable. Cell phones went anywhere from $500-$1,000, depending on its capabilities and the services it offered. I had my arm elbow deep in that game as well. I made more than enough money to cover my legal fees. So I used the abundance of cash I collected on the yard, along with the Greendots and other money wire transfers to stack an account Khadida hooked up for me. Even though I was getting it in a major way, I couldn't allow myself to become overly confident. Being in prison, I had to be mindful of the fact that while making the kind of paper I was making, I was also making enemies—the haters. Haters made it their business to put a boss's business on blast.

I knew the po-po had eyes on me and were watching my every move, so I stayed slick with my activities and delegated responsibilities out to gangstas I trusted and had the utmost confidence in. Crip gangstas I knew, whom I'd personally done background checks on.

My top worker/enforcer was a savage homie from my set named Lil Paul Blue, and he collected cheese from all the cats who were trying to re-up on a new sack. He also paid off the handful of runners we utilized to hold work for us, or transport contraband from one housing unit to another. I made sure I hit all my goons off with a lil something to line their pockets with too. Kush and meth kept my wild goons turnt all the way up, high as fuck and battle-ready for real! They were getting it for free, which ensured they would get on a bitch-ass hater's head for me if I so much as breathed the command. I remained true to my decision not to serve any Mexicans or white boys, not out of prejudice, but because if they put shit in the game when it came to paying a debt, then it ain't just one person my goons gotta bust on; nine times outta ten it would end with us having some type of a race war. I was getting too much paper to be risking that kind of shit.

The homies and I were mobbing around the yard chopping it up and chilling when I saw the cat Droop Loc over by the program office. He had a bedroll in his hand and was wearing some shower shoes. *He musta just got out the hole. No wonder I ain't seen that fool on the yard lately. I wonder what he got into.* When we rounded the track and neared the spot where he was posted up at, I stopped and excused myself from the crew. I broke away from my pack and went to confront Droop Loc about his apparent staring problem.

"What's happenin' wit' it, cuz?" I asked, stopping when I was just out of arm's reach.

"Ain't nothin'. What's up wit' you, cuz?" he responded and held my eye contact—no tension, no hostility.

He ain't actin' like he want it wit' me, I thought, but decided to press the issue anyway.

"I noticed you checkin' for me a few times a few days back. What's up with that?" I searched his eyes for any sign of deception and watched his hands out the corner of my eyes. *If he buck up and drop his bedroll, I'm bankin' him on the chin!* I told myself and prepared for whatever.

He smirked and chuckled under his breath.

"I ain't got no beef with you, Baby Shug. I just pay attention to detail and keep tabs on the real ones." His response was unexpected, but I played it cool and maintained my composure. "I've been hearing about you. From what I've heard so far, it seems like you got your shit together. Do your homework, cuz. Ask around, and when you ready to do some big business, get at me," he said and chucked the deuces up before walking off, nodding in Lil Paul Blue's direction.

"You know him?" I asked my top worker when I rejoined my crew.

"Yup, that's the homie Droop Loc from 76 East Coast. He just settled an excessive force lawsuit against the state worth two hundred racks. He hella papered up. That's why they keep puttin' him in the hole for the pettiest shit. They mad that they had to break him off like that."

Two hundred racks, huh? I most definitely need to be doing business with that fool! I thought as I walked with the homies.

If Lil Paul Blue was vouching for him, then Droop Loc was straight. The more I thought about it, the more I wanted to put a dent in some of that two hundred thousand he got broke off. *Fuck it, why not? I ain't got shit to lose, and I got everything to gain!* My mind was made up before the yard closed. Droop Loc was going to be my number one customer, or my new worst enemy, if he black-eyed the game.

The next morning at five minutes after nine, the CO manning the gun tower inside the building popped my door open and informed me that I had a visit. It took about fifteen minutes to get myself right. I spotted Khadida as soon as I stepped into the crowded visiting area. She rocked a banana colored tube dress that boldly showcased her voluptuous dimensions and proudly displayed the banging definition of her outline: tits pushed out proud, her hips sensuously flaring out, and that ass poking out like it had an attitude all its own. Her silhouette was sexy as fuck!

"Hey baby, I missed you." She greeted me with a hug before planting a wet kiss on my lips. Our tongues tussled for a while, and I squeezed her ass cheeks a few times.

"I missed you too. You look beautiful, baby. I like how this dress is fittin' your frame, ma." I pulled the chair out for her and smiled when she sat down and that big ass spread out, threatening to spill over the plastic blue bucket seat. We kicked it and talked shit for the first hour of the visit.

"A'ight now, baby, you been duckin' and dodgin' me every time I get on you about this supposed good news you say you got for me. All week long you've been puttin' me on pause when I try to squeeze the information outta you on the phone. You keep sayin' you wanna tell me in person because you want to see the expression on my face. Well, here I am," I told her with a smile on my mug.

All week long, the most reoccurring thought running through my mind was: she's pregnant. It had been close to a month since I first pushed the dick up in her. I know that's a little soon, but it wasn't impossible, so the thought of her telling me that she was carrying my seed was at the forefront of my speculation. In all actuality, it was more my wishful thinking than anything else.

She stuck the tip of her tongue out, teasing me before speaking.

"What would be the one thing I could tell you that would be the single most pleasing thing to your heart? I mean, if you only had one wish that you could make come true, what would that one wish be, Shug?" Her tone was a little more serious as was her body language. The expression on her face told me she was expecting a well thought out response.

I took my cue from that and sat up straight in my chair, pinching my chin in deep thought and giving serious consideration to her question. After a full minute of weighty contemplation, two answers stood teetering on my life's priority balancing scales: my freedom and my brother's health. *If she's pregnant and that's the news she plans on revealing to me, I hope my answer doesn't hurt her feelings,* I thought before saying, "If there was one thing that I could make become a reality, then the one thing most pleasing to my heart would be for me to see my brother back healthy again, out of that coma and living his life to the fullest."

Her eyes widened with surprise and a smile decorated her face, a perfect set of white teeth peeked at me from behind her parted lips. It was obvious from the expression on her face that she was touched by my answer. I could tell she was expecting a completely different type of response from me.

"Well, I pray that happens, and I honestly believe that Wah

will make a full recovery. But that's not the surprise," she said, rubbing my arm affectionately.

"That's a'ight, baby, don't trip. What is the surprise though?" I asked, anxious.

She perked up and sat up in her chair, her posture erect as she grabbed both my hands.

"Well, I wanted to be the one to tell you to your face that the investigators discovered some evidence that could not only get you back in front of a judge, but evidence that quite possibly might get you exonerated of all charges, baby."

I pulled away from her and backed my chair up with a look of disbelief. My heart beat hard like four 15's in the back of a box Chevy.

"For real! Are you serious, Khadida?" I asked, sliding back up to the table, trying to calm down. But I was beside myself with emotion, and I couldn't slow my breathing for shit.

The smile on her face spread, and she was glowing with delight.

"I wouldn't play with you about something like that, baby. Supposedly, they have two surveillance tapes in their possession, surveillance tapes that show that you were not the shooter."

My eyes narrowed to slits, and a beaming smile stretched across my face. I tried to swallow the news she just hit me with, but I was choking with joy. I wasn't expecting anything like that to come out of her mouth. A feeling of unbridled elation carried me to my feet and made me pick her up in a bear hug and swing her around. The entire visiting room looked at us like we were crazy. When I stopped spinning her, I kissed her until the CO at the podium got on the intercom and told us that we were doing too much.

Khadida told me all about her last meeting with our legal team and the discovery of new evidence. When she finished, I was nearly in tears. *I might fuck around and get out from up under these two life sentences!* I thought with a smile on my face that refused to go away. I was barely able to suppress my emotions. My thoughts instantly went to my ex, Miko. *I'm gonna murk that sorry ass bitch as soon as I get out! I don't give a fuck what happens after that. If it's the last thing I do, I'm killing that bitch Miko!*

CHAPTER 32

Wah

It started when the nurse left the room and closed the door behind her. A gust of cold air rushing over my face made my eyes dry up, causing me to blink in an effort to generate moisture. Suddenly, my body had an involuntary reaction, and I abruptly sucked in a mouthful of air and swallowed it hard. I felt my lungs inflate with oxygen and my chest cavity expand to its limits. *What the fuck is happening to me!* I wondered fearfully, then regrettably swallowed again. Swallowing hurt like hell; the pain was almost unbearable. It felt like I was suffocating. *Am I choking to death? Calm down, Wah. Calm down and breathe,* I told myself and breathed deep through my nostrils. That's when I noticed the smell of disinfectant inside the room wasn't vague anymore; it was strong and pungent. I blinked again and instantly knew something was different. *What the fuck!* My sense of smell was stronger than it had been since getting shot. I sneezed hard and felt warm snot shoot out onto my chin before it dribbled down onto my neck. I tried to wipe the snot away, but my limbs felt heavy as hell, like they had weights attached to them. *But my arms are moving!*

After struggling for what seemed like hours, my wrist landed heavily on my lips, missing my intended target. My coordination was all fucked up. *But you're movin', Wah!* For the first time in nearly two years, my body was reacting to the commands that my brain were issuing out. *It's hella cold!* I thought after feeling myself shiver. The room was dark, the climate inside was borderline frosty. I closed my eyes and took a few deep breaths as I mentally prepared myself to move mountains. My hand still lay across my lips, unmoving. I could feel my breath against the skin on the back of my hand. I felt a sharp pain in my stomach. *What the fuck is wrong with my stomach? It hurts!* I used every bit of strength I could muster and moved my hand in the direction of my stomach. I felt the plastic tube-like hose against my hand. It took a few minutes of fidgeting around with my fingers, but I eventually wrapped my fingers around the tube and tried to pull it out of my stomach. I could feel my strength draining rapidly. Trying to remove the tube from my stomach was a monumental struggle. After several more futile attempts, I gave up and sank back into the pillows depleted of energy. *I give up! I can't do this shit!* I was completely exhausted and physically spent. As happy as I was about moving on my own accord, I was equally as angry that I couldn't do a damn thing about my circumstance. *Fuck it!* I was so exhausted I just leaned back, closed my eyes, and went to sleep.

Hours later, I woke up to a group of hospital staff huddled around my bed, rubbing my extremities and pulling at my body parts.

"Welcome back to the world of the wide awake, Mr. Mitchell!" a tall doctor in a white outfit with a shock of gray hair greeted me cheerfully.

"What?" It felt like I was spitting out dirt when I spoke for the first time in nearly two years. Then it hit me! *I just spoke! I ain't in a coma anymore!* I cracked a smile that hurt my entire face, but it felt so fucking good to me!

Once the medical staff got over their initial shock and surprise, they ran all types of tests on me. The bullet wounds had completely healed, leaving me with six shiny patches of skin covering the holes. Thankfully, I didn't have any serious or long-term damage to any of my internal organs. The rehab process was a ma'fucka! It was literally like teaching a grown ass man how to walk and function all over again. Luckily, working out and exercising was something I excelled at. A vigorous workout routine was something I was familiar with due to my years of incarceration back in the day.

My recovery was slow at first because I'd been lying on my back for damn near two years. The first thing I noticed was that I'd lost a lot of weight and a good amount of muscle mass. At first I wanted to eat everything. I stayed hungry as hell, but the size of my stomach had shrank so much, I could only consume a small amount of solid food at a time. I drank a bunch of Boosts and other liquid protein drinks, and slowly but surely I started putting back on some of the weight I had lost. Regaining my ability to talk wasn't that big of an issue. Once the pain of my being parched went away, my verbal abilities came back easily. After the first ten days I was walking again, albeit on wobbly legs at times. I wanted to hurry up and get the fuck outta this hospital, but I understood the realistic chances of my being able to leave wasn't all that likely until I was fully physically fit enough to do so. When I wasn't working out or eating, I was sitting up in the bed reading books or flipping through magazines trying to keep from thinking about Tocarra too much. Thinking of her left me feeling lonely and abandoned. Emotionally, I was in a fucked up place when a chubby, light-skinned nurse interrupted my solitude and pushed the door to my room open with a wheelchair in front of her.

"Are you ready for your physical therapy session, Mr. Mitchell?" The wheelchair was a precautionary measure, something the hospital staff insisted on.

"I ain't using that wheelchair anymore, nurse," I told her as I climbed out of the bed and made my way toward the door, trying to walk as normal as possible. She stood back with a questioning look on her face, as if she wasn't sure that my walking all the way to the physical therapy area on my own was such a good idea. I showed her a look of determination, letting her know I wasn't budging.

My workout routine started with twenty minutes of stretching. Afterward, I knocked out a few sets of arm and leg exercises using a resistance band. I swam and ran in a pool for another forty-five minutes, an exercise that helped redevelop my motor skills. Then I got on the weights and beasted up on them for an hour or so. Repairing my frame and fully regaining my strength was of the utmost importance because I had some serious goon business that needed handling. Every rep I did, every set I knocked out, I did so with painful memories motivating my physical and mental drive. Whenever I felt like quitting, or like I didn't have anymore gas in the tank, I thought about Miko and those six shots, and I used that bitch as motivation to push myself over the top. After my workout, as I made my way back toward my room, I thought about those bullets tearing into my skin and digging into my body, and letting the rage from that antagonize my anger. *It's a wrap for your ass, Miko. I swear I am going to personally kill your punk ass for all the shit you've done!*

My murderous thoughts were interrupted when I turned into the doorway of my hospital room and came face to face with two of the flyest females I'd ever seen. *Damn, who the fuck are they?* My eyes first took in the lovely vision of the Keyshia Cole lookalike, and I smiled with approval as my pupils traversed her curvy canvas. My smile widened when I saw the shocked expression on her face. I glanced over to the taller, curvier chick and was even more impressed. *She got a Megan Good face with an Amber Rose frame. Damn, baby is gorgeous!* She too was slack jawed with her mouth open. We stood there looking at one another in awkward silence for a few seconds before I did what came natural.

"Hello ladies, what's really good? Either you got the wrong room, or I died and went to heaven. I'm thinking it's the former, because heaven ain't got 'em thick and beautiful like y'all." My dimples were on full display, and I was really feeling myself having just worked out and showered. "I'm Wahdatah by the way," I told them and smiled wider, dimples deepening.

"I'm uh . . . hi um . . . my name is Khadida, and this is my sister Khassandra. I thought you were . . . how did you . . . Oh shit, I'm trippin' out for real!" Keyshia Cole's twin put her hand flat against her chest and sat down on my bed to keep from losing her balance. To say that she was shocked to see me out of the coma was an understatement.

"Didn't you come visit me a while ago?" I asked Khadida before my gaze veered back over to Khassandra. Her big, round protruding ass momentarily hijacked my focus. When I glanced back over at Khadida she just looked at me and nodded.

After breaking the ice by exchanging small talk, I closed the door and we chilled in my room and got acquainted. It was good meeting my brother's new woman and hearing her update me on his status. I soaked up everything she was saying, but for some reason my eyes couldn't keep from wandering over to Khassandra and taking in her exquisite beauty. *The bitch is beautiful as hell and got a bangin' ass body!*

We ended up talking for another couple hours before Khadida announced that they had to head back to LA. As soon as they bounced, I stretched out on the soft, comfortable hospital bed and tried to take a midday power nap. After twenty minutes of restless tossing and turning, I finally gave up on the nap and lay there with my eyes closed, letting my thoughts roam, killing time. I thought about Shug and his situation and smiled, knowing he had a good legal team working on getting him exonerated. Then I thought about Tocarra, and my smile faded and sadness enveloped my mood. *Where the fuck you at, baby? Why the hell you ain't here with me?* Thoughts of Tocarra emotionally put me in a bad space that I didn't like being in, which led my thoughts to Miko. I envisioned putting both my hands around her throat and choking the life out of her punk ass. The smile immediately returned to my face. Then I thought about putting a gun to Miko's forehead and slowly pulling the trigger. My smile expanded. I thought about standing over her body and emptying the clip into her face. The smile on my face stretched ear to ear, and I kept imagining different ways of killing that 'ho Miko until sleep finally overtook me.

CHAPTER 33

Miko

With a stern look on her face, Miko followed Tiyatti and Anthony into the house. Dressed in a pair of dark gray wool slacks with a matching vest over a black sweater and a pair of black leather Ferragamo boots, her long, silky mane was pulled back into a ponytail. Her flawless appearance belied the downright ugly intentions deeply rooted in her heart. Cream and Suspect stood off to the side with the two bags of money Rooster and Jarvis attempted to run off with, their mugs on mean and chrome canons on display.

Miko stopped in the middle of the living room and turned to Cream.

"Did you tie both of those ma'fuckas up and stuff 'em in a sack like I told you to?"

"Yup, they downstairs in the chamber tied up tight as tennis shoes," Cream answered.

"Good, take this chump down there with 'em!" She spat the order out like she was trying to get a foul taste out of her mouth. Anthony nudged Tiyatti forward with his pistol pressed against his back and steered him to the door leading to the torture chamber.

Tiyatti didn't know what to think. He couldn't wrap his mind around what he did, or didn't do, that had him in the predicament he found himself in, with a pistol poking him in his spinal column in a room full of heartless killas.

Cream twisted the doorknob, opened the door to the torture chamber, and stepped inside. One by one they entered the room of horrors. The smell of death was strong and heady; the scent was palpable in the concrete torture space.

Tiyatti walked on wobbly legs as he descended the stairs, fear gripping his heart and unkindly squeezing it. Timidly, he walked down the steps leading to the sunken bowl of the windowless room. He eyed the stack of rolled up rugs sitting across the room against the far wall and immediately deduced that the rugs were probably intended to conceal dead bodies. A blur of movement to his right caught his attention out his peripheral and hijacked his focus away from the rolled up rugs. Two sleeping bags writhing about wildly several feet to his right, with a noticeably taller person in one bag and a shorter person in the other.

Panicky and fearful, Tiyatti began looking for a third sleeping bag, and breathed a sigh of relief when he didn't see a third one. He thought about turning and forcefully pushing past the people behind him, but quickly dismissed that notion, knowing the chances of him bullying past four armed killers were practically impossible. Suicide by stupidity. He watched Miko pull a pair of gloves out from her vest pocket, then slip them over her fingers until they fit tightly.

"Where's the gun?" she asked Suspect, who pulled a .38 snub nose pistol out of his back pocket.

Tiyatti figured it out as he watched Miko take the gun and pop the cylinder out. One by one she plucked each bullet out until only one remained. She slapped the cylinder back into place. Using the palm of her open hand, she spun the cylinder, listening to its metallic clicking. She smiled with satisfaction when it stopped—a lone bullet mysteriously resting somewhere in one of the cylinder's six holes. In a final act of despondency, he pled his case, desperately hoping to talk his way out of the precarious predicament.

"Ay look, Miko. I didn't have anything to do with what Rooster and Jarvis tried to do. I called you as soon as I heard 'em talkin' about it." He paused to take a deep breath, then looked up at Miko and continued to plead his case. "I mean, you were on the phone with me when they started shooting at me! You have to know I wasn't involved in that shit. They were trying to kill me, man!" Tiyatti pointed emphatically at the two twisting sleeping bags on the floor. "Those two ma'fuckas were trying to take *your money*, but they were trying to take *my life!*"

Miko looked at Tiyatti with a gleam of disgust in her eyes. "I remember the phone call quite clearly, Tiyatti. I also specifically recall making it very clear to you not to let them take my money." She looked at him with deeper intensity and walked up on him until her lips brushed against his ear. She whispered so that only he could hear her. "You were hired to protect *my money* and to take care of *my assets*, but when the opportunity presented itself for you to do just that, you failed to step your game up and upgrade." She stepped back, and the evil look she gave him blended well with the wicked grin on her beautiful face. The double entendre was a secret only the two of them would share.

He wanted to say something in his defense, but the look in her eyes told him it was useless. Then Tiyatti knew in his heart that it wasn't about the money at all. Her having him standing there under the gun was 100% a result of him rejecting her sexual advances. Tiyatti dropped his eyes and took a deep breath, then shook his head in defeat at her scandalous ways. He was absolutely correct, too. Miko was indeed a woman scorned, bitter and spiteful because he turned down her advances.

Tiyatti jerked his head up and made one last frantic plea.

"Look, Miko, I'm sorry. I swear I didn't mean any disrespect. All I wanna do is walk away from this street shit and start my life fresh. You don't owe me a dime. You don't have to pay me or nothin'. I'll go about my business like we never even met." He didn't realize he was only digging a deeper hole for himself with every word he spoke.

She misconstrued the meaning of every one of his words. Miko was a picture of calm on the surface, but inside she was enraged and incensed that a lowly worker had the audacity to look her in the face after having sex with her and tell her that he'd just go on about his business like they'd never met. Infuriated was an understatement; it didn't come close to describing what she was feeling.

"Walk away from this? Are you serious!" she scoffed at him and shook her head. "Nah, it doesn't work like that, baby boy. You know entirely too much about my business. You know too many details when it comes to my day-to-day operation. I can't allow you to up and walk away like that. I can't do it, and it's not going to happen like that, Tiyatti. Put simply, your hands ain't dirty enough. You walking away is out of the question, boo. You understand?" Her voice was soft and sexy in sound, sinister in purpose.

He looked over at the two squirming bags on the floor and saw an opportunity, grasping for straws he desperately reached for it. Rooster and Jarvis had emptied their pistols at him and tried to gun him down in cold blood. Notwithstanding how Miko felt about him, Rooster and Jarvis were the reasons he was in this predicament in the first place.

"You said my hands ain't dirty enough for you to allow me to walk away from all of this, right? What do I have to do to get my hands dirty? What do I have to do for you to be satisfied enough to let me walk away from the game?" Hope wrapped around his every word, and optimism braided into his every emotion.

Miko stood with her arms folded across her chest looking like a boss.

"You wanna get your hands dirty, huh? You wanna do something that will right your wrongs and fix the problem? I don't know . . . do you really think you're up for some cold-blooded gangsta shit?" She posed the question with a devious smirk.

"Whatever I gotta do I'll do. I just want to walk up outta here with my life. I swear, whatever I gotta do, Miko, I'll do it." Tiyatti looked down at the squirming bags again and a foreboding sense filled him. Getting his hands dirty would have something to do with Rooster and Jarvis over there wiggling around on the ground.

"Have you ever killed anybody before, Tiyatti?" she quietly asked, turning the small pistol over in her hand.

"Nah, nah, I ain't never killed nobody before, but I will if I have to!" he answered and stilled himself for her response.

Miko held the .38 in her gloved hand and took a step back, then signaled to Cream with a nod. Cream reached behind him and picked up a black thirty-six ounce aluminum baseball bat with the word 'Slugger' stenciled in white letters across the fat part of it.

"Here you go," Cream said, holding the bat out to her, handle first. Miko grabbed the handle with her free hand. Tiyatti looked at the bat in Miko's hand and then back up to her face.

"Whatchu gon' do with that?" he asked, already knowing, but still unable to resist the urge to question her intentions.

Miko chuckled.

"I ain't going to do shit with it. You the one who finna do something with this!" She waved the bat back and forth menacingly.

"What! What do you want me to do with it?" Tiyatti asked, wide-eyed and shook.

"You said you wanna get out the game, right?" she posed the question.

Tiyatti remained silent.

Click!

Miko pulled the hammer on the .38 all the way back and aimed it at his face. "I asked you a question. Do you want to get the fuck out the game or not!"

He squeezed his eyes shut and turned away from the gun.

"Yeah." His voice was barely a whisper. "Yeah, I want to get out the game." He sobbed and mumbled, defeated.

"Well then, the way I see it is"—Miko used her other hand and pointed the fat end of the bat at the two sleeping bags thrashing about on the floor—"the only way you're leaving up outta here alive is if you take this bat right here and go beat on Rooster and Jarvis' bodies until they stop moving, permanently. Beat on them until they are dead, or I assure you, Tiyatti, you will be dying today too." She looked at him and smiled innocently, with a pleased look on her face, her voice no longer laced with malice. "When you're done killing those two ma'fuckas over there, then your hands will be dirty enough for my taste," Miko said and extended her arm with the handle of the bat pointed at Tiyatti. He slowly reached his hand out and begrudgingly took the bat from her outstretched arm. "Beat them until they stop moving, permanently." Miko reiterated her expectations and stepped back.

Tiyatti gazed over at the violently thrashing sleeping bags. He closed his eyes and conjured up mental pictures that angered him, images that provoked his fury and riled up his rage. He thought about Rooster standing in the doorway emptying his gun at him, the bullets narrowly missing his head and crashing into the wall behind him. He thought about how afraid for his life he had been at that moment. He thought about his mother dying at too young an age and leaving him and Devontay to fend for themselves in a world so cruel and unforgiving. He thought about Miko and the room full of heartless goons staring him down with pistols in hand, forcing him to commit the gruesome callous-hearted act. He thought about how Miko's sexual seduction caused him to betray Duchess and break the bond of their relationship. All of those thoughts combined pissed him off properly enough, infuriating him past the point of no return. All the pain and fear and hurt that festered in his heart for so long finally bubbled up and boiled over. With bat in hand he walked over to the sleeping bags flopping around like fish out of water and poured his pain, anger, and agony out on them. He took to the taller of the two first, Rooster.

Bap! Bap! Bap! Bap! Bap! Bap! Bap! Bap! Bap! Bap! Bap! Bap! Bap! Bap! Bap!

He heard bones cracking and smashing under the violent pressure of the crushing blows he delivered. His beating was nonstop, and the hard body in the sleeping bag soon turned soft under the continuous brutal assault. Vicious blow after vicious blow rained down until finally the body stopped moving all together. When he finished, Tiyatti breathed hard, beads of sweat coated his brow as he tried to restore his breathing pattern. Realizing he had just killed a man for the very first time, Tiyatti became enraged at the fact that Miko had again forced him to do something he could never undo. That thought pissed him off further. He looked down at the smaller of the two sleeping bags and turned his full attention and anger to it. Jarvis. He summoned all that pain and anger and agony again.

*Bap! Bap! Bap! Bap! Bap! Bap! Bap! Bap! Bap! Bap! Bap!
Bap! Bap! Bap! Bap!*

The bat came down without mercy over and over again. So preoccupied with the savage beating he was issuing, Tiyatti didn't notice Cream and Suspect moving away and walking up the steps, out of the chamber. He didn't see Anthony following close behind them. So busy was he with his brutal beat down, he paid no attention to Miko as she slowly walked backward up the six concrete stairs, where she kneeled and quietly set the .38 on the top step. He never heard the door close shut. He never heard the lock click.

*Bap! Bap! Bap! Bap! Bap! Bap! Bap! Bap! Bap! Bap! Bap!
Bap! Bap! Bap! Bap!*

Tiyatti continued beating on the lifeless body inside the sack until he was depleted of energy.

Clang!

He dropped the bat at his feet and warily staggered away from the unmoving bags, leaning his back against the wall and breathing like he had just run a race. He closed his eyes and tilted his head back until the back of it touched the cold concrete wall. Sweat profusely poured down his forehead. His heart pumped fast and raced with adrenaline. His breathing came in short, rapid huffs and puffs.

Miko and her goons watched the handheld tablet as the video of Tiyatti committing the second of two homicides played out on the screen.

"Having me put that hidden camera down there was genius, Miko!" Suspect exclaimed, jubilantly. "Are you sure it didn't turn on and start filming until after we were out of the room?"

"Stop asking dumb questions, Suspect. Of course I'm sure." She cuffed the tablet and tucked it under her arm.

"The show is over, y'all. Let's bounce and get the hell up

outta here." She informed the others of her decision and turned to leave.

"Why? What's the rush, Miko?" Suspect asked, wanting to see more.

"The rush is the dead bodies up in this bitch! I wanna be long gone before the police show up. Make sure you wipe this entire house down and remove any trace of our ever being here. Use bleach too. I don't even want a dog to know that we were here before." She turned to Cream and said, "We're not using this spot anymore either, so I need you to scout out another torture house that I can use too, a'ight?"

"A'ight." Cream was good with that.

While Cream and Suspect began wiping the torture house down with bleach and wet rags, Miko and Anthony walked out to the Maybach sitting curbside. When Anthony closed his door she calmly told him, "Wait fifteen minutes and use that disposable cell phone to call the police. Let them know that a heinous crime has occurred, and they need to get to the torture house as soon as possible."

CHAPTER 34

Tiyatti

What the fuck! Tiyatti thought, after opening his eyes and realizing he was alone in the windowless concrete room, alone with two dead bodies he had just killed. Perplexed, he looked around for signs of a trap. *It's a setup!* Panic and fear swelled in his heart. He looked up at the closed door and made his way over to the staircase. Slowly, he walked over to the steps leading to the only exit. *The gun!* Before his foot hit the first step, he saw the gun on the top step, his eyes narrowing with confused curiosity and suspicion. At the fifth step, he bent down and scooped up the snub nose pistol, figuring it might come in handy on his way out the torture house. He popped the cylinder and checked to see how many rounds he had at his disposal. *One fuckin' bullet!*

"What the fuck is really goin' on?" he asked aloud, reaching out and trying the doorknob. It twisted, but the door wouldn't open. He put his shoulder against the door and leaned his weight on it, pushing with force. Nothing. Again he pushed with more force, ramming his body into the door, but the door didn't budge. "Ay, open the door!" he yelled as loud as he could while beating his fist on the door. No answer. *What's that!* He thought he heard a noise on the other side, so he started beating on the door with all of his might again. "Open the ma'fuckin' door, man. It's locked! Let me the fuck outta here!" He listened with his ear to the door. Silence.

"Hello?" Nothing.

Tiyatti looked at the gun in his hand and briefly considered shooting the doorknob off. *But what if it doesn't come off, and I end up needing that one shot later?* He tried working out the different scenarios in his head, but nothing seemed to add up. He tried the door again with one final desperate push, putting all of his weight on the door. After realizing the door wasn't opening, a thought occurred to him. *The bat!* He turned and his eyes wildly looked around the torture chamber until he located the aluminum bat. He stuck the gun in his waistband and in one fluid motion, jumped down the steps and went to retrieve the bat. In seconds he was back up on the top step with renewed hope. He stepped to the side and began striking the doorknob with brute force. He swung the bat as hard as he had been swinging it when he was beating on Rooster and Jarvis' bodies.

Thwack! Thwack Thwack! Thwack!

Yes! The doorknob fell off after the fourth swing. Tiyatti was awash with hope. He put his weight on the door again to no avail. He tried it one more time and pushed again, and then he kicked the door with all he had. He swung the bat again trying to hit home runs with it. It was useless. The door wasn't opening. Tiyatti stood on the platform fuming at the situation he found himself in.

Thump! Clang!

He flung the bat across the room, and it solidly hit against the pile of rolled up rugs next to the wall. The bat loudly clanged on the ground and rolled away, finally coming to a stop several feet from the rolled up rugs. The rolled up carpet sitting on the top slowly unfurled, and a stiff corpse rolled out onto the concrete floor.

"What the fuck!" Tiyatti muttered when he saw the stiff body, its head full of reddish brown dreads splayed out on the floor. A single bullet hole pierced the center of the forehead, with a fresh trail of blood running down onto the face and into the right eye. *Rooster?* Tiyatti's neck twisted sideways in bewilderment as he walked down the steps toward the dead body. *Damn, he looks just like Rooster!* He neared the dead body. Instinctively, his eyes went to the other rolled up carpet. He unrolled it with his foot and watched in shock as Jarvis' dead body spilled out.

"Jarvis!" he exclaimed in a whisper, confused as ever. Incomprehension clouded Tiyatti's brain, making his brow furl with uncertainty. He picked the bat up, prepared to use the bat if necessary and walked toward the sleeping bags, not knowing what to expect. *If Rooster and Jarvis are over here, then who the . . .*

Tiyatti squatted next to the smaller of the badly beaten lifeless lumps and slowly began unzipping the sleeping bag with his left hand, clutching the bat in his right hand at its midway point. He pulled at the zipper and peeled the top back, then leaned in to sneak a peek. *Damn, whoever you are you're hella fucked up!* He looked down at the badly beaten face. It was then he fully realized how much damage he had actually done. *You did some serious work with that bat, Tiyatti!* He couldn't help complimenting his handiwork. He'd done major damage to the unlucky person in the sleeping bag. The cranium was crushed and caved in on one side, and the long hair was bloody and matted, sticking to the face. *Hold on, there's something familiar about you,* Tiyatti thought as he looked on. After taking a closer look, his stomach wretched violently with nausea. The sickest of feelings smothered him, and his breathing became difficult. It almost became impossible to breathe. He started choking with revulsion.

"No! Nooo! Nooooooo!"

He dropped the bat and fell to his knees, pulling the sleeping bag further back in an attempt to expose more of the badly beaten corpse. He reached down and moved the hair back, peeling the bloody clumps of hair off the skin until Duchess' brutally battered, crushed face was clear to him. Tiyatti rocked back onto the heels of his feet and threw his head back in anguish as tears began pouring from his eyes. His chest filled with the worst kind of hurt a man could ever know, and he let it out in a loud howling roar.

"Noooooooooooooooooooooo!"

The agonizing realization that he'd just beaten his pregnant girlfriend to death gradually sank into his understanding until it hit the bottom of who he was. The pain at the center of his heart was unbearable. *I killed her! I killed the love of my life! I killed my unborn child!* At that very moment he wanted to be as dead as Duchess was. He reached down and gingerly cupped her head in his hands, then leaned forward until his forehead touched her caved-in face. The thick, sticky blood covering his hands was still warm.

"Aww baby, baby, baby, I'm so sorry! Please forgive me, baby! Please, please, please forgive me, Duchess!"

Through a steady stream of tears and the most excruciating pain he ever experienced, the presence of the other sleeping bag caught his attention.

"No! No! No! No! No!" Tiyatti gently set Duchess's head down and crawled over to the other sleeping bag. "No! No! No! No! No, please don't be . . ." He used the back of his forearm to wipe snot from his nose and the tears from his eyes; his vision blurred from crying, and he blinked the tears away.

When he unzipped the sleeping bag and saw Devontay's crushed face and head, he violently vomited all over the concrete floor.

"Aww naw! Noooooooo!" He sobbed hard and cried out, "Noooooooooooooooooooo! I'm so sorry, baby brother!" Tiyatti painfully cried his sorrow against Devontay's bloody skin, as he lovingly caressed the side of his little brother's face that wasn't smashed in. No string of words could remotely come close to describing his pain. He wept harder and cried uncontrollably between the dead bodies, the three people he loved most in the world: his brother, his girlfriend, and his unborn child. *What the fuck did I just do? I killed my family! I don't deserve to be alive!*

With unflinching conviction he reached into his waistband and extracted the snub nosed pistol, gripping the gun tightly. He kissed his brother on the head, then kissed Duchess's smashed-in face. His unsteady, blood-soaked hand clutched the gun as he reached out and touched the deformed-looking baby bump in her stomach. "What the hell did I do? What the hell did I just do!" Tiyatti bent over, crying harder than he ever cried in his life. His spirit was broken. His soul had a hole in it that could never be filled. The tip of the .38's barrel touched his temple and his blood-slicked finger squeezed the trigger.

Click!

His chest heaved and he sobbed loudly, squeezing the trigger again.

Click!

Again his chest swelled with grief, and he wished death would hurry and come claim him too.

Click!

He wanted to die so bad it hurt. He put the gun to his head again, but then an image of Miko flashed behind his closed eyes, and hatred suddenly enveloped his entire being. *I'm going to kill your ass, you dirty bitch! If it's the last thing I do, I am going to kill you, Miko!* The idea of killing Miko altered his thought process, changing his mind, making him want to live so bad that it pained him.

CHAPTER 35

Miko

Miko sat in the back of the Maybach while the luxury whip floated through traffic, filled with a sense of great pleasure over her latest accomplishment. She thought about her father and how ruthless a kingpin he had been. She thought about the pain she felt her entire life over his death. The pain she felt every day growing up without her father in her world—the same pain that made her a savagely wicked queenpin—pain that fueled the ruthless blood running through her veins.

She looked down at the screen in her lap and watched Tiyatti wallow in his pain, and it made her feel better. His was the deepest form of pain possible, yet it provided her with the deepest form of pleasure possible. The slit between her legs moistened with delectation over the power she felt at that moment, knowing it was by her sinister cunning that she had inflicted the cruelest, ultimate form of tormenting sufferance. Sometimes killing wasn't enough; it was too petty a penalty for those who offended her in the worst way. In her mind, one must be made to endure the most awful type of punishment for their violations and transgressions, for their disrespect. One must be forced to live with their most painful circumstance, the most agonizing of conditions with no way of ever escaping it.

Tiyatti crossed the line infringing upon her core fundamental belief: *"Never let a man check you, never let a man disrespect you, and don't you ever let a man threaten to wreck you!"* For his disrespect he paid the ultimate price. She looked down at the screen while the Maybach slithered like a snake through midday traffic. A victorious smile spread across her face when the police stormed the torture house. Tiyatti was locked in a room with four dead bodies. If he didn't kill himself, he would definitely be spending the rest of his life in prison living with the unending agony of what he'd done, what she'd duped him into doing. *You shoulda upgraded when you had the opportunity, ma'fucka,* Miko thought coldly, laughing softly in the back of the luxury whip before tossing the tablet down onto the seat next to her.

"Anthony?" she called out to her driver.

"Yeah?" he responded with dutiful patience in his voice.

"Book a flight to Paris tonight. Suddenly I'm in the mood to do a little shopping and sightseeing," she said, leaning back into the supple leather and closing her eyes. As the luxury whip sailed through the streets, Miko felt as if she were floating on cloud nine.

CHAPTER 36

Miko

After returning from her two-week long stay in Paris, for the next two months Miko Dunbar took the necessary corrective measures to thoroughly clean house in a sinister, brutal manner. Any worker not fitting into her future plans either came up missing, or was murdered in cold blood. If they had a suspect background, or so much as a cloud of suspicion hovering about them, she had them eliminated. The streets were playing for keeps, and she didn't plan on losing. When the dust settled and the smoke finally cleared, Miko's drug empire was drastically reduced in size as far as the number of workers she employed was concerned, but the money flow never stopped, and the profits grew to levels never before enjoyed by the queenpin.

The key to her success was the new direction in which she chose to go after having a long sit down with the shrewd and clever Javier. Acting on the Columbian drug boss's suggestion, Miko put an end to her workers selling petty product and took her low level workers off the streets and out of the crack houses, which in turn greatly reduced her risk of exposure to law enforcement agencies. It also presented a much smaller target for her enemies to aim at. Now her crew exclusively sold whole bricks to gangstas who had deep pockets and proven track records.

Javier's astute thinking and prudent advice was what attracted Miko to the ruthless Colombian drug boss in the first place, that, and his dark olive complexioned skin and strikingly good looks. Javier Mesas was a cartel boss who sold thousands of kilos a month, trafficking tons of cocaine through Mexico and up and down the West Coast, while also flooding cities in the states of Arizona, Texas, Colorado, New Mexico, Washington, Oregon, Nevada, and Montana. The forty-year-old Colombian drug boss ascended to the highest of heights in the brutal game of drug trafficking by instituting savage and ruthless methods to kill off and snuff out his competition. Like Miko, Javier was the son of a kingpin, and his father had been gunned down in the game, too. So, being an ambitious-driven drug boss was in his DNA. Javier's unsympathetic callous get-down was rubbing off on Miko. His uncle did business with her father Kiko Dunbar back in the day, and it was because of that relationship that she was able to insert herself into the game and establish a major connection with Javier. They met every other month since she began copping large quantities of cocaine from him nearly two years ago. As a result of their mutual attraction, they fast became lovers. Javier had a weak spot for exquisite, beautiful women with good pussy. Normally, they'd meet up and sleep together the night a shipment landed and the transaction was completed. So it was a surprise when she got a phone call from him several days after their last shipment a week ago.

"What's going on, Javier?" Miko asked, curious to know why he was calling so unexpectedly.

"Nothing much, Miko. How's business up there?" he responded.

"It's good, thanks for asking, but I know you didn't call simply to inquire about the state of my business affairs, Javier." She wasn't overly concerned, but she wanted to know what was really going on, nevertheless.

"Very perceptive. You are right, Miko, my dear. I actually called to extend an invitation for you to come down to Colombia and spend a weekend with me. I have a very uh, how do you say, important gift for you, a gift that I am sure you will come to greatly appreciate in the months and years to come."

Miko wasn't quite prepared for his invite, but covered her surprise up well. "An important gift, huh? Spend the weekend with you?"

"Yes, a gift I believe you will come to greatly appreciate." His tone was serious.

"And you can't bring this important gift that you speak of to the States?"

"Yes, I could, but this is the type of gift that first has to meet with your approval before it goes to the States. Otherwise, it may end up being a complete waste. Trust me on this, Miko. I haven't steered you wrong yet, have I?" Thoughts of their most recent hookup, and his thick Colombian accent made her pussy wet. Her interest was piqued.

Miko thought about it for a second before replying, "Okay, when, where, and how?"

"I'll send a car to pick you up, and my private jet will fly you down Friday. I'll have my people pick you up at your home, if that's okay with you?" Javier was a boss for real; everything he did was top flight or first class.

* * * * * *

Javier's private jet touched down on U.S. soil and an entourage of hardhearted Colombian killers stepped off the Hawker 900XP midsize business jet. An hour later, a small caravan of luxury vehicles pulled up and came to a stop in the circular driveway in front of Miko's grand estate. Several heavily armed Colombian goons spilled out and dutifully posted up at the bottom of the steps in front of the coliseum-styled pillars next to the hunching lions squatting at the base.

Ten minutes later, Miko came sashaying out in a pair of Chanel skinny jeans that left nothing to the imagination and a matching short-sleeved blazer with a pair of checkerboard Chanel pumps on her feet. Anthony was at her side, always within arm's reach, prepared to react with deadly force at the slightest act of aggression.

An hour and a half after the Colombians showed up at Miko's mansion, she was sitting in one of the plush leather seats of the Hawker 900 XP with a glass of Chardonnay in her hand, tilted toward her full, sensuous lips. She let the expensive wine wet and tantalize her palette, taking pleasure in another sip of the rich, exquisite liquid as the multi-million dollar jet cut through the clouds heading south in the direction of Colombia.

That evening, Javier met Miko at the entrance of his villa dressed in a black Giorgio Armani silk suit specially tailored to hang from his frame in an elegant manner. After helping her to her feet, he greeted her in the most chivalrous fashion, kissing the back of her hand, a kingpin courting a queenpin.

It was Miko's first time visiting Colombia, the cocaine capital of the world. She raised her eyebrows with appreciation on more than one occasion as her eyes took in the opulent surroundings of the extravagantly designed villa. She admired the forty-foot-high palm trees lining the red brick pathway leading up to the giant double doors. She marveled at the luxurious plush rolling green lawns that were perfectly manicured and greener than a golf course. With admiration she took note of Javier's strong security detail. The small army of killers patrolled the grounds with military-style assault rifles cradled in their arms or slung across their shoulders. They walked with vicious-looking dogs by their sides, appearing every bit as intimidating as the assault rifles.

This is how a boss bitch like me is supposed to be living! she thought enviously, smiling approvingly at the man-made lake that covered at least four acres.

After exchanging pleasantries and a personal tour of his Colombian kingdom, Javier stopped in front of one of the many rooms on the second floor of the rich Italian marbled hallway.

"You know, Miko, you and I have made a lot of money together, and lot of beautiful music together, if you know what I mean." He smiled and nudged her arm after winking at her.

"True, it has been a very profitable, as well as a very pleasurable partnership that you and I have. You've been good to me in a business sense, and even better in the bedroom." Her smile was disarming, and the fire in her eyes burned bright with lust as thoughts of the well-hung drug boss ramming his long, thick love muscle in and out of her from the back, wet her pussy and moistened her panties.

"That is why I have such a vested interest in you, Miko," he told her and squeezed her soft body against his well-defined rock hard frame.

"The feelings are mutual, Javier." Her pussy beat like it had a heart in it.

"I asked you here because my sources in San Diego have informed me that the police are preparing to serve an arrest warrant on you regarding a badly mutilated individual they seem to believe you had something to do with." He saw the teeter-totter of emotions in her eyes. The disappointment at him sticking his nose in her business versus her appreciation for him being up front about it and presumably offering his assistance concerning it. He was a true kingpin, one whom she'd both admired and learned from. Miko wasn't a fool, she wasn't so stubborn and set in her ways that she couldn't be open to other alternatives that were going to help her get to the next level in the game.

"I'm listening," she said, wanting to say more, but her instincts telling her to say less and listen to whatever options he presented. Miko listened with the attentiveness of a prisoner during sentencing as Javier laid his proposition out. When the Colombian kingpin finished speaking, Miko wore a devious smile on her beautiful face while wicked thoughts danced around in her head. *If I take Javier up on his offer, then it will definitely make me the coldest bitch to ever do this shit. It will definitely put me on a level no other bitch has ever been on!*

CHAPTER 37

Wah

I wasn't in the best shape of my life, but after vigorously working out every day for the past eight weeks, I was in damn good shape. All things considered. My physical frame was a ripped 190 pounds, and I was feeling hella strong again. I felt strong and I looked strong. My features were back up to par, too; waves glistening and pronounced, giving my close cropped cut that ripple effect. My edge up was precise, and my half-inch deep dimples were still a main attraction on my handsome mug. My heavily tattooed brown frame looked like a thug-painted masterpiece. The day had finally come for my release from the hospital, and I was as ready as I'd ever been to step into the streets and face the unknown.

Khassandra picked me up in a cotton candy blue Lexus IS 250 with tan Louis Vuitton leather interior. *Damn, she fine as hell!* I thought when she slid up next to the curb.

"Thanks for scoopin' me up, Khassandra. Good lookin' out," I told her and settled into the plush leather passenger seat. Her coming to pick me up from the hospital was more her idea than mine. She made it known from day one that she was crushin' on me hella hard. I let it be known that I still had feelings invested with Tocarra, and until it was clear to me that Tocarra and I were no more, I couldn't allow my emotions to get caught up with her or anybody else. But at the same time, I'd been in a coma for nearly two years, so smashing her cookies was gonna happen, and sooner rather than later!

"Where would you like to go?" she asked, rocking a pair of oversized Chanel shades. A bronze and black maxi dress complimented her shapely body. The nails on her fingers and toes were elaborately decorated and meshed well with her ensemble. The girl had style. I gave her directions to my old crib, and we chopped it up as she dipped in and out of traffic until we parked in front of the place where I took those six shots from Miko's .380.

As soon as I stepped out the Lexus, I knew somebody had moved into the spot where I used to rest my head. *I know that punk bitch got my money! She probably got my briefcase full of bling and the diamonds too! As soon as I get my hand right, I need to go find that 'ho!* I left behind some very costly belongings, as well as some important personal paperwork and other things that had a lot of sentimental value. I needed to know where my shit was! Suddenly I saw a flurry of activity out of my peripheral and instinctively my hand went to my waistband. *Shit!* I thought when I realized I wasn't strapped. I breathed a sigh of relief when I recognized my old neighbor Irene coming out her crib.

"Wahdatah, is that you? Oh my goodness! It is you, Wah! Aaggghhhh!" she screamed her joy out loud. "It's so good to see you, boy! It's so awful what happened to you. I didn't think you were going to make it when the ambulance took you away. Wow, it's so good to see you again! You really look amazing, Wah!" She hurriedly made her way over to me. Irene had been my neighbor for years, a pretty looking cougar in her mid-forties, with a Vivica A. Fox vibe. She used to stay on me, trying to test the sexual waters.

Irene was good people, and on more than one occasion, she had watched my pad when I went out of town to handle business. She may have been in her mid-forties, but her face indicated mid-thirties, and every curve on her body screamed twenty-five! I saw Khassandra cut her eyes at Irene before placing her hand on her hip with attitude.

"What's up, Irene? Yeah, it didn't look good for your boy at first, but I was blessed and came up out of it all right. What's good wit' you though? How you been?" I asked after hugging her.

"I've been good, Wah, but right now I'm just happy as hell to see you alive and well. Oh my goodness! I can't believe that you are standing here right now!" she said, ignoring Khassandra completely.

"Well, it definitely feels good to be alive and well, that's for damn sure," I told her and turned to Khassandra. "This is my friend, Khassandra. Khassandra, this is my neighbor and good friend, Irene." They exchanged cordial hellos that made it clear they wouldn't become friends anytime soon. I broke the uncomfortable silence with a question. "Ay, Irene, who's living up in my crib? And what happened to all of my stuff?"

"A young black couple moved in shortly after your, um . . . the incident. But after I read in the paper that you were in a coma, I had all of your belongings put in a storage facility. It was the least I could do. Hold on, I'll be right back." Her response surprised me, in a good way. She turned and bolted into her house, then returned minutes later with a key and a slip of paper in one hand, and an envelope in the other. "Here." She held her hand out with a smile. I was blown away by her revelation. The fact that she went out of her way to put my stuff in storage was a good look. It meant a lot to me.

"What's this?" I asked as I took what she offered.

"This is the storage facility's address and location. Here's the key to it. Oh, and I put a few dollars in the envelope, so you can pay for a rental truck to help move all of your stuff, and you do have a lot of stuff to move. And oh, here go your car key too." She laughed when she said it, and pulled the key to my Dodge Charger out her bra.

My heart swelled with momentary elation. I wasn't mentally ready to go through all my personal shit right then, so I put off going to the storage facility. But once I got my shit out of storage and got my affairs in order, I would be able to rest easy and plot my next move. I looked at the key and rifled through the envelope full of bills. I stuffed the envelope in my back pocket and looked down at the car key in my hand. My thoughts immediately went back to the day I got shot. *I'm coming for your ass, Miko! Believe that! I'm coming for your ass, bitch!*

CHAPTER 38

Baby Shug

For the past sixty days I woke up every day knowing I was about to be released from prison. It was just a matter of time before my exoneration became official. Khadida had done well by me and hired a top notch legal team who went hard in the paint for me. The street savvy investigators somehow managed to discover, not one, but two well-concealed surveillance cameras capturing the actual murders of Camron and Drape being committed by a lone female shooter, a light-skinned bitch they identified as some chick named Jracia Coleman.

I knew I was about to get out of prison, and I was fully prepared for the occasion, but like I heard so many of the older convicts doing life in prison say: "It doesn't matter if you have a day, a decade, or a life sentence to serve, getting out of prison wasn't guaranteed until your feet touched down on free concrete." So until I bounced up outta here, I was still in the mix and still a major part of the penitentiary bizness.

Other than Khory and a handful of my most trusted comrades, nobody on the yard knew about my upcoming release. I wanted it that way because I had some unfinished business with a busta who needed to be handled pronto. After doing a background check on Droop Loc and verifying that his money was good and his get-down was reputable, I made it my priority to establish a business relationship with him. As a result, my bank account had an extra zero added to it. He confided to me that he had an issue with another Crip on the yard he claims told on him. Droop Loc showed me the paperwork to prove it, and then asked if I could be of assistance in rectifying the situation. I gladly accepted, for a small fee, of course. We agreed on five racks, although I would've done the deed for free. Anyway, like I was saying, I had some unfinished business to tend to, which brought me to Roc.

Roc was a Crip from West LA that I'd been serving trees to for a minute now. His money was hella good, and it was always on time.

"What's crackin', cuz?" I dapped him hard on top of his fist and embraced him with love.

"Ain't nothin'. Whaddup wit' you, cuz?" he responded likewise, dapping me back.

"You still tryin' to make that happen, homie?" I skipped over the preliminaries and cut straight to the chase, speaking in code.

"All da time, cuz. I stay tryin' to make it happen, you feel me?" he said, and we slapped hands and laughed.

We went back and forth with each other for a few minutes talking in code while trying to negotiate a deal. Roc wanted a half pound of kush for $2,500. My ounces went for $400 a pop on the yard, but since he was purchasing such a large quantity, I was letting them go at a lower rate. We continued to haggle until finally settling on $2,800 for eight zips.

"You gon' let me bump the sounds before I buy the music so I can see how it go?" he asked. That was code for: could he get a fifty dollar balloon of kush up front to personally test out before wiring the money to me?

"No doubt, Roc. You got that comin', cuz," I told him, slapping his right hand with mine. We literally sealed the deal with that handshake. I slickly handed the sample balloon off to him when our hands slapped together. He pulled his hand away with the fifty dollar balloon in it and cuffed it somewhere near his front pocket. As soon as he did it, I saw a CO moving toward us from about twenty yards away, and my eyes widened with nervousness. *Oh shit, here come the po-po!* The CO was fast approaching, slipping on a pair of black gloves as he neared us. I looked Roc in his eyes and talked through clenched teeth. My face read panic, but I tried to sound calm when I spoke.

"One time is comin', cuz. The po-po headin' our way, and he glovin' up like he about to shake us down! Swallow that shit, Roc!" Roc nonchalantly raised his hand to his face and inconspicuously stuffed the balloon in his mouth. When he heard the sound of jingling keys from the CO's belt, he swallowed the balloon knowing he could shit it out later and retrieve it from the toilet. He wasn't trying to catch a case, or get wrapped up and dragged to the hole on a fluke.

"You two, get against the wall. Now!" the CO barked the order out with authority.

I knew the drill, so I turned and placed the palms of my hands flat on the wall and stood with my legs shoulder length apart. Roc did the same, only he felt the need to be vocal throughout the process and verbalize how he felt about the situation. He made clear his disdain for what he felt was a case of convict harassment—*gangsta profilin'* is what he called it.

"What the fuck is you fuckin' wit' us for, man? All these white boys and Mexicans on the yard, and your Uncle Tom ass pick out two blacks to shake down. This is gangsta profilin'! You ain't gon' find nothin' on us, man. You pussy for real, bruh. Ol' Uncle Tom ass ma'fucka."

The CO ignored Roc's insults and continued to carry out his duties. He performed a clothed body pat-down search on Roc and told him to bounce. Roc got off the wall and started walking in the opposite direction. The CO searched me the same as he did Roc, only with me, he muttered a message while squeezing my pockets and running his hands over my arms and legs, checking for contraband.

"I confirmed all the Greendot numbers and handed the package off to your cellie," he whispered so only I could hear. He didn't have to say much; it wasn't necessary. I understood clearly.

"A'ight then, CO," I responded as I came off the wall after the search, same as I always did after my pipeline let me know the large sack of contraband had touched down.

An hour later, Roc was walking laps around the prison yard when he fell to his knees and rolled over onto his back, where he started shaking from a seizure. His mouth foamed with a thick, frothy white lather. The balloon he thought to be full of kush weed was actually filled with hella potent heroin. I poked half a dozen holes in it before leaving my cell. The acid in his digestive track quickly ate away at the tampered with rubber material, and the heroin poisoned his bloodstream immediately. The yard went down on a Code-One medical, and a team of medical staff responded with promptitude, but it was too late. Roc eventually expired due to complications related to an overdose.

With only eight months left on his seven year sentence, Roc didn't make his date with freedom. Like the old heads said: "It doesn't matter if you have a day, a decade, or a life sentence to serve, getting out of prison wasn't guaranteed until your feet touched down on free concrete." Roc's bitch ass wouldn't be seeing freedom in this lifetime.

When they resumed program and let the yard back up, I passed Droop Loc on the track while mobbin' with my wolf pack. We exchanged winks and head nods. That's how shit went down on the Level-IV prison yard.

Once they re-called the yard, I walked toward the building

with a smile on my face, knowing it was just a matter of time before I'd be getting at another ma'fucka who needed killing. *Miko, your days on this earth are numbered, bitch! It won't be long before karma comes a callin' your name, 'ho!*

CHAPTER 39

Miko

A week later . . .

Miko paced back and forth in front of the mass gathering of gangstas with a satisfied smirk on her flawless face. Looking amazing in a cherry-red Elie Tahari denim ensemble that clung to her every curve, and a pair of black Louboutin pumps that flashed red with every step she took, the queenpin addressed the room full of street hardened thugs who had been sitting in silence waiting for their boss to talk about the latest rumors filtering out into the streets. There had been much rumblings in the hood; the streets were talking. Whispers about a high-priced contract being put on the heads of her enemies was one of the most talked about topics in the town. She called for the meeting of mobsters with hopes of financially motivating the criminal-minded hoods who were hungry in the game and willing to do just about any and every thing for fortune and fame, or to make their name ring. The room full of goons waited with bated breath for the order to be declared, for the contract to become official. All eyes were on Miko, as the gorgeous queenpin prepared to address them.

"I appreciate all of you making an appearance today. The fact that you're here today reaffirms what I already know, that I have the right type of young, hungry soldiers on my team. Gangstas who are willing to kill for money and who are willing to kill for me. I'm not going to sit here and waste your time with small talk and phony promises." Miko was a strong speaker when the occasion called for her to be. Her flawless beauty and the uncut thuggish way in which she came at the thugs worked to her advantage; it made the young, pussy-thirsty thugs want to rally around her. The fact that she paid her workers good money was icing on the cake. She continued talking and letting her words provoke their greed and instigate their avidity. Her eyes scanned the sea of mean mugs, making eye contact with as many of her workers as possible; Dough Hound, Wainy-Bo, Pokey, Wu Rock, Sham, Black Boy, Sam Savage, Big Boonie, and Sleepy, to name a few. They were the top hitters in her organization, who she believed could get the job done. She looked at them intently and challenged every one of them with her unfeeling eyes, and her curvaceous silhouette enticing their thirst.

"Some of you may have heard the rumors, some of you, maybe not. So, for the record let me make it clear what the deal is." She turned and walked to the chair behind her and grabbed the black gym bag sitting on it, then she turned back and faced the crowd of killas before turning the bag upside down, letting the stacks of big faces fall heavily to the floor around her Louboutin pumps. A rush of murmuring *ooh's* and *ahh's* immediately filled the room. A few gangstas tried to maintain their cool and keep their composure, acting as if the sight of a million dollars cash didn't faze them in the least bit. Miko recognized it for what it was and smiled knowingly before continuing. "Yeah, that's right, one million ma'fuckin' dollars!" she said coolly, taking pleasure in the raised eyebrows throughout the room. "I am offering a million dollars cash money for the death, or capture, of Wahdatah "Wah" Mitchell and Marcellus "Baby Shug" Braxton. Dead or alive, either will get you half a million apiece, a million for the both of them." She eyed each man in the room closely before speaking again. "My sources tell me that Wah was just released from the hospital, and Baby Shug is due to be released from prison any day now. If you need to know more, I suggest you pull out a pen and paper, or grab your phone or whatever the fuck else you need to take notes." Miko stepped over the pile of money stacks and continued telling the room full of thugs everything there was to know about Wahdatah and Shug. When she finished talking, the questions came at once. Miko decided to answer them all at once.

"I don't have time to sit here and answer all these questions that y'all are hitting me with. It's simple though: you kill Wah and Shug and I give you a million dollars for your troubles! That's it, that's all, period point blank, plain and simple, end of discussion." Miko turned and walked out the room, leaving the room full of young thugs clamoring with excited talk about which of them was going to kill the brothers, and how they were going to do it.

Anthony stood next to Cream and Suspect and the pile of money, holding his hand-canon tight while they stuffed the stacks back into the gym bag. In a matter of minutes, the room full of greedy gangstas dispersed and went about preparing to hunt for Wahdatah and Baby Shug—a million dollars cash money, their murderous motivation.

CHAPTER 40

Wah

Shug was supposed to be getting out tomorrow, and killing Miko was at the top of our list of priorities. Considering everything we had been through and the savage journey we were about to embark upon, I wanted my brother by my side. I needed his extra set of eyes watching my back when we did our dirty. He was the only person I could trust. Besides, he had as much right and reason as I did to be hands-on with killing Miko. I took a couple of minutes to clear my subconscious fog before throwing the sheets off and sitting up in bed. A sneak peek at the time read 7:23 a.m.

When I looked to my left, I smiled at the vision of loveliness lying next to me. Khassandra was half naked on her stomach in a pink Victoria's Secret bra and panty set with the sheer black lace trim on the sides. *That fat, round, meaty ass is eatin' those panties up! I better get some of that pussy now. Come tomorrow, I'ma be too busy to be focused on fucking.* I grabbed my half hard dick. After making it clear with her on how things stood between Tocarra and me, there wasn't any gray area concerning my feelings, or where my loyalties lie. I didn't know what was going on with Tocarra, but I knew my heart was still hers. At the end of the day though, I'm still a man. A man who was in a coma for damn near two years with no pussy. *The pussy was hella good last night, and I'm confident it's every bit as bomb this morning. I need that; it's callin' my name!* I reached over, took her hand, and put it on my erection. It was long and hard in her hand.

"Ummm." She squeezed it, purring lustfully.

We rolled toward each other at the same time and met face-

255

to- face in the middle of the bed. My fingers twisted on the bra clasp and her large, plump breasts poured out when the brassiere came undone. The warm, soft, titty flesh pressing against my skin only added to my excitement. Our lips hesitated as we craned our necks and repositioned ourselves. I tenderly sucked on her bottom lip, and then she sucked on mine. Our tongues tussled as the passion in each of us grew hotter. Wet sounds followed each delicious kiss. I slid my hand down into her panties and stuck my middle finger between her shaved slit, now wet and slick with her desire. *Damn, she hella wet!* I quickly slipped another finger in. My middle and index finger poked and probed her teasingly as our kissing intensified. I flicked the tip of my thumb across her swollen clit while she bit my lip and thrust her hips toward me. She moaned in my mouth and squeezed my dick harder. She squeezed and pulled on it with a sense of urgency, like she was anxiously trying to extract something from it and only had a few seconds to do so. We separated long enough for her to frantically climb out of her panties.

Seconds later she was sitting on top of me leaning forward, offering her tits to my tongue. My tongue flickered out and flitted across her erect nipple, and then I felt her reach back and grip my dick at the thick base. Her wet heat slid down my rock hard length, and slowly she threw the pussy on me with the most incredible rhythm in her hips. *Damn her pussy feels good!* I reached up and cuffed her titties at the crease underneath, pushing the soft, fleshy globes together so I could suck both nipples and lick my tongue across them simultaneously. She rode my dick hella slow, grunting while grinding her hips hard as she went up and down. She popped her tight pussy on me in a way that made me wanna push deeper and poke a hole in her heart from the bottom. Think of something else, Wah! Think of something else! I told myself, trying my damndest not to nut. After a couple of minutes, I let one of her titties go and concentrated on sucking the one still in my possession. She rode my dick with more aggression, like she was the one who was fucking me. I took my free hand and roughly rubbed the surface of my fingertips over her clit, adding to the pleasure. My fingers rubbed furiously as she humped harder and threw the pussy faster and faster.

"Agh! Agh! Agh! Agh!" Khassandra was going all out on it. My dick was harder and longer than I ever remembered it being. She snatched her titty from my mouth and put both hands on my chest then bounced up and down on my beef grunting and moaning louder, her tits swinging every which way. She rode the dick like a jockey coming down the stretch! Her head jerked up and she threw the pussy at me hard, yelling with pleasure as her body shook. Her first orgasm flooded her pussy and thoroughly drenched my dick. Her humping slowed as her frame shook and jerked with satisfaction. She continued to milk my manhood while I toyed with her pearl tongue, intensifying that good feeling in her guts. *This bitch got the creamiest pussy ever!* Goose bumps dotted her skin, and before she knew what hit her I wrapped my arm around her waist and put her on her back in one motion. Through it all, my hard dick never came out of her soaking wet pussy. With long, hard, fast, deep strokes I pounded her pussy out as my heavy nuts smacked against her sticky ass cheeks each time I hit the bottom.

"Ungh! Ungh! Ungh! Ungh!" I was grunting now while she lay back and absorbed the dick down, purring like a cat. For fifteen minutes I plowed into her pussy and tried to climb into her guts, fucking her as hard as I possibly could. *I'ma dent her ma'fuckin' uterus!* I vowed as I banged away.

"Oooh! Oooh! Oooh! Oooh yes! Yes! Yes! Motherfucker, yes! Fuck me harder, baby! Fuck my pussy harder, Wah!" Her legs were wide open and cocked all the way back with her knees pressing against her shoulders, she was holding onto her ankles allowing me an all-access pass into that ass.

We both looked down and watched with nasty pleasure as my long, hard dick pulled out, glistening with her juices before slamming back in to the hilt, nuts slapping against the crack of her ass. *Left right center! Right left center! Center center right! Center center left! Left right center!* I ran the rhythmic cadence in my head as I mercilessly beat her pussy up. I was banging her hard from every direction; my deep stroke was relentless. She bared her teeth like fangs as her eyes rolled back into her head and started screaming and cumming at the same time. I felt a surge of cum shoot up from my nuts, through the length of my dick, and into the depths of her tight, gushy wet pussy. I kept beatin' the pussy up until I was on empty and my dick went limp. Good, hard animalistic sex! It was exactly what I needed to start my day off right. We lay tangled up in each other's limbs catching our breath, basking in the beauty of good wake-up sex.

Later that day, I went to the storage facility and almost cried when I realized the money and the bling were gone. I grabbed a few essentials and shook the storage facility, mad as fuck, wanting to kill some shit up. I had several outfits, a knot of dough I'd tucked away, and a pair of 40 Glock pistols I kept in the stash box.

While driving back to the hotel, I made a mental note to thank Irene for having the foresight to put my car up after I got shot. The triple black Mopar Charger had been sitting under a carport near her apartment with a tarp covering it for nearly two years. As soon as my pockets got spoiled, I was gonna show Irene some love. But first I had to start laying my trap for Miko's punk ass.

CHAPTER 41

Wah

The next day . . .

Khassandra stood on her tip toes and kissed me, then hugged me when she saw me tuck the 40 Glock in my waistband. We'd eaten breakfast and chopped it up for a while before I got ready to bounce to go pick up Shug.

"Be careful, Wah," Khassandra told me, before turning to go take a shower.

While riding the elevator down, I thought about Tocarra and wondered what happened to her. The feelings I had for her were still strong. I was still in love with her, despite the fact that I had been in a coma all that time.

Once I plopped down in the Charger, I leaned back and fired up the piece of blunt in the ashtray. *What the fuck I wanna listen to?* I thumbed through the selection of music and settled on Meek Mills' "Dreams and Nightmares." I whipped the bully car in and out of traffic until I was in the courthouse parking lot. My watch read 9:20 a.m., still early, but it was better than being late. I let the thug music ruffle them white folk's feathers for a minute, before I lowered the music and shut the Charger down. Before exiting the ride, I put the 40 Glock back in my stash box, knowing I was gonna be around a gang of law enforcement while at the courthouse.

Fifteen minutes passed, and I was leaning against the Charger when Shug pushed the glass doors open and stepped into the warm California sunshine a free man. My face lit up when I smiled. He blocked the glare of the sun from his eyes and looked around searching for me. When he saw me, his smile grew bigger than mine. We walked toward one another and embraced in a bear hug; it was a poignant moment for us both. The emotions flowing between us were hella strong and powerful. Tears filled my eyes. I didn't want to say shit, because I knew my voice would crack with emotion.

"Man, I missed the fuck out yo' ass, bruh!" His voice was full of sentimental feelings.

Fuck it, this all love! I let the floodgates open up and a couple tears fell down my face as my emotions poured out.

"I missed the fuck out of you too, homie!" Our embrace lasted a full minute before we finally broke the hug up.

"Man, I thought I lost you, Wah!" He put his arm around my neck and pulled me close, hugging me again.

"Nah, bruh. It's gon' take more than six shots to take me out the game!"

We chopped it up for a couple minutes, then squared off and started slap-boxing in the parking lot before we burst out laughing and got in the car, settling into the plush, black leather seats.

"I see you still got the Charger, huh!"

"Absolutely, bruh. My neighbor Irene put it up for me and kept an eye on it while I was gone."

"That's what's up." He checked his reflection in the mirror.

I poked and pushed a few buttons until the door to the stash box slid open. "Stick your hand under the dash and pull both those thangs out, bruh," I told him as I twisted the ignition. The Charger came to life and roared loud with power. Meek Mill was spitting about "Tony Story" when I merged into traffic.

He turned the twin 40 Glocks over in his hand as we blended in with the rest of the world. "That's what I'm talkin' 'bout! Both these ma'fuckas is sweet, Wah. I see you ain't waste time gettin' strapped, huh?"

"Fuck nah! You know what it is. They playin' for keeps out here, bruh, and you know what they say: It's better to get caught with it than get caught without it. I came out the coma ready to clack on somethin'!"

Bomp! Bomp! Ba-Ba Bomp! Bomp! Bomp!

I leaned on the horn a couple times when I recognized one of my homies from way back doing his thug thang downtown pushing a money green Monte Carlo on gold 24s with the brains blew out. He acknowledged me with a head nod and chucked the deuce up and did it moving.

"So where you posted up at, Wah?" Shug asked, inspecting the 40 Glock clip.

"Ha-ha, you real funny, Shug. I see you still got jokes, huh?" I looked over at him after checking the rearview.

He looked at me with innocent surprise on his face. "Whatchu talkin' 'bout, man? I just asked a simple question: where you layin' your head at?"

"Man, miss me with that shit. You know where the fuck I been restin' my head at. I know damn well Khadida told you I been fuckin' her sister since I got out the hospital."

"What? You smashin' that already, Wah? Damn, I'm impressed, bruh." He had a guilty smile on his face.

"Fuck you, Shug."

He playfully mushed the side of my head and broke out laughing hard, and then he got serious and asked, "You like her, bruh?"

"Yeah, she cool. But keepin' it all the way one hundred witchu, homie, I'm still feelin' Tocarra." He got quiet when I said that, and something didn't feel right to me about his silence.

The mood in the Charger went from light to heavy just like that. I snuck a peek in the rearview, waiting for his response and saw a black Nissan Altima three car lengths behind us. It had a couple of shady looking cats riding in it, looking like they were with the bizness. I made a left turn, and then a right turn to confirm my suspicions.

"Get on yo' gangsta, bruh. I think we got company behind us," I told him and took one of the Glocks from him.

Shug got hyped while checking the 40 Glock again. He rolled the window on his side down, looked over at me and said, "Remember the drive-thru when we clacked on ol' boy in the Camry?"

"Yup," I told him, narrowing my eyes, focusing on my surroundings.

"Let's do that shit again, bruh. Bend the corner over there by that McDonald's and head up into the drive-thru. As soon as we get behind the wall, I'ma jump out and hide behind that dumpster. When they drive past me, I'ma air they bitch asses out and run to that parking lot across the street over there by the high school next to the college. You come scoop me after you get back in traffic."

It's gotta be that bitch Miko and her people! I surmised, before I ran the scenario through my thought process. "Okay, but we only got one shot at it, bruh. It can't be any mistakes, Shug. It ain't no tellin' what type of artillery they rockin' in that Altima."

"Let's not make none then, bruh," he said and got ready.

I banked a right and rolled up into the McDonald's drive-thru. Shug jumped out the Charger already bent over and creeping low toward the dumpster by the wall. The Altima slowed down and rolled into the drive-thru behind me. My eyes locked on the rearview, and I saw the eyes of the driver mean muggin' the back of my whip. Then it got ugly. Gunfire discharged and ripped the day wide open with thunderous explosions.

CHAPTER 42

Cream & Suspect

Cream walked out the front door followed closely by Suspect as they bounded down the steps and made their way over to the dark blue Chevy Tahoe. They passed an array of expensive luxury whips situated side-by-side along the driveway of the mini-mansion they shared. He adjusted the Desert Eagle in his waistband and arranged the large black leather Hugo Boss coat, so it adequately covered the chrome canon in his dip. He stuck his hand deep into the pocket of his black True Religion jeans and fished out his car keys.

"Call Miko and let her know we about to be in motion, bruh," he said over his shoulder to Suspect and hit the chirp on the Tahoe, unlocking the front doors.

"A'ight," Suspect told him, thumbing his cell phone before putting it up to his ear.

Cream put the Tahoe in traffic while Suspect went back and forth with Miko. After hanging up with her, Suspect checked the text message he received.

"Oh shit!" he exclaimed, smacking the back of his hand against Cream's arm. His excitement arrested Cream's attention.

"What's up?"

"I just got a text from Sham, and he said him and Wu-Rock got eyes on Wah and Baby Shug down at the courthouse." *Shoot on sight!* Suspect sent the text to his young soldier, Sham, telling him to take the shot if he could. Suspect called Miko and told her the news.

"That's where we going then," Cream told him, busting a U-turn in the middle of the street. He stepped down harder on the accelerator and pushed the truck with urgency in the direction of the courthouse. With fifteen miles behind them, Cream whipped the Tahoe through the crowded downtown traffic trying his damndest to link up with Sham and Wu-Rock.

"Fuck!" Suspect smashed his fist into the dashboard in frustration. "We shoulda went around the other way over there by the City College off Park."

"It's too late now, bruh. We stuck here for the time being. Call Sham and ask him what it's lookin' like on their end."

Ring. Ring. Ring.

"What's good?" Sham answered the phone.

"We stuck in traffic about five blocks away from the courthouse, but we on our way. What it look like where y'all at?" Suspect put Sham on speakerphone.

Sham's voice was calm and collected.

"Baby Shug just came out of the courthouse, and they're standing next to a black Charger choppin' it up in the parking lot."

"What the fuck is y'all waitin' for? Go kill they asses then!" Cream ordered, pissed off that traffic was moving so slowly. Cars were bumper to bumper in the congested streets.

Sham ignored the condescending hostility in Cream's voice and explained why they hadn't got off yet.

"We can't do anything right now. It's a gang of police walking around in the parking lot! The courthouse is swarming with po-pos and legal people." Nobody spoke on either end of the phone for a few seconds. Then some action jumped off. "They on the move! They finna get in traffic! They just got in the Charger heading east, bruh!" Sham's voice was turnt up.

"Don't lose 'em, Sham. You hear me? Don't lose 'em! First chance you get I want you to smoke they asses!" Cream barked out as he inched the Tahoe forward, desperately looking around for a way to get out of the traffic jam, so he could double back around and cut Wah and Shug off.

"Stay on the phone, Sham! I want a play by play while it jumps off!"

"A'ight," Sham replied.

"What kind of heat are y'all workin' with?" Suspect asked, trying to stay as involved as possible.

"I got a Tech-9 with two extended clips and a .357. Wu-Rock got a Beretta, plus we got the Chopper in the backseat. Why? What's up?"

Cream jerked the steering wheel hard left, busting a tight illegal U-turn as soon as the car in front of him gave him enough space. He looked up at the street sign.

"What street are you on, Sham?"

"Hold up. They pullin' into the McDonald's drive-thru across from the City College!" Sham declared loudly, mentally preparing himself to commit multiple murders.

"Get behind 'em and follow 'em up in there. Air they bitch asses out, Sham!" Suspect ordered the execution. "Murk both of them ma'fuckas, homie!"

"Follow 'em in there, Wu!" Sham told Wu-Rock, the driver of the Nissan Altima.

"Yeah, there they go! Got y'all bitch asses now!" Sham said gleefully, brimming with wicked delight when the Altima pulled into the McDonald's drive-thru behind the black Charger. Then all hell broke loose on the other end of the phone.

Pap! Pap! Pap! Pap! Pap! Pap! Pap!

A gun sounded off with a thunderous barrage of gunfire. A couple seconds of silence followed and the thunder clapped again.

Pap! Pap! Pap! Pap! Pap! Pap! Pap!

Bbbtttaaattt! Bbbtttaaattt!

The Tech-9 sounded off with two booming bursts and got the last word in.

Cream stepped on the gas a little harder, gripping the Tahoe's steering wheel a little tighter while breaking a handful of traffic laws along the way as he whipped the SUV wildly through traffic. The cars ahead of them came to an abrupt stop, and once again Cream and Suspect were stuck in traffic, mad as hell.

Feeling helpless, Cream banged his fist against the steering wheel with angry impatience. He craned his neck to the left looking up the block and saw the huge golden arches of the McDonald's up ahead about half a block away. *There they go right there!* he thought, excited. A black Charger was speeding away up ahead. He picked the Desert Eagle up out his lap and whipped the truck from the line of traffic-jammed cars, jumping the Tahoe onto the sidewalk. He wrestled with the steering wheel until he was back on the street in front of the logjam. His foot smashed down on the gas until the Tahoe was doing seventy in a thirty-five headed for the back bumper of the Charger.

"What the fuck happened to Sham and Wu-Rock?" Cream hollered as he mashed on the gas, looking over at the phone in Suspect's hand.

"Watch out, Cream!" Suspect yelled to his brother, eyes wide with fear.

Boooooommm! Crash!

A car trying to avoid the chaos in the street hit the Tahoe with so much force it caused the big body truck to slam into the back of a parked car, where it careened left and veered across the slip of island between the streets. The Tahoe ended up on the other side of the street, stalled in the middle of the road, steam coming from under the hood. The airbag had deployed, and Cream and Suspect were in the front seat dazed and nearly unconscious.

In seconds, police were swarming around the wreckage around the Chevy Tahoe with guns drawn, ready to kill something.

CHAPTER 43

Wah

Pap! Pap! Pap! Pap! Pap! Pap! Pap!

Shug ran around the back of the car and hit the light-skinned driver up with his first barrage, making it so the Nissan couldn't flee the scene. The driver slumped over dead against the steering wheel as bullets punched holes into his clothes. Dude in the passenger seat got caught completely off his guard. He was talking on speakerphone when Shug started bustin' on the driver. Instead of returning shots from his own Tech-9, he hesitated and tried to duck and hide from the 40 Glock's spray. His hesitation allowed Shug to approach the driver's side with the Glock turned sideways while he busted off shots inside the Altima as the passenger lifted a Tech-9.

Pap! Pap! Pap! Pap! Pap! Pap! Pap!
Bbbtttaaattt! Bbbtttaaattt!

Over half of Shug's slugs hit the passenger in his upper body. The last bullet hit him in his ear, tearing a tunnel through his head before exiting through his other ear and cracking the glass in the window behind him. The Tech-9 sprayed two quick bursts into the right side of the driver's slumped frame; it was a reflex response after the 40 Glock hit him up. People screamed and hollered for help while others smartly ducked for cover and hid from the gunfire going off around them.

"Somebody call 911. They're shooting!" an older white lady cried out.

"Get down! Get the hell down!" a fat white dude hollered to the crowd of terrified people in front of McDonald's.

Shug blended in like one of the terrified pedestrians and

271

bolted across the street, running left between two buildings until he was in the parking lot of the high school.

"Are you good? Are you straight?" I asked when he jumped in the Charger.

"Yeah I'm good. Them fools in the Altima ain't though," he responded, wiping the prints off the Glock.

"Did you recognize any of 'em?" I asked, pondering whether I should start the bully whip. My mind was clicking with suspicion. It wasn't a coincidence people were gunning for us minutes after Shug was released. The only people who knew Shug was being released were Khadida and Khassandra. For a split second I wondered if they were somehow involved with the ambush. *After dealing with a foul bitch like Miko, I ain't putting anything past a bitch!* I thought instinctively.

"Nah bruh, I don't know who the fuck they was, but I wasn't trying to ID 'em either."

That's when Shug turned in his seat and brought me up to date on what Miko had been doing over the last two years while we sat parked in the high school parking lot waiting for the coast to clear.

"I know you been out the loop for a while, Wah, being in that coma. But from what I been hearing through the prison grapevine, that bitch Miko is doin' it real big out here right now. Her name is ringing bells hella loud, and she built a little empire with a small army of Eastside Pirus on her team. I didn't mention any of this on the phone because you already know how I feel about discussing illegal shit on a cell phone. It's a lot of good dude's stretched the fuck out because they said the wrong thing on a cell phone and exposed too much game in the process."

I listened as he told me everything he knew or had heard about Miko's drug empire, and what she had accomplished since we took our fall. He told me about her cousins, who had been doing bids on a manslaughter charge at the time the shit between us went down. Then he told me about Miko's crew supposedly being responsible for killing three of my lil homies who called themselves the Young Glock Gang.

"One of 'em is still alive," Shug said. "When they brought me down here to the county from the pen, that's all them fools in the county jail were talkin' about—some cat they call Bony James."

"What! I know Bony James! That's my lil homie, bruh! Bony James is wit' the bizness, Shug. He hella solid."

"Well, right now he hella up against it. They got him on double murder charges."

"Ugh, that's fucked up. I hate to hear that," I remarked, feeling bad for the homie.

"Nah, what's fucked up is that the murders they tryin' to put on him are murders Miko's cousins committed. The law tryin' to hit him with that death during the commission of a crime shit."

I looked around making sure the coast was clear before I pushed the Charger out the parking lot, then stepped on the gas and merged into traffic. I looked over at Shug and said, "I think I'ma move into Granny's house until I get my finances right." Silence filled the car. *This the second time he's done that,* I thought, feeling funny again. "What's all that silent shit about, Shug?" I asked when he clammed up.

Boooooommmm! Crash!

I heard a loud crash, and I looked up in the rearview and saw a Tahoe twisted around another car with steam coming from under the hood in the middle of the street half a block behind us.

Wheeeew! Wheeeew!

273

Sirens screamed as flashing lights filled up the rearview, which made me slow down and square up in the seat. *Oh shit! We just killed two people, and the guns we used are still in the car with us!* I thought about testing the waters and outrunning the cop cars, but my instincts told me to stay cool and remain calm. I poked and pushed on a few buttons again until the door to the stash box slid open. Shug hid the Glocks and sat up proper in his seat.

When I looked into the rearview again, I saw the cop cars surrounding the Chevy Tahoe that had been involved in a crash. *Damn, that was hella close!* I thought, letting out the breath I had been holding. They had their guns drawn and were yelling out orders to whoever was in the Tahoe. *I wonder who the fuck that is in the Tahoe? Whoever it is, better them than me.*

CHAPTER 44

Wah

The welcome home party for Shug lost some of its luster after the botched ambush. Instead of going big and taking it to the club like we planned, the four of us decided to stay in and chill. We smoked blunts and sipped Hennessy, chopping it up playing spades and dominoes before watching *American Sniper*. It was a small personal get together, just the four of us having a good time enjoying life without the bullshit. The shindig lasted late into the night until we decided to call it quits and go our separate ways. Shug and Khadida went to their room, which was right across the hall from our room. As soon as they bounced, Khassandra and I retired to the bedroom, where I fucked the shit out of her for a few hours until she fell asleep with my dick buried in her pussy.

The next day Shug and I decided to drive to LA and help the girls pack some of their belongings. Shug and Khadida were moving in together. I didn't want Khassandra staying with me at Granny's, so she was going to be staying with them for a while. I was posting up at granny's house by myself until I decided on something long term. While we were in LA though, we hit the malls up and got a lot tighter in the process, having a gang of fun and getting to know each other better.

Shug being with Khadida was a good look. She was the female version of him, minus the violence, and they gelled well together. I was happy for him.

As far as hook ups went, Khassandra was cool. We got along for the most part, and the sex was the bomb, but I couldn't stop thinking about Tocarra and how much I missed her.

As soon as we got back from LA, I was flossing in the

Charger with Shug after coppin' some trees. I continuously stole peeks in the rearview mirror. After how that shit went down with the two clowns at McDonald's, my antennae were up and I was on high alert. I believe in coincidence, but I didn't believe in coincidences that came in the form of two heavily-armed thugs in an Altima trying to murk me!

I was in the neighborhood Drape lived in before he got killed, so I decided to go pay the homegirl Silky a visit and see what she was talkin' about. It had been damn near two years since I last saw her. If the streets were talking, then I was sure Silky had been listening, and she probably had a lot to say about it. I parked the Charger next to the curb, and Shug looked over at me with a quizzical expression, and then down at one of the 40 Glocks in his lap. He didn't recognize Drape's street, but being a Crip, he knew he was in enemy territory. "Who stay over here?"

After checking the 40 Glock in my hand, I looked out the rearview one last time before replying, "The homegirl Silky. Drape used to live in these apartments too." He opened the door and got out, then sucked his gut in and tucked the gun in his waistband. I put security on the Charger and slipped my strap into the small of my back, then pulled my shirt down, concealing the bulge before I joined Shug on the sidewalk. We walked up to the gate, and I pushed it open with my right hand. Shug followed behind me as we took the stairs two at a time.

Knock. Knock. Knock.

"Who is it?" a deep voice demanded to know from behind the door.

Who the fuck is that? I wondered, touching the pistol just in case the fool behind the door had foul intentions.

"It's Wahdatah. Where Silky at?" I responded coolly,

bracing for drama. I could hear the chain unhooking and the door unlocking.

"Aagghh! It's so good to see you, homeboy!" Silky screamed out her delight. "I thought you were dead, Wah! They said you got shot and died right after Drape got killed!" She hugged me hella hard and teared up when I slipped my arm around her waist and hugged her back.

"I got shot, but I didn't die, Silky. You know a ma'fucka like me is bulletproof, ma." I tried to make light of it, so I wouldn't become emotional with her. *Damn, the homie Drape been dead for two years!* The thought of my tight man Drape resting in peace still hurt my heart in a real way. Thoughts of him, Moolah, and Thun-Thun's wild ass entered my mind and started fuckin' with my feelings. *Don't get emotional and tear up, Wah!* I checked myself, then cleared my throat and introduced her to Shug. She, in turn, introduced us to the dude she was entertaining, a young goonish looking gangsta she called Pokey.

"Y'all want something to drink?" she asked while on her way to the kitchen.

"Hennessy wit' ice," I said.

"Same for me," Shug told her.

We looked at each other and started laughing, recognizing that we were still on the same page after all this time. I took the pistol from the small of my back and set it on the couch next to me. Out the corner of my eye I saw the dude named Pokey fingering his phone.

Silky brought our drinks, and I looked over the top of mine after raising it to my lips, casually scanning the room with my eyes. Pokey was acting hella suspicious, his eyes darting from us to Silky, and then back to his phone. *What the fuck is wrong with him?* I wondered. Growing up amongst dark-hearted thugs who kept a trick or two up their sleeve, made you learn how to recognize when a ma'fucka was acting suspect with his mannerisms. *This Pokey clown is definitely on some shady shit! Don't get caught slippin'. Trust your gut, Wah!*

When he looked up and turned his gaze in my direction again, I looked away like I wasn't paying him any attention. Minutes later when Silky and I became immersed in conversation, Pokey conveniently got up and left the room. As soon as he disappeared, I looked over to Silky.

"How long have you known ol' boy, Silky? And where he from?" My voice was low, so only she and Shug could hear me.

She looked at me with a perplexed expression.

"I've known him for about two weeks, and he's from Skyline. Why? What's up?" she whispered back in a conspiratorial tone.

I put my finger up to my lips and stood.

"Shhhh." My instincts were telling me that Pokey was bad bizness. He was up to something, and I wasn't about to be second-guessing my instincts again. I second-guessed my instincts outside of the jewelry store, and it got Moolah and Thun-Thun murked. I second-guessed my instincts when that bitch Miko came to my house, and because of it, I got six bullets in my body, and I nearly lost my life. *What the fuck is this shady ma'fucka up to?* I tiptoed to the only closed door in the small apartment and put my ear against it. I gripped the 40 Glock tight in my hand in case Pokey opened the door and caught me ear-hustling. My eyes narrowed to slits as I listened in.

"I'm tellin' you, Dough Hound, both of them fools is sittin' in the living room right now! I woulda busted on 'em if I hadn't left my strap in the car. Miko said a million dollars dead or alive, and I'm claimin' that shit, homie! What?" Pokey stopped talking and listened for a second. "Yeah, I could get my burner out the car and slump 'em myself, but then I'ma have to smoke the bitch too, and I ain't trying to murk no female, homie." Pokey listened to the party on the other end.

"Fuck it then, the bitch gotta go too. Wrong place wrong time," he responded. ". . . Yeah, I'll call you when it's done. A'ight then."

Quickly, I crept back into the living room and took my seat. I didn't think I'd have enough time to tell Shug and Silky what I had overheard while Pokey conspired to kill the three of us, so I improvised on the go, leaning my glass back and downing what remained of the Hennessy. Just as I set the glass on the coffee table, Pokey appeared from the back with his left hand in his pocket.

"Let me get a refill, Silky, a'ight?" I said, wanting to get her out of the line of fire. *He said he left his gun in the car, but he got his hand in his pocket. I ain't taking any chances!* My hand was on the Glock, ready to bust it.

"I'll be right back, y'all. I gotta go grab something out my car. I left the charger to my phone in my car, and my battery gettin' low." Pokey made the announcement while making his way toward the door.

I stood with the 40 Glock in my hand and pointed it at Pokey's chest. "I suggest you sit yo' bitch ass down, potna. You ain't goin' nowhere, bruh!"

"What the fuck is wrong with you, man!" He turned his head toward Silky. "Damn, Silky. This how you let your people get at me? Pullin' pistols on a ma'fucka and shit?"

Silky didn't know what the hell was going on, but she knew me, and she knew how I got down. So she rolled with it and let it play out like it was supposed to.

"If you don't knock off all them fuckin' theatrics and sit yo' bitch ass down somewhere, I'ma put a slug in yo' head and let you think about that for a minute."

Pokey mugged me for a second and saw that my grip on the 40 Glock was steady. He let a defeated breath out and sat his bitch ass down on the arm of the couch closest to him with a look of despair. Shug and Silky looked at me, waitin' for an explanation, so I gave them one.

"I heard this pussy on the phone talkin' to some fool named Dough Hound." I glanced over at Shug, "From what I gathered, bruh, the bitch Miko got a million dollar price tag on our heads." Then I looked over to Silky. "It sounded like this Dough Hound cat told him to take us out the game, but Pokey here left his thumper in his whip. Ain't that right, Pokey?" I said and eased over to where he was sitting. The grim-faced goon pled the fifth and kept his lips closed and poked out.

"Is that shit true, bruh? Did that bitch Miko put a million dollar price tag on our heads?" Shug asked and palmed his 40 Glock.

Pokey kept his mouth shut and mugged us hard, as if we were the ones who had offended him. "I'm not going to ask you again, cuz. Play tough if you want to; I won't hesitate to knock your noodles out, potna," Shug promised, waving the Glock like a tambourine. Something about the way Shug got at him loosened his lips.

"Yeah, it's a million dollar contract on y'all, half a million for each one of you." Pokey put his head down and closed his eyes, disappointed in himself for going against the grain.

While he sulked in his cowardice, I put the 40 Glock against his head and squeezed one off before he knew what hit him. Silky jumped back with a shocked expression, while Shug and I went to work.

"Get a sheet so we can wrap him up," I told Shug.

He left and reappeared seconds later with a satin bed sheet in his hand. We rolled Pokey up like a blunt and stuffed his ass in a large duffle bag Silky brought from her closet. I was about to drag his dead ass out the front door and down the steps when Shug stopped me.

"We can't go out that way, Wah."

"Why not?" I asked in midstride, with the duffle bag's nylon strap in my right hand.

"Because they got cameras out there somewhere. That's how they found out it wasn't me who killed Drape, remember?"

"Oh shit, you right. I forgot about that." *What the fuck we gon' do? We gotta get rid of this fool!* I thought about it for a second, then remembered the time I forced that bitch Carmelita up onto the window ledge in Drape's crib. *Perfect!* "I'm finna go get the Charger and bring it around back. Throw him out the back window, and I'll put his punk ass in the trunk," I told Shug and turned the doorknob.

After wheeling the Charger around into the alley and parking it beneath one of Silky's windows, Shug dropped the heavy duffle down two stories, and it hit the ground with a loud ass thud. I stuffed him in the trunk and closed it. *Now we gotta find a place to bury this fool.* Then it hit me. *Under the lemon tree!*

"Let's shoot over to Granny's house and put his ass under the lemon tree," I told him after he got in.

"I don't think that's a good idea, Wah," he said, slipping on his seatbelt.

I started the Charger and burned rubber down the alley. "Whatchu talkin' 'bout, Shug? Where else we gonna bury his body?" I asked when I was halfway down the alley. He got quiet, and I got that feeling again. *What the fuck is wrong with him? Why does he keep clamming up?* I pulled the Charger over and parked it next to a fence, then turned in my seat and faced him. "Talk to me, bruh. Why I keep gettin' the feeling that it's some shit you ain't telling me?"

Shug bit his bottom lip and averted his eyes. A heavy silence filled the tight space in the Charger's cockpit. Shug turned toward me and let out a deep breath. "When I was in the county jail after you got shot, that bitch Miko came to visit me.

"What!" I responded with dumbfounded anger.

"Nah, not like that, Wah. The bitch came unannounced and unexpected." He hesitated for a second before continuing. "I'm sorry, bruh, but she came to brag about killing Tocarra. She said if I ever got out, or if you ever recovered from the coma, we could find Tocarra's body up under the lemon tree." He went on to tell me about Tocarra's efforts to follow Miko and tag her in an attempt to clear his name and everything that happened afterward.

What! Tocarra's dead? Why the fuck he ain't said nothin' about it before today! I was stunned with pain. I recalled Tocarra playing back the recording of Miko recounting all the foul shit she had done. My emotions started choking me as tears welled up in my eyes. To hear him say that Tocarra was dead hurt me in a way I wasn't prepared for. I grinded my molars and chewed on my anger, trying to swallow what I was feeling. It didn't work. The thought of Tocarra being dead pained me in an unfathomable fashion. Tocarra was a good girl who got tangled up in a goon's world when she met me. I felt responsible for her death. It hurt like hell to the depths of my soul to know that Tocarra lost her life simply because she became a part of mine. Then I thought about her body under the lemon tree. *Fuck nah! I'll be damned if I let her rot under the lemon tree! She deserves better than that. It's the least I* can do since it was me and my lifestyle that ultimately got her killed. I heatedly revved the engine and flexed the muscle in the Mopar.

"You foul for not telling me about that shit, Shug!" I told him and put the Charger in traffic, heading toward Granny's crib. *I love you because you're my brother, but you leave a lot to be desired when it comes to keepin' it one hundred.* I felt disappointed, mad that I'd been misled.

When we arrived at the house we carried Pokey's corpse inside, and I was overcome with a nostalgic feeling; being in Granny's house without her being in it fucked with my emotions in an even deeper manner. It hurt in a way I can't explain. To know I would never see my granny smile again, that I would never hug her or hold her hand again, hurt like a ma'fucka. It peeled that invisible scab of sorrow back and opened the fresh wound of hurt all over again. Granny was more like a mother to me since my moms got killed when I was so young. Granny was the only woman I had ever truly loved outside of my moms and Tocarra. And to think that both of them had been killed and buried under the lemon tree only added insult to my injury.

After a few sentimental minutes inside the house, I shook off the emotions and we went outside to handle our business. On the way out, I grabbed the shovel from the garage before heading over to the lemon tree. It was the place where I spent quite a few of my childhood moments. For so long it had been my sanctuary, the place of so many enlightening moments in my life. Now it was the place of two of my most painful memories. It was hard, but I had to do what I had to do.

This is gonna be some hard shit to see! I thought, mentally preparing to dig Tocarra's body up. There was a small swell in the ground that hadn't been there before. Sticking out of the dirt was what looked like the corner of a suitcase. Tears filled my eyes. *Why'd you have to go after that bitch Miko, baby?* I wondered, while my heart broke again. The thought of Tocarra's body stuffed in a suitcase made me sick to my stomach. I was overcome with emotion when I thought of her body bent in half and folded up inside the suitcase. I had to take a couple minutes to get my shit together.

After setting the 40 Glock on the ground near my foot, I took a deep breath and got after it. The shovel stabbed into the earth and pierced the hard-packed soil. It took about five minutes for me to dig around the suitcase and clear out all the dirt around the huge luggage piece. Shug grabbed one end while I grabbed the other end, and together we pulled hard to unearth the rest of the suitcase. It was heavy as hell and stank of a rank, corroded odor. *Hold your breath, Wah! This gon' be ugly!* I warned myself and held my breath and tugged hard on the zipper, slowly unzipping the suitcase. When it was zipped all the way back, I peeled the upper half of the suitcase back and braced myself for the worst. *What the fuck!* My eyes almost jumped out their sockets. There was nothing but dirt inside the suitcase, no body, no bones, no clothes, nothing whatsoever—nothing indicating a body had ever even been inside of it!

"Bruh, there ain't no dead body in this suitcase!" I looked up and said to Shug.

"I know, I see. But it's a suitcase here, and we damn sure didn't put it there. So obviously, at one time or another somebody was inside of it." He shrugged and shook his head, just as confused as I was.

While he looked down at the dirt-filled suitcase, I looked at the side of his head and let my thoughts wander. *Are you lying to me, Shug? Did you do something to Tocarra, and now you trying to cover up your dirty? Nah, he was locked up until I got out the coma. He couldn't have done anything to her.* I stood there stuck on stupid. *What the fuck happened to Tocarra! She gotta be alive! If she ain't in this suitcase, then she must still be alive!* I made a mental note to check all the hospitals, jails, and morgues to see if there was any record of a Tocarra Rhodes-Robinson ever having been hospitalized, admitted, or arrested anytime over the past two years. *She ain't under the lemon tree, and she never came back to the hospital, so where the hell could she have gone?* I wondered, dumfounded as I tossed the duffle bag with Pokey's body in the hole under the lemon tree and started throwing dirt on him. *Tocarra gotta be alive!* I thought with a renewed sense of hope and threw dirt on top of the duffle bag much faster. *After I kill that bitch Miko, I gotta find out what happened to Tocarra and see where the hell she been all this time!*

CHAPTER 45

Miko

The raid executed on Miko's estate included six uniformed police officers from the San Diego Police Department, a team of Crime Scene Investigators and two detectives. One by one, Miko's employees were searched, handcuffed, and escorted to black and white patrol cars, where they were quickly whisked away and questioned extensively down at the station.

An hour after the arrival of law enforcement agents, Miko Dunbar herself was led away in handcuffs and ushered to a cop car, where she was tucked into the backseat before being driven downtown to the county jail for booking. As far as she was concerned, the ride in the back of the police cruiser was a necessary inconvenience she had to tolerate and endure. Javier warned her that the cops would be coming for her soon, and she was fully prepared when they showed up. Her attorneys had already been notified, and the necessary funds for her bail had already been wired to their offices, where they were in the process of cashing it out, per her orders.

Her face was a blank; she was unfazed by it all, while sitting in the back of the cop car, turning her emotions off and robotically going through the motions as the cops assisted her out of the backseat. Throughout the entire booking process, Miko remained stone-faced; the humiliating strip search, the degrading visual inspection of her body cavities, the fingerprinting process that messed up her elegantly designed manicure.

Miko's one phone call lasted all of thirty seconds. She called her attorney and simply told him, "Have me out of here before the sun goes down. I don't want to miss the sunset."

CHAPTER 46

Wah

Armed with the news that Miko had a million dollar price tag on our heads, Shug and I plotted on the best way to permanently knock her punk ass out the box. We racked our brains and contemplated schemes to lure the scandalous bitch into a trap. When we least expected it, the opportunity we had been waiting for surprisingly presented itself to us; it was all over the news. The dumb bitch had been arrested. Which is why I was posted up in the cut, making sure our plan played out perfectly.

I leaned back in the shadows of the doorway and pulled my fitted cap a little lower over my eyes, trying to block out the brilliant sun's glare. I held my cell phone chest high in one hand like I was texting somebody, while my other hand rested against the 40 Glock in the back of my waistband. It was blistering hot and muggy as hell outside. The sun wasn't showing me any love. *It's hotter than the middle of Africa out here! It gotta be at least 100°!* I thought, while my eyes unassumingly darted from the screen on the phone up the street to the building I had been spying on for the past forty-five minutes.

"Awwck twooh!"

I coughed some snot up from my chest and spit a chunky green loogy onto a small patch of dirt near a skinny tree on the edge of the sidewalk ten feet away. *I'm sweatin' like a runaway slave. This is crazy!* I took my hand away from the pistol and used the back of it to wipe my face. After wiping the thin coat of perspiration from my brow, I adjusted the black Yankee's fitted on my dome and fixed my eyes on the target.

* * * * * *

Miko stormed out the county jail with an attitude and a pissed off expression, irate that the Sheriff's Department intentionally kept her jailed long after her bail had been posted. She took the phone out of her purse and angrily swiped at it and called Anthony.

Ring. Ring. Ring.

"What's up, boss? Where are you at?" Anthony answered.

"I'm in front of the jail. Hurry up and come get me outta here!" Miko was still heated at the circumstances she found herself in. The hot sun beaming down on her didn't help matters.

"A'ight, I should be there in twenty minutes or so," Anthony assured her as he prepared to leave his residence.

"Thank you." Miko softened up a bit in an attempt to calm her frazzled nerves. "Oh, and Anthony . . ."

"Yeah?"

"Make sure that other thing is taken care of too."

"All right, Miko. It's as good as done," Anthony responded obediently. He placed the cell phone back in his pocket once she ended their call.

* * * * * *

The muscle-bound silverback ma'fucka I had been waiting on finally emerged from the building and bounced down the steps like the world was supposed to be afraid of his big ass. When he reached the bottom step he stopped and pulled his phone out, then talked for a minute before stuffing the phone back in his pocket. He got up close to the white Maybach sitting at the curb and cursed, then kicked the flat right rear tire. He pulled his phone back out and made a call, talking for a couple more minutes before ending the call and kicking the flat tire a second time.

Satisfied that my part was done, I made my way to the Charger and waited for Shug to call me.

* * * * * *

Miko was sitting on a nearby bench when her phone started ringing in her purse.

"Yeah," she answered, curious to know why Anthony was calling her back only seconds after they had spoken.

"We got a problem, Miko."

"A problem? What kind of problem do we have?" She stood up, as if that was going to soften the blow.

"The Maybach has a flat, and we took the spare out last week when you had me put those bags of money in the trunk."

"Great, what else could go wrong?" Miko would've strangled her smart phone if it would have fixed her problem.

"Sorry, boss, I'll try to—"

She cut him off and said, "Don't worry about it, Anthony. I just spotted a taxi up the street, so I'm gonna take a cab home. I'll be damned if I'ma wait out here under this hot ass sun any longer than I have to." She shielded her face by placing her hand to her forehead like a visor. "Go ahead and take care of that other thing that we talked about. Tell our friend good-bye, and after you've taken care of that, I want you to meet me at the house, okay?" Miko ended the call and flagged down the yellow cab moving in her direction.

The taxi eased up to the curb and stopped in front of her. She hurriedly pulled the back door open and quickly ducked into the backseat.

"Where to?" the cab driver respectfully inquired.

Miko gave the female cabbie the address to her mansion and got as comfortable as possible in the backseat. She checked the battery life on her phone and felt like things were looking up. Thank goodness! The battery was at 80%, so she busied herself responding to all of the texts and missed calls her phone received while she was locked up.

* * * * * *

Ring. Ring. Ring.

"What's poppin'?" I answered my phone as I pushed the Charger through traffic.

"It's good, Wah. It worked!" Shug was hella turnt up that our plot to trap Miko was working.

"That's what's up. Did you get the address?" I asked, reaching for the ink pen on the dashboard. Shug repeated the address, and I hurriedly wrote it down.

"I'll see you when you get there, bruh," he told me.

"Likewise, family. Be safe," I responded.

"Out."

"Gone." I hung up and tossed the phone on the passenger seat next to the 40 Glock. With a little more urgency, I whipped the Charger in the direction of Miko's mansion. Shug was already on the way. If all went well, he would be there when I got there.

* * * * * *

He did his best to make himself look smaller as he blended in with his surroundings and camouflaged himself in a baggy oversized doctor's garb. The surgical mask covering his face was the touch that helped him blend in perfectly.

Beep. Beep. Beep. Beep.

The machines monitoring the patient's vital signs and other significant medical information beeped steadily in room 1469. A couple of nurses walked by chatting incessantly in hushed tones, both dressed in colorful scrubs as they giggled over their dialogue. After giving one final look out the window to ensure his presence wasn't being scrutinized, he quietly shut the door behind him and closed the blinds. He walked softly until he was standing next to the half-jackknifed bed and looked down at the horribly disfigured patient before him. There was no sympathy in his voice when he leaned over and whispered in the ear of the man lying in the hospital bed.

"Snitch ass ma'fucka, this is for Miko. She wanted me to personally tell your bitch ass good-bye!"

The patient's body tensed up and jerked violently when he realized what was going on. He tried to scream, but his yell stopped at the huge palm sealing his mouth shut.

"Unghh!"

Pfftt! Pfftt!

Both bullets entered the front of Capone's head and came out the back of it, then went through the pillow before coming to rest somewhere deep in the hospital bed's mattress. The machine emitted its shrill sound, and the crooked graph on the apparatus flat-lined. Anthony, however, had already left the room, strolling toward the elevator. When the elevator opened on the first floor, the black hulk emerged from the conveying space in an expensive silk suit and a $1,200 pair of gators. The oversized doctor's garb and mask were balled up and lay in the corner of the elevator. He had gladly done Miko's deadly bidding, and he took great pride and pleasure in doing so on a regular basis. The queenpin had given him a job fresh out of prison that paid handsomely. It was a convict's dream come true, working for the top drug dealer in the city days after being released from the joint. As soon as he closed the car door behind him, Anthony unscrewed the silencer and threw it inside the glove compartment, before pushing the newly fixed Maybach in the direction of Miko's mansion.

CHAPTER 47

Miko

The taxi slowed to a stop at the top of Miko's circular driveway, and the cab driver waited patiently for the passenger to dig through her purse until she came up with more than enough money to cover the fare. Miko handed the driver a hundred dollar bill.

"Keep the change," Miko told her and smiled, before opening the door and stepping out. She looked at the vast grandiose estate and closed her eyes, breathing in deeply through her nostrils and basking in the new found feeling of wealth and affluence.

"Thank you." The cab driver smiled and folded the big face in half before stuffing it in her bra.

The heels on Miko's pumps click-clacked lightly against the exclusive flooring as she quickly climbed the steps leading to the posh manor. When she got to the top of the steps, she looked around and wondered how long it would be before the help showed up. She twisted the doorknob and pushed the door open, putting her hand out to balance herself against the wall in the foyer as she removed her shoes.

Boop! Bop! Thump!

Miko's head exploded with bright lights when Shug snuck her in the temple with a vicious two-piece that knocked her out cold. Her body crumbled to the floor. Her head hit the marble hard. For a few seconds she shook at Shug's feet as if having a seizure, before her body locked up in slumber.

"Nah, bitch, wake your punk ass up, 'ho!" Shug kicked her in the stomach with brute force and brought her out of the unconscious state she was drowning in. Miko bent in half in agony and struggled mightily to find her bearings as excruciating pain shot through her abdomen. Her brain was swimming in dizziness.

"Please! Please! No, stop!" she cried out desperately.

Wah thought about his mother being shot by Miko at point blank range and pushed Shug out the way. He thought about the intense pain of those six shots he took from her pistol that put him in a coma. Then he thought about his boy Drape being murdered in cold blood, so Miko could set Shug up and send him to prison. His anger was deep, his anguish even deeper. *It's your turn to suffer now, bitch!* He picked the dazed queenpin up in his arms and lifted her entire body up over his head.

Thoomp!

Wah viciously slammed Miko's soft body face-first onto the immovable marble floor and smiled when her face smashed into the ground. Her grill cracked sickeningly loud against the ground. All her top and bottom front teeth broke off in her bloody mouth. She was out cold again.

Baby Shug looked around and saw a Grandfather clock with a giant glass face on it. He rushed over to her limp frame and grabbed a handful of Miko's long, silky hair, then dragged her across the room and ran her headfirst into the glass on the Grandfather clock, making sure she touched both jagged glass edges before pulling her back out. He forcibly slung her limp body to his right and watched her land hard and awkwardly at the foot of the spiraling staircase.

Perfect! he thought when he saw her right arm flail out at her side. He placed her limp left arm against the bottom step, making sure her hand was flat on the first step palm up and her elbow on the marble floor.

Stomp!

Crack!

Shug jumped in the air and stomped his foot down. Miko's forearm snapped in half, the thick, bloody forearm bone poked through her skin. She made a noise that sounded like a whimpering scream with no energy behind it; Miko was a bloody, beaten, broken mess.

Wah stepped between them and put his hand against Shug's chest.

"Don't kill that bitch yet, Shug. I want her punk ass to know it was by our hands that she took her last breath." Shug kicked the unconscious queenpin in the head, not giving a fuck if she died now or later, just so long as she died. To see his ex-fiancée lying there broken and bloody brought a sense of elation to him he had never felt before. Personally, doing karma's dirty work felt rewarding to his soul.

"I'ma go and get some water to pour on that bitch's face, so we can wake her up. That bitch easily got another hundred bones in her body that I need to break, and you can best believe I'ma try to break every single one of 'em," Shug said and turned, walking toward the kitchen. "You want something to drink while I'm in there?" he asked Wah in a nonchalant manner.

"Nah, I'm straight, bruh," Wah assured him.

Minutes later, he watched as Shug poured a bottle of Vitamin Water onto Miko's face. Then shit got twisted.

Boom!

The front door opened and slammed shut. Anthony entered the mansion and saw Wah and Shug standing over his badly beaten responsibility.

"What the fuck . . ." He reached for the thumper in his shoulder holster and busted off three shots at them.

Pop! Pop! Pop!

Wah and Shug reached for their guns when Anthony squeezed off. They dove for cover, returning fire immediately.

Pap! Pap! Pap!! Pap! Pap! Pap! Pap!

Shug dove back into the kitchen as he fired while Wah dove headfirst behind a beam, then hurriedly dipped into the hallway to his right with his gun in hand.

Pop! Pop! Pop!

Anthony was a good shot. Bullets struck where Wah and Shug were, only they didn't penetrate the thick walls they hid behind. The bodyguard darted to his left and ducked under the staircase where Miko lay woozy and hurting bad, damn near dead.

"Get up, Miko! Get up!" he desperately encouraged her and thought about grabbing her leg and pulling her closer to him.

Pap! Pap! Pap! Pap! Pap! Pap!

"Shit!" Anthony hollered out as shots from Wah's 40 Glock peppered the wall close to his face. Wah had the best angle. Shug couldn't see Miko's bodyguard from his position.

Pop! Pop! Pop! Pop! Pop! Pop! Click! Click!

Anthony unloaded into the wall Wah was hiding behind when his pistol clicked on empty. He quickly reached into his sock and reloaded. Wah heard Anthony drop one clip out and replace it with another when a thought crossed his mind, and he came up firing.

Pap! Pap! Click! Click! Click!

"Fuck! I'm out of ammo, Shug. Throw me a clip, bruh!" Wah screamed desperately when his gun clicked empty three times.

Anthony saw his chance and took it, running as fast as he could in Wah's direction with his pistol raised and ready to explode. Wah saw the big, burly bodyguard with the huge hand canon coming his way, and his eyes got hella big.

Pap! Pap! Pap!

The first shot hit him in the chest. The second shot hit him in the stomach, and the third shot hit him in the right side of his forehead above his eyebrow. He crumbled heavily to the floor, sliding several feet before coming to a dead end, literally.

Shug, panicked and his heart filled with the worst kind of fear as he yelled, "Wah! Wah! Talk to me, Wah!" Shug held the 40 Glock in his grip as he left the kitchen heading Wah's way.

"I'm good, bruh. His big, dumb ass went for the banana in the tailpipe! I still got half a clip."

The look on Shug's face was one of supreme gratefulness.

"I thought he got you, bruh! You fooled the fuck outta me, man!" Shug hugged Wah fiercely, relieved that he was okay. Anthony lay on the floor with three bullet holes in his body and a pool of blood forming around his huge frame.

"C'mon, bruh. Let's finish this bitch off and get the fuck up outta here!" Wah told him.

They walked back to the front room and got the shock of their lives.

"Oh shit! What the fuck happened? Where that bitch go!" Wah exclaimed, bewilderment plastered on his face. He was stunned and stuck on stupid. Shug stood there with his eyes wide, silent with befuddlement.

Miko's body was no longer at the foot of the spiraling staircase. Only a small pool of blood and a bloody trail were on the ground where she once lay beaten and broken near death.

CHAPTER 48

Wah

When we came out the hallway, and I saw that the bitch Miko was gone, I almost flipped the fuck out and fainted. Then a thought hit me: *The way we left that bitch, as bad off as she was, there's no way somebody in her condition could just get up and walk away.*

Miko was a dangerous bitch. She managed to get the drop on me once before and pumped six shots in me. I wasn't putting anything past her grimy ass. *That bitch must've crawled up the steps!* I looked down at the bloody smear she left behind and instantly knew she pulled herself up the steps.

"She couldn't have gone far, bruh," I told Shug and followed the blood trail with the Glock ready.

"What we gon' do about him?" Shug asked, jerking his thumb toward the dude I killed.

"What about him. Fuck that fool, he dead. Leave his ass where he at," I told him.

We headed upstairs in search of the bitch who murdered my mother. When I got to the top step, I saw bloody crawl marks indicating that she'd dragged herself into the master bedroom. *It's a fuckin' trap!* I thought when I saw the door wide open. It looked like a setup to me.

"Be on your tiptoes, Shug. Just in case that bitch got hold of a gun or something."

We followed the trail of blood leading to a walk-in closet with double doors that had gold fixtures on them. I stood off to one side. Shug was standing on the other side. We flung the doors open at the same time, guns up with our fingers on the triggers. I was ready to put a bullet in her face, Shug was too.

Miko was sitting with her back to the wall under a giant glass-encased painting of herself. In the painting she was dressed in a snow white Dior pantsuit with black trim and exotic platinum and diamond pieces of jewelry hanging from her neck, wrists and earlobes. She had a white brim on tilted to the side and stood knee deep in a pile of money stacks. The caption on the painting read: **"A REAL BO$$ BITCH"**

Miko sat under the framed picture with her hands at her side. Her breathing was haggard and difficult when she spoke.

"Pweese, pweese don't kwill me," she pleaded, before dropping her chin to her chest in defeat.

"Don't start beggin' now, bitch!" Shug told her. He walked up on her, roughly snatched her up by her hair until she stood on wobbly legs. The bone on her right arm grotesquely stuck out of her skin with jagged edges that still had meat particles hanging off it.

Blam! Blam! Blam! Blam! Blam! Blam! Blam! Blam!

He put his hand around her neck for a better grip and repeatedly smashed her face into the exquisite painting of herself until the framed picture fell off the wall and landed at his feet.

"This is for my mama, bitch! This is for Camron! This is for Monisha!" Shug was overcome with rage as he continued bashing the front of Miko's face and head against the wall, until it cracked the plaster and left a web of fractured cracks running every which way. He finally let her go when the wall cracked, her unconscious body crumbling to the floor with a soft thud. Her broken forearm looked hella bizarre and out of place, poking through her skin as it lay unmoving by her side.

I was tired of playing with the bitch. As far as I was concerned, she didn't deserve to breathe the same air as me, so I walked up to her, kneeled next to her body, and put my mouth to her ear.

"This is poetic justice, bitch. For my mama!" I whispered and squeezed off two shots.

Pap! Pap!

I shot her in the face and blew her brains out the back of her head. I stood up and inhaled deeply. It felt as if a hole in my soul were being filled with something. *Sweet revenge! Killing her felt so much better than I thought it would.*

"I'm finna drag this bitch downstairs and put her and that big ma'fucka in the trunk of her car, bruh. A'ight?" Shug said, grabbing Miko by the ankles and dragging her out the closet.

I heard him, but I wasn't paying him any attention. I was looking at the area of the wall where the painting used to be.

"Yeah, do that," I muttered, noticing a thin line running vertically down the wall next to the network of cracks caused by Shug's continuously smashing her head into the wall. *What the hell is this?* My knuckles double tapped the wall firmly, and I heard what sounded like a deeper bass in some spots more so than in others.

"Shug, check this out, bruh," I hollered before he made it to the steps. He walked up next to me, and I repeated the knocking process again, and then he did it too.

Knock-knock. Knock-knock. Knock-knock. Knock-knock.

"What do you think it is?" His voice was full of interest.

"I think it's something on the other side of this wall, bruh," I said with conviction, looking around the closet for something that would help me open the wall up. I couldn't find anything that would tear the wall down like I wanted it to. "I'll be right back." I went around the huge house searching until I found a hammer in one of the cabinets under a bathroom sink.

While I went to look for the hammer, Shug dragged Miko and the big dude outside and stuffed them in the trunk of her car. After stuffing both corpses in the trunk, Shug met back up with me in the walk-in closet. I had been beating on the wall with the hammer for fifteen minutes, and just like I thought, there was something on the other side of the wall—an empty space. In less than an hour, I had a hole in the wall four-feet high and two-feet wide. Sweat dripped down my face like a prizefighter in the twelfth round of a championship fight, and my muscles were tight and hella swollen.

I ducked down and went to see for myself what was so important to Miko that she had to conceal it behind a wall. Just before I stuck my head in the hole I stopped. *What if Tocarra is back here!* My brain warned me that it might be Tocarra's dead body. *Man, if she back there, go get her out!* I told myself and went through the wall headfirst.

After falling inside, I dusted myself off and started hyperventilating.

"Shug, c'mere. Look at this shit! Hurry up, ma'fucka. Look at this shit, bruh!"

Shug climbed in behind me and hollered like a 'ho. We slapped hands, hugged, and then started doing the Dougie on the other side of the wall!

"I'm riotch, biotch!" I yelled at the top of my lungs and beat on my chest like a silverback gorilla. *This shit is too good to be true!* I thought while drowning in exhilaration. The hidden room was about the size of a prison cell and filled with countless stacks of money. Innumerable stacks of hundreds, fifties, and twenties lined the back wall from the floor halfway up to the ceiling.

"Ooh shit! Look, Wah!" Shug pointed to the ground where the wall met the money. Wedged between the wall and the money was a briefcase that looked identical to the metallic briefcase from the jewelry store heist. I instantly knew what we had to do.

"Call Khadida and tell her to leave the taxi cab in a parking lot somewhere and go rent a SUV, a Navigator, or Escalade and get that ma'fucka over here now!"

He called, and in minutes she was on the way. It took us a while, but after hours of nonstop work, we had every single bill in a bag, box, or suitcase. Fifteen minutes later, we had the Escalade full of dough. If it didn't fit inside of the Escalade, we stuffed it in the Charger.

Shug drove the Maybach to an abandoned lot while Khadida followed. I trailed behind her in the Charger with my gun ready to get empty if she tried to take off with the money! Shug wiped the Maybach down and set fire to it, and we watched it burn from a safe distance until I felt like it was fully engulfed in flames. Shug told Khadida to scoot over and jumped behind the wheel of the Escalade. We drove in a two-car caravan over to Granny's house, richer than we'd ever been! Shug had a good chick riding shotgun with him. Knowing Khadida was by his side when he was broke and at his worst let me know that she was the one for him. In my eyes, she deserved to be by his side when he was rich and at his best.

I bent a corner on my way to Granny's crib and passed Drape's block. Images of the people I loved most began playing like a horrifying movie in my mind. My eyes filled with tears when I thought about the good times with Granny, Drape, Moolah, and Thun-Thun. *I miss the hell out y'all, man!* Those tears toppled over my eyelids and slowly slid down my cheeks before falling onto my shirt when I thought about Tocarra. *Where the fuck you at, baby? You suppose to be by my side right now, Tocarra! Why you ain't here when I need you the most?* Another wave of tears fell from my eyes when I looked up and saw Shug and Khadida in the rearview in the Escalade behind me. Jealousy entered my guilty heart. *One of these days I'll find out what happened to you, Tocarra. I promise you, baby. One of these days I'll find out,* I promised silently as I pushed the Charger through traffic.

As I turned down the street I grew up on, I remembered the many priceless moments I enjoyed with all those I ever loved who were now deceased. I thought, *No amount of money in the world can replace the joy of sharing life with the ones you love the most.*

EPILOGUE

Wah & Shug

Trey Songz' "Bottoms Up" was beating out the speakers as Khassandra fed bills into the money counting machine and marked each stack with the proper money band after it came out. Khadida's fingers punched the calculator keys like a classical pianist as she did the math on the stacks and wrote down the totals. She repeated the process twice to ensure the counts were accurate. Shug and I sat across the room on separate sofas wrapping the money up tight in cellophane to make sure the condition of the money stayed protected once we put it up.

"What that count look like, baby?" Shug asked Khadida as he stuffed another cellophane-wrapped $100,000 bundle into the suitcase next to him.

"So far I've counted eleven million four hundred thirty-six thousand," she said, scribbling the numbers down on a piece of paper, not wanting to lose her count. Khassandra placed another stack of money in front of her and turned back to the money machine.

After stuffing another stack into the suitcase next to me, I looked over at Shug and said, "Have you thought about what you want to do with your half of the money yet, bruh?" I stood up and walked across the room and poured Hennessy into two glasses and waited for him to finish wrapping a bundle so he could answer. I handed him a glass and sat down with mine.

He hit the blunt he plucked from the ashtray and sipped his drink before saying, "Yeah, I know what I'ma do with my half. After I get a new crib, a new whip, and a new wardrobe, I'm sewin' up the entire Westside, bruh. With that bitch Miko out of the game, somebody gotta supply the demand, you feel me? I figure why not me, why not us?" He sipped some more Henny then looked at me. "What about you? Have you figured out what you want to do with your half?"

"I guess it's true what they say, homeboy: 'Great minds think alike, Shug.' I wanna lock some blocks down too. From the South all the way to the Eastside, I wanna control every sack that gets bought or sold in that part of the Southeast Planet. I'm thinking of opening up a strip club too."

"Is that right? A strip club, huh? You come up with a name for it yet?" he asked and downed the rest of his drink.

A smile formed on my face as I tasted my Hennessy. "Yeah, I got a name in mind."

"Oh yeah, what's that?" he asked and hit the blunt.

Trey Songz' voice continued flowing out the speakers. "I'ma call it Bottomz Up, bruh," I told him and added, "Why the fuck not? It's like music to my ears!" We laughed and he passed me the blunt. We started singing the song together, hella off key, but it sounded good as fuck to me!

Most people would've been satisfied with what we had and would have quit while they were ahead, but we weren't like most people. Whether we were ahead in the game or not, we weren't the quitting kind. We weren't built like that. Our gangsta mindset and the thug lifestyle were deeply rooted in our DNA.

Cream & Suspect

Cream and Suspect walked one behind the other dressed in a dark blue county jail two-piece with the words San Diego County Jail stenciled across the back and down the front right pants leg. They looked noticeably bigger and more thuggish than the other inmates walking ahead of them. With their bedrolls tucked under their arms, the long line of hard-faced criminals slowly walked down the narrow hallway passing modules full of numbered cells that housed numerous inmates. Killers and other hardened felons with big chips on their shoulders and 'fuck the world' dispositions were posted up at the windows in their cells, mean-mugging the line of men walking by.

Together, Cream and Suspect heard the muffled roar of love and respect from the Eastside affiliated gangstas who worked with or for them at one time or another. But not every gangsta in the cells had love in their eyes. A few men had hatred in theirs, two thugs in particular.

Bony James

Bony James stood next to his homie gritting his teeth and cracking his knuckles as the line of new inmates walked by. The look on his face was a homicide charge waiting to happen.

"Damn, Bony, your whole demeanor changed up when them fools walked by. Do you know one of them cats or something?" a tall, swoll, Ving Rhames lookalike asked.

Bony James chewed on his molars and reached down to touch the heavily bandaged bullet wound on his back. "Yeah, actually I do. I know two of them bitch ass ma'fuckas," he said with venom in his voice.

The Ving Rhames lookalike glanced over at Bony James. "What they do? And do the homies have a green light to bust on sight or what?" the goon asked a little too eagerly.

Bony James' voice was a bone-chilling whisper.

"Them the ma'fuckas who shot me and killed the homies Goldie, Jayquan, and G-Mack. Hell yeah, it's on sight!" Bony moved away from the window and looked around the cell for something he could tear apart and make a knife out of. After determining the metal writing table would do, he turned to his homie and said, "Tell all the homies it's a green light on the two new ma'fuckas named Cream and Suspect."

Tiyatti

From a cell in another module, Tiyatti watched with a mask of uncut hatred as the line of new inmates walked by with their bedrolls in their hands. He shot daggers at the two muscularly built thugs at the back of the line. When they passed by the unit he was housed in, Tiyatti turned and reached for the nine-inch long, one-inch wide, thick strip of steel under his mattress. He quietly went down to one knee in the back of his cell and began grinding the point on the shank he'd started working on two days ago. The deep groove on the concrete floor assisted in putting a sharpened point on the end of the homemade jailhouse knife. Tiyatti worked the steel fast and furiously against the concrete with the most hurtful kind of pain as his motivation. Thoughts of a pregnant Duchess carrying what would have been his first child and his little brother, Devontay, fueled the rage eating away at his heart. *I'm finna stab every ma'fucka associated with Miko Dunbar's crew. I don't give a fuck if they were there or not. If they Miko's people, they gon' get it!* Tiyatti declared inwardly as he gripped the knife tight and tested the sharp point against his mattress. *Perfect!* he thought when an inch-wide hole appeared after his first stabbing motion.

And I'm starting with you, Cream and Suspect. You ma'fuckas are dead first chance I get!

READING GROUP DISCUSSION QUESTIONS

Note from the author: These questions are meant to initiate discussion, provoke thought, and spark debate. Your participation is tremendously appreciated, and I hope my writing was pleasing to the reader in you. Please feel free to post a review online. Thank you for the love. And don't worry, you won't have to wait long. Deeply Rooted 3 is coming soon!

1. Do you think the Young Glock Gang was justified in how they responded to Miko's business tactics?

2. How do you feel about Tiyatti becoming involved in the street life? Do you know someone like Tiyatti? Someone who felt they had no other choice but to turn to the streets in order to survive? If the opportunity presented itself, what would you advise he do?

3. Did Tiyatti bring what happened to him on himself? If so, how?

4. Was it foolish or honorable for Tiyatti to confess his infidelity to Duchess?

5. Do you feel Miko's treatment of Tiyatti was solely a result of her being rejected by him, or do you think that him knowing too much really did play a part in how she did him? Explain.

6. Did Capone get what he had coming to him, or was it too steep a penalty to pay?

7. What do you think happened to Tocarra?

8. Was Miko a thorough enough queenpin, or was she too cold-blooded?

9. How do you feel about Miko's death?

10. Do you think Wah and Baby Shug will ever become successful legitimate businessmen? Or are they destined to live and die in the streets? What would you like to see become of Wah and Shug?

A sneak peek into:

DEEPLY ROOTED 3

Prologue

Two ski-masked thugs waited patiently in the cut with high-powered assault rifles clutched tightly in their grip. It was unusually cold outside. The nonstop driving rain tumbled down sideways in sheets. The weather had been nasty like that all day, but this was one of those rare occasions that presented the two thugs in the bushes with a once in a lifetime opportunity—a Dodge Durango weighted down with dope and a stash house hiding hundreds of thousands of dollars. The rain was an unexpected occurrence, a watery annoyance they were forced to endure. But the idea of being rich beyond their wildest dreams was waterproof, so they tolerated the adverse conditions and stayed crouched low in the bushes with their guns at the ready.

The taller of the two men blinked water droplets off his eyelashes and wiped the face of his watch off: 3:21 a.m. What the fuck is takin' these fools so long? The thought raced through his mind as he nervously licked at the rain on his upper lip. He shivered under his hoodie while his teeth clattered loudly in the night. Then he turned on his haunches, looked behind him, and made eye contact with his partner in crime.

"Didn't you say it was supposed to go down at three?"

The shorter thug nodded and said, "Yup." Fat water drops fell off the front of his ski-mask, dripping down onto the glistening wet AK-47.

"Where the fuck they at then?" the tall thug spoke, aggravated.

"I don't know. I'm sittin' out here in the fuckin' rain witchu!" the shorter thug equally retorted.

They continued to wait in the bushes in silence armed to the teeth. Moments later, their patience was rewarded when a pair of headlights flashed bright against the wall above their heads.

"That's them right there!" the short thug announced in an excited whisper as the Dodge Durango headed in their direction. Each thug re-gripped his gun, preparing for the ambush.

The brakes on the Durango squealed when the black truck eased to a stop at the curb in front of the dilapidated house. A sagging fence encircled the all-dirt front yard. The headlights shut off, and the individuals inside the truck waited in silence. The driver racked his pistol and chambered a round. The goon in the passenger seat did the same, then pulled the navy blue Nike beanie down low on his head in anticipation of the cold and wet conditions awaiting him outside. The third thug in the truck sat in the back with the duffle bags full of bricks. He held a Tech-9 with a modified extended clip attached to it. The murder weapon was capable of spitting out a hundred hollow tip rounds in mere seconds.

Incessant rainfall continued pelting the exterior of the truck with chubby drops of water. Their suspicious eyes scanned the area around the stash house as they waited. The soft leather interior sighed under the weight of the driver when he leaned forward and peered intently at the bushes lining the outer wall of the house next door. *Is that somebody over there squattin' in the bushes?* The question flashed through his overly cautious mind. His keen eyes narrowed to slits as he examined the shrubbery across the way. The stash house's front door opened, and light from inside the house flooded the porch with brightness. His eyes instantly went toward the light. *About time!* he thought while choking his pistol.

A thug in a blue and gray Seattle Seahawks hoodie appeared on the porch with a chrome thumper in his hand. A second thug emerged from the house following closely behind, his barrel-chested silhouette filling up the doorway. The three men inside the Durango sat up with a start.

"It's time to go, y'all! Get on your shit!" the driver announced and grabbed the door lever. He pushed the door open with his shoulder and stepped out into the cold, rainy night. The passenger door opened, and the thug wearing the navy blue Nike beanie stepped onto the street with his gun pointing at the ground, safety off. The thug in the back climbed out last with the Tech-9 in his right hand and the duffle bags full of dope in his left. The three of them walked away from the Dodge Durango, ready to commit murder as sheets of rain fell unremittingly from the sky.

Both stash house workers met up with the three thugs from the Durango in the middle of the muddy front yard. The noisy clanging of empty soda cans sounded off in the bushes next to the house. *What the fuck!* The driver of the Durango swung his arm in the direction of the bushes with his finger on the trigger, ready to pop off shots. The Tech-9 swung that way as well, the wet, black steel glossy under the moonlight. The man who had been in the passenger seat pointed his pistol at the bushes too. The two goons who emerged from the house did the same; all five guns were aimed at the bushes. The rain fell harder. A loud thunder clap bombarded the night, and a flash of lightning lit the sky up with a burst of brightness. It was the perfect diversion for the thugs who were once hidden in the bushes.

"Drop yours or get dropped by mine, ma'fucka!" a voice barked from behind. Cold, wet tips of AK-47 assault rifles touched the necks of two of the three thugs who had been in the Durango.

Pfftt!

The goon in the Seattle Seahawk's hoodie shot the thug holding the Tech-9 in the ear, slumping him in the muddy front yard. His body sloshed loudly on the wet ground, along with the two duffle bags.

Pfftt! Pfftt!

Quickly, he turned and hit the barrel-chested thug who had followed him out of the house with two slugs to his wide body. The barrel-chested thug crumbled in a heap and died at the shooter's feet as his blood began mixing with the muddied, watery surface beneath him.

"Walk y'all ma'fuckin' asses inside, or you gon' die like they did!" the tall thug who had been in the bushes ordered, while poking the driver of the Durango in the small of his back with the end of his AK-47, ushering him in the direction of the house. His partner stabbed the man who had been in the passenger seat in his upper back with his AK, forcing him to follow the crowd.

The two men from the Durango evil-eyed the thug in the Seahawk hoodie as they walked past him. Their eyes held a look of disgusted hatred, repulsed that they had been set up by one of their own, a cowardly homie who had just murdered two of his own in cold blood.

"Who the fuck you lookin' at like that!" the guilt-ridden thug in the Seahawk hoodie verbally banged on the two men as they passed by him. He never gave them a chance to respond.

Pfftt! Pfftt!

The silent shots slumped both of them on the spot. The driver of the Durango died first and collapsed in the mud. The man wearing the navy blue Nike beanie tried to run and took one to the back of the head and fell on top of the dead driver.

"C'mon, let's go get the money!" the man in the Seahawk hoodie ordered in a heartless tone.

With that aspect of their goon business taken care of, the jackers took their time as they went inside and bagged up the dough. They walked to the Durango lugging the two large duffle bags and a trash bag full of money to the truck before returning to the front yard. After dragging the dead bodies into the house, they wiped everything down in an attempt to remove their fingerprints from the scene of the gruesome crime. As soon as the Dodge Durango jumped off the curb and sped up the block, the rain suddenly stopped. A parade of muddy boot prints trampling through the front yard and littering the sidewalk in front of the stash house left behind a revealing account to one with a knowing eye.

* * * * * *

Baby Shug stood next to his right hand man, Kirky, looking down at part of the grisly murder scene before him. He swallowed the sour taste of rage filling his mouth like thick saliva and fought to hold back the angry tears threatening to fill his eyes. Getting ripped for twenty-two bricks and half a million dollars hurt his pockets and pained his pride profoundly. But that pain dimmed in comparison to the hurt his heart felt over the loss of his crew. Four of his workers had been brutally gunned down. He knew all the dead men well; they weren't just his workers, they were some of his closest homeboys. Men he had grown up with, men he shared an extensive history with.

With his hands pushed deep inside his front pants pockets, Baby Shug stood meticulously eyeballing everything around him. He closely studied the interior of the house before stepping outside into the cold, crisp morning air. He rubbed the palms of his hands together and took a deep breath, his eyes following the dried trail of dirty boot tracks. The scene was speaking to him; the multiple sets of muddy boot prints outside in the front yard told him there were at least three jackers. It became obvious to him that two of the stickup kids had been lurking in the bushes. He ascertained that the string on the ground tied to the empty Pepsi cans across the yard was more than likely used as a distraction.

The fact that the bodies had been dragged into the house after being slumped outside told him that it might've been an inside job, since one of his stash house workers wasn't amongst the dead. Stickup kids with no personal ties would have left the dead bodies in the front yard where they fell. The trail of dirty boot prints leading up to the curb and disappearing where the transport truck would've been parked convinced him that it was indeed an inside job.

"Ay, Kirky, c'mere," he called out to his trusted underboss, hoping his gut was wrong.

"Yeah dat. What's up, Shug?" Kirky said, easing up next to him.

"Call School Boy and Gun Smoke and tell 'em to come down here and help Meech get rid of these bodies. Have them clean the stash house up too and make it look like it's new," Shug instructed, before turning and walking toward the 2014 gun metal gray Range Rover.

After two failed attempts, Kirky called out to him, "Ay Shug!"

"What's up?" Shug stopped with his hand on the Range Rover's door handle and turned to face the young savage goon he'd taken under his wing when he decided to seriously get in the drug game months ago.

"They ain't answering their phones, cuz."

"Call 'em again," Shug told him and released the handle. He leaned against the Rover's door, waiting with his arms folded across his chest and the heels of his boots resting against the curb.

Kirky called again and waited for an answer. Nothing. He looked up at Shug, shook his head, and awaited further instruction. Shug pulled his own phone out and called School Boy, and then Gun Smoke. No answer. He tried again, same result. No answer. His homies not answering their phones was highly unusual, very suspect. Instantly, his gut convinced him that they were involved and were probably already long gone in the wind.

Shug turned to Kirky with a mean mug on his handsome brown face and pointed his finger at him.

"I want you to personally go find those ma'fuckas, Kirky. Ya heard me? Find 'em and bring they asses back to me alive and breathin'."

"A'ight, say no more. I'm on it, Shug," Kirky assured him and went to help Meech deal with the bodies and the stash house.

Shug looked down at the three sets of muddy boot prints on the sidewalk, and a voice deep down inside reiterated to him that School Boy and Gun Smoke were involved, and they more than likely had help doing their dirty. He looked over at the stash house and slowly shook his head one more time before climbing into the Range Rover. After closing the door and getting comfortable, he shut his eyes and let mental images of better days with his homies play behind his closed eyelids. Moments later when he opened his eyes, he blinked the tears back and cleared his blurry vision before pressing the start button. He knew he'd have to kill a few of his own Crip homies, homies he grew up with, men he shared extended history with. *I'm gettin' tired of killin' people! But these dumb ass ma'fuckas keep puttin' shit in the game, forcing my hand. Homie or not, you take my money, I take your life! When I find the ma'fuckas who got me, it's gon' be all bad for them. No mercy. No mercy whatsoever!*

CHAPTER 1

Wah

As soon as I heard the doorbell sound, I finished doing what I was doing and bounced down the spiraling staircase like a boss. The bottom of my pebble-colored Timb's smashed the soft, expensive carpet as I descended the stairs like Obama coming out of Air Force-One. I stopped at the bottom of the stairs and checked my reflection in the dark glass to my left. *That's what the fuck I'm talkin' 'bout!* I thought with satisfaction. I wore a crisp, loose- fitting, black denim 'fit, platinum and diamonds shining in all the right places; something chunky hanging off my neck, something heavy holding down my wrist, and my left earlobe looking like it had a miniature disco ball on it.

Khassandra squealed her delight when she heard the doorbell chime and rushed out the kitchen with her apron bunched up in her hand. She danced excitedly next to me as I approached the door prepared to greet our guests. I opened the huge double doors and invited my folks in. It was always good seeing my brother. We'd grown a lot closer since killing that bitch Miko, and I found myself thoroughly enjoying spending time with the man who I once considered my worst enemy.

We were both knee-deep in the dope game now, but had discovered early on that it would be next to impossible for us both to successfully and effectively run a drug empire as a single entity. The fact that I was a Blood and he was a Crip wouldn't allow us to function smoothly as one unit. We were brothers, true that, but that didn't mean shit as far as the streets were concerned. In San Diego, Bloods and Crips had been feuding since the 70s. For decades, Bloods had been

1

killing Crips, and Crips had been killing Bloods. And it wasn't a damn thang Shug or I could do that was going to change that part of the game. No amount of money and no amount of drugs would ever erase the memory of the many murders that made the feud between the Bloods and Crips run so deep with hatred. It was a beef deeply rooted in the black community and constantly in motion 24/7. We understood that reality and pushed forward in spite of it, on two different paths, but both heading for the same destination: super boss status!

"What's poppin', bruh?" I embraced Shug with a solid dap on his fist and a warmhearted bear hug.

"Ain't nothin'. What's good wit' you?" he asked and showed me the same kind of love.

Everybody exchanged heartfelt hugs and hellos. We clowned around for a few minutes, making small talk before naturally pairing up and breaking off. The two sisters moved away to chit- chat and fuss over some of the new highly stylized décor of my mini-mansion before Khassandra took Khadida upstairs to show off the walk-in closet and tout her ever-growing expensive handbag collection and the extensive shoe game she was so fond of.

As soon as I couldn't hear them anymore, I walked over to where Shug was standing and draped my arm across one of his shoulders.

"How's business on the Westside?" I asked after a couple of seconds of peering through the tall windows.

"Business is good, Wah. I still got Kirky out huntin' for School Boy and Gun Smoke. Aside from that, everything is straight. The money flow is major and the drama is minimal. No doubt about it, bruh, the Westside been good to me," he said with a sincere smile.

I took my arm from around his shoulder and walked over to the bar, returning with two glasses of Hennessy and two blunts. He accepted the drink and blunt and we posted up in front of the floor-to-ceiling glass room overlooking the Pacific Ocean from atop the cliffs. The mini-mansion in La Jolla was my most costly purchase to date, my prized investment. We stood in silence for a minute, sipping, smoking, and watching the sun set in the distant horizon. I watched the waves relentlessly crash against the rocky shoreline, the thick white foam licking at the dark wet sand before retreating into the immense body of water. The view was incredibly serene. Combined with the side-effects from the kush and Hennessy, it had a tremendously calming effect on me.

"How about you, Wah? How's business been on your end?" Shug asked, before pulling on his blunt and swallowing a mouthful of Henny. He never took his eyes off the majestic spectacle of the reddish-orange sun in the distance as it slowly sank somewhere on the other end of the earth.

"Er'thang is good on my end, bruh," I told him. "Seyku got the blocks rockin' right, and the strip club is poppin' the most, even better than I expected. Every baller in the city be down there makin' it rain in that bitch." I inhaled another chest full of smoke and swallowed some more drink.

Shug grew silent for a second and drew in a deep breath. When he spoke, his voice was barely above a whisper.

"Remember that thang we spoke about, about gettin' off the diamonds and the jewelry?" he asked

"Yeah, I remember. What about it?" I asked.

"Well, a cat I did some time with last year hit me back and assured me he knows somebody with deep pockets and more than enough paper to purchase every piece of bling we got. He claims that he can put us in touch with this cat, for a small finder's fee, of course."

"Is that right? A small finder's fee, huh?" I quizzed with suspicion in my voice and one of my eyebrows cocked. "Exactly how much money is he talkin' about for this *finder's fee*?" I asked, swishing the drink around in my glass. *Don't do it, Wah! Don't do it! It sounds too good to be true!* the voice in my head warned me. I ignored it and listened to what Shug had to say.

"He wants a thousand off every hundred racks we get, Wah. If you really think about it, all things considered, that really ain't shit, bruh."

I sucked in some more smoke, swallowed a mouthful of the dark amber-hued liquid and pondered Shug's proposition. Thoughts of the shootout with Joey Cheese and his soldiers flashed through my mind, followed by more thoughts of the gunplay with the New York thug Keitho and his people. Naturally I was suspicious, but I was also growing tired of holding onto the diamonds. The sooner I could get them shits off, the better. So despite my reservations, I was willing to at least consider testing the waters again.

"Can you trust this dude you did time with, Shug? I mean, do you believe he's on the up and up. Is he solid?"

"C'mon now, Wah. Fuck kinda question is that? If I didn't feel like I could trust him, I wouldn't be fuckin' wit' him like that, and I damn sho' wouldn't be introducin' you to him if I didn't think he was solid." Shug spoke a little louder and wore an unpleasant expression after I questioned his get-down.

"I didn't mean it like that, bruh. I'm just sayin' . . . I don't want to be fuckin' around wit' somebody that we might have to murk later in the game because they on some shiesty shit, you feel me?" I reminded him of the previous incidents that popped up in my head a few seconds ago. "Millions of dollars worth of diamonds seem to have a way of bringing out the worst in people, you know? Remember Joey Cheese and that fool, Keitho?"

"I feel you, Wah, but at the same time, every day we do deals with shady ma'fuckas, and every one of those deals got the potential to cause one of us to maybe have to murk somebody. That's just how the game goes, bruh." He wasn't telling me anything that I didn't already know.

We looked at each other, and an unspoken understanding passed between us. When you conduct business with unsavory characters, shady shit is subject to occur. Grimy goings-on were an understood aspect of the equation. But this was a lot of money we were talking about. I had to think about it some more before I made a decision. I downed the remaining drink in the glass.

"I'll let you know something before the night is over, a'ight?" I told him.

The setting sun winked at us one last time before disappearing into the darkness, leaving behind a colorful display in its wake.

"No doubt," he responded.

With that established, we faced each other and dapped it up. We stood near the floor-to-ceiling glass window and chopped it up about other shit related to the thug life, until Khassandra's heels click-clacking on the marble floor interrupted our session.

"Sorry to break up the love fest, y'all, but dinner is ready."

She turned to walk away, and we both watched her shapely, round ass seductively wobble in the form-fitting, low rise, light blue Seven jeans as her back pockets rhythmically bounced up and down slowly. When she disappeared around the corner, we looked at each other and exchanged smiles, slapping hands in appreciation of the voluptuous visual. Like I said before, Khassandra looked like Megan Good but had ass like Amber Rose.

We sat down and feasted on the meal Khassandra spent the better part of the day preparing. New York strip steak, greens, yams, macaroni and cheese, with sweet buttered rolls. For dessert, her version of a triple-layered red velvet cake. The food was the bomb, as usual. Not only was Khassandra beautiful, sexy, and built like a video vixen, she could cook her ass off as well.

The conversation at the dinner table was plentiful and flowed freely. The four of us clicked like dice, and it had been that way from the start.

Weeks after killing that bitch Miko, Shug and Khadida purchased a six-bedroom, two-story home in an affluent, racially diverse upper middle class neighborhood in a more prosperous part of the city. I copped a six-bedroom, nine-bath, exquisite multi-leveled estate in La Jolla. Khassandra moved in with me shortly after. We were kicking it, but I made it clear to her off top that ours was not a regular-type relationship. Although I respected her and kept it one hundred with her, I made it perfectly clear I still had feelings in my heart for Tocarra, and it would remain that way until I learned more of her whereabouts, or put some type of closure to what she and I once shared—what we still shared.

After the four of us finished eating, Khassandra and Khadida went about cleaning the dishes while Shug and I retreated behind the closed door of my lavish first floor office.

We sat down and chopped it up some more, reminiscing about the past, laughing and clowning about some of our childhood memories. Shit that had been serious beef to us at one time, but in hindsight was comical, considering how strong our relationship is now. Then the conversation got a little more serious, a lot more sentimental.

"You really do miss her, huh?" Shug asked when he saw me looking at the framed picture of Tocarra and me on the wall. Something about the way he said it and the images flashing through my head at that moment squeezed on my heart and provoked my emotionality.

I looked over at Shug, then my eyes went back to the picture on the wall, and I flashed back to that trip to New York, to the day I had a stranger take the picture of Tocarra and me, when we were out sightseeing in Times Square. It was one of only a handful of pictures I had of Tocarra. Although I had known I was going to kill a man that day, the framed picture captured a special moment in time; it represented one of the brighter instances of my life. Tocarra and I were sporting mega-watt smiles while hugged up in Times Square. We had just talked about taking our relationship to the next level, and the picture captured the essence of our happiness together.

"Yeah, I do miss her, bruh. I miss her like a ma'fucka, Shug." I continued staring at the picture and thought about the day I met Tocarra. We were verbally sparring over the taxi cab after my getaway from the jewelry store heist with the briefcase full of bling in my hand. *Our very first conversation took place inside the back of that cab. It flowed easy like water going downstream.* Then I thought about the day we took that particular picture. I remember making love to her early that morning and how good it felt when she was in my arms. I thought about how good it always felt anytime I was around Tocarra. Discreetly, I blinked back my emotions. My eyes remained dry, but inside I was crying. *Where the hell are you, Tocarra!* My not knowing where she was or what happened to her after she left my bedside to go look for Miko was still fucking me up in a real way. Despite all the time that had gone by, my love for her still remained.

"When are you going to move on, Wah?" Shug asked in a quiet voice. "I know you loved Tocarra and all, but obviously she gone, and she ain't trying to be found. Otherwise, she'd be here with you. You got a good woman living right here up under your own roof, and you ain't even seeing that for what it is, bruh, because you so stuck on Tocarra and the past."

I don't think he meant any harm by what he was saying, but it made me see him in a way I didn't like seeing him. Tocarra had been acting on his instructions and in his best interests when Miko did whatever she did to her. Yet, here he was telling me to forget about her like she wasn't that important. Since coming out of the coma I've discovered that Shug had some serious honesty and loyalty issues. It's possible his past dealings with Miko had a lot to do with that, but I wasn't feeling how his expression of the truth didn't always make the most sense.

"I can't move on, bruh. Maybe you can't understand it, but something deep down inside me is telling me not to give up. She wasn't in that suitcase under the lemon tree, so something keeps telling me that Tocarra is still alive." I stopped talking for a second and thought about her some more. I snapped out of the daydream and looked at him. "Did you know that before I met Tocarra I had never been in love before, Shug? Tocarra was the first woman to ever conquer my heart, bruh, and she still got it. She still got my heart, homie!" My emotions overwhelmed me for a second. I sat up in my chair and downed the rest of my drink, then I stood and walked over to the photo that provoked so many emotions inside me. The trees and the drink were tampering with my mental temperature. I stared longingly at the beautiful, brown-skinned woman in the picture and got lost in how she made me feel. I reached out and caressed the glass where Tocarra's face was with the tips of my fingers. *I wish like hell I knew where you were and what happened to you, baby!* It hurt my heart thinking about her and our short time in each other's lives. Shug sat behind me quiet, letting me have my moment. "Do you know what the only thing that's missing from this picture is?" I asked and turned to him, my voice low and serious.

"What's that, Wah?" he asked, using his hand to fan the cloud of smoke from the half-smoked blunt he fired back up.

"The one thing I wanted most in my life, Shug, the one thing that I felt like I never truly ever had in all of my years growing up."

"And that is?" When he asked, I could hear in his voice that he was genuinely curious about what my answer would be.

"A family of my own, bruh. All I ever wanted was a family of my own, Shug." My voice cracked as the drink and smoke continued to instigate my emotions. I regained my composure. "When we were in New York, Tocarra confided in me that she couldn't have kids because her ovaries were compromised. But I always felt that just because a doctor said it, that don't make it gospel." I drifted off in thought while a collage of our past lovemaking sessions played behind my closed eyes. A sad smile creased my lips before I went on. "I was tryin' my damndest to make a baby with her every day, bruh! When we were house huntin' she got sick like she had morning sickness or something. I don't know what it was, Shug, but my gut was telling me that Tocarra might've been pregnant!" *Maybe it's just my wishful thinking.* I blinked back my tears and breathed in deeply, trying to fend off the thoughts of *what if?* I hadn't ever spoken openly about my feelings like that before, but I felt like I could trust my brother with the truth of my heart. Shedding tears wasn't something I did a lot of in my adult years. The pain of not having a father present in my life while growing up, and my mother being murdered when I was so young, took a heavy toll on my psyche and had such a tremendous effect on my mental, that my emotional pool was almost dried up. I did more crying in my younger years than any kid should've ever had to do. I didn't have many more tears to give to the world. One last time I looked at the picture of Tocarra and me, smiling and loving life in New York, and I swallowed the emotion welling up. It was painful not having her around to share my success with, to share life with.

Sometimes not having my soulmate by my side while life was being so good to me seemed hella unfair. Sometimes I felt guilty fucking with Khassandra the way that I did, but Khassandra knew how I felt about Tocarra, and I didn't make any apologies about it. So it was what it was—convenient. I liked Khassandra, but I was still in love with Tocarra.

Maybe Shug is right. Maybe it's time I accept the prospect of a tomorrow without Tocarra in it. Maybe it's time for me to move on with my life and just let Tocarra be a memory to me. I sat back down and blazed another one up, guilt-ridden about the thought. In an attempt to get my mind off Tocarra, I thought about the diamonds. *I'm tired of sitting on all that bling anyway.* After a couple minutes of mulling it over, I reached a conclusion about the diamond deal. I looked at Shug and announced my decision. "Go ahead and holla at your boy, bruh. Let's do the deal with the diamonds, homie." *Fuck it, why not?*

"You ain't said shit, bruh. That's what I'm talkin' 'bout! Let's get this money, Wah!" He pulled his phone out and called the dude he had done time with, some cat named Droop Loc.

When he finished talking, I looked him in his eyes and told him, "I hope these dudes we hookin' up with is legit, bruh. Real talk, because I'm gettin' tired of killin' people, Shug."

"Man, it's all good, Wah. Trust me, bruh. I got this," he assured me.

That shit sounds good, I thought before speaking. "I trust you, Shug. It's the shady ass ma'fuckas in the game who I have a problem trusting. A part of me is telling me that we should pass on this one, but if you got faith in this fool, then fuck it, let's do the damn thang," I told him, while the voice in my head kept telling me I was making a mistake. I ignored my thoughts and let them drift off to Tocarra again. *Where the hell you at, ma? Why the fuck I can't find you?*

Author Bio

Ice Mike was born and raised in San Diego California. He is an author, a poet and an advocate. Having spent much of his life deeply immersed in the criminal lifestyle, he chose to leave the criminal/gang world behind in hopes of showing others that it's never too late to alter ones course in life or change ones path and purpose. Ice Mike hopes to one day open a writing academy that helps disadvantaged youth develop and cultivate their gift of writing, so that they too can realize their fullest potential.

If you would like to know more about Ice Mike, go to:

E-mail: icemikewritenow@gmail.com
Facebook: icemikewritenow
Instagram: icemikewritenow
Twitter: icemikewritenow
Website: www.dufflebagbooks.com

41696216R00194

Made in the USA
Middletown, DE
23 March 2017